The
Grey
Pilgrim

J. M. Hayes

Poisoned Pen Press

Copyright © 1990, 2000 by J.M. Hayes

B+T 1|25|01 15L

Significant portions of *The Grey Pilgrim* were originally published by
Walker Publishing Company, Inc. in 1990.

First US Trade Paperback Edition 2000

10 9 8 7 6 5 4 3 2 1

Library of Congress Catalog Card Number: 00-103989

ISBN: 1-890208-50-7

Poisoned Pen Press
6962 E. First Ave. Ste 103
Scottsdale, AZ 85251
www.poisonedpenpress.com
info@poisonedpenpress.com

Printed in the United States of America

For, and in memory of, my parents,
who, in spite of overwhelming evidence
to the contrary, believed their son
might amount to something.

And in memory of
Don Graybill and Steve Martinez,
great friends and fellow pilgrims.

There Honour *comes, a Pilgrim grey,*
To bless the Turf that wraps their Clay...

—William Collins
Ode, Written in the Beginning of the Year, 1746

No Nation but Our Own

The Last Great Papago Rebellion began on Wednesday, October 16, 1940 in an insignificant village deep in the Southern Arizona desert. The place was called *Stohta U'uhig*, "White Bird," though no birds of that hue were present then. The place wasn't on any maps, except a couple produced in limited quantity for the Bureau of Indian Affairs (BIA) that failed to place it accurately anyway. It was also known as Jujul's village because he'd been its Head Man and Priest for longer than most people could remember.

Jujul's name was pronounced in the Spanish fashion. It sounded to English speakers like "who who'll."

He was standing near his adobe hut in the midst of a small crowd. His villagers were typical, curious sorts, drawn to the unusual. The unusual was present. A black automobile with a crudely painted tribal police crest on its door had brought a policeman in an ill-fitting uniform and a curiously pale man, a representative of the BIA, to White Bird.

Jujul would have liked to examine the automobile. He'd seldom been so close and had never actually touched one, but there was pressing business. Luis Azul and the fat little Gringo stood in the shade of the paloverde in front of Jujul's home. Luis was scraping at the dust with his feet, refusing to meet Jujul's gaze. The White Man had shed his suit coat and draped it over a pudgy arm. His collar and vest were open and his tie loose, but it wasn't enough. He was soft, unaccustomed to heat or exertion, and he was paying for it. Perspiration soaked his clothing and mixed scents with the remnants of his floral aftershave. The result was nauseating.

The fat man looked back and forth between Luis and Jujul. He wanted to get this business over with. He said something to Luis and Luis, still refusing to look Jujul in the eye, translated again.

"Mr. Larson says I must repeat his words, and this time I must be certain you understand them. It is a simple matter, he says. You must give him the names of all your men who are between twenty-one and thirty-five years of age so that they can be registered. It is a new law which goes into effect today. Everyone must obey it, even the Gringos. *Siwani* Jujul, I do not think the White Men will necessarily take our people for their army. I think this is only their way of counting us so they know how valuable we will be as allies if they go to war and need our aid. *Siwani*, the tribal council has agreed to this. It is truly a thing which must be done."

Jujul was tall and slender for a Papago. His face was the color and texture of fine old leather and the scar on his right temple was almost invisible beneath his thick white mane. He was an imposing figure, and since he was tall enough to look down on the White Man and his servant, the tribal policeman, his contemptuous glare was even more impressive.

"*Pia'a*," Jujul told Luis. "No. Tell him I said no. He is without authority here. This is the land of the Desert People. It is not America. It is not Mexico. This place is no nation but our own. I who am Chief Medicine Man of this village, deny the right of either of you to be here, other than as our guests. We shall not take part in this registration thing. If you continue to insist on it, you will no longer be welcome among us."

"*Siwani Mahkai*, I beg you, do not provoke him." Luis replied. "This place is America. There will be trouble if you do not agree to this. The Gringos may be a crazy people, a foolish people, but they are strong. They will make you obey."

Luis worried at the brim of his campaign hat with his dark brown hands. Jujul had seen Catholics do the same with the beads from which they hung the curious symbol of their faith. Luis was very uncomfortable.

"Tell him," Jujul demanded.

Luis reluctantly translated, softening Jujul's words as he did so. There was no way to soften the final answer. Jujul watched, intrigued, as the White Man slowly became a red one, his face flushing to almost the color of the skin of the Desert People where they did not expose it to the sun.

"Arrest the son of a bitch," Larson shouted, spraying the dry wind with his spittle.

"*Siwani* Jujul," Luis stuttered, "Mr. Larson says that I must arrest you."

"And how will you do this, Luis? Unless there are a great many more of your policemen hiding in the machine that brought you, then I think you are too few. I think, also, if you draw your gun on me, Raven or Wheat Rows or another of my men will shoot you. So, tell me, how will you do this?"

Luis was suddenly more than just nervous. He was afraid.

Edward Larson was twice Jujul's weight and half his age, and he was also irrational with rage. He came very close to taking a swing at the old man, but a second glance at the chief's sinewy muscularity was enough to dissuade him. Instead, he ordered Luis Azul to use whatever force was necessary to take the old man into custody. Luis explained what would happen if he did anything of the sort. Larson hadn't really noticed the other villagers up until then, and when he did, he briefly experienced a kinship to Custer. He let Luis lead him back to the tribal police car. Since no one followed, he allowed himself the luxury of shouting threats that most of them couldn't understand while waving his chubby fists.

Jujul and his people stood and watched quietly. The policeman maneuvered Larson into the car, got it started, and began to back down the rutted track they'd followed to the village, searching for a place that was wide enough to turn around. Everything might have been all right if Larson hadn't felt the need for one last gesture. He stuck his fist out of the passenger's window, aimed it at Jujul, and raised a single finger.

Jujul was not particularly familiar with the White Man's ways, but he recognized Larson's unexpectedly crude insult. He bent down and selected a smooth round stone. He had hurled them at cattle and predators since he was a small boy. He had used rocks to keep animals from places where they were not wanted or steer them where they were. He was very accurate with this one. The windshield in front of Larson's startled face went suddenly opaque behind an intricate web of radiating cracks.

Jujul only threw one stone, but scores of others hailed down on the car as his villagers joined the fun. Luis Azul panicked and backed into a thicket of creosote in his hurry to point both himself and the car in the opposite direction He did not, however, panic enough to expose the driver's side to the stone throwers.

"Stop!" Jujul shouted. "Let them leave." It was important to him that only their pride be injured. Few of his people heard him. Fewer still obeyed. He started forward, to place himself between his people and the automobile, uncertain whether he could get there in time. The auto's rear wheel spun, throwing its own share of rocks and gravel. The engine roared and the wheel finally grabbed hold. The vehicle lurched back onto the path, almost stalled, then sped away with a clashing of gears accompanied by the derisive jeers of his villagers.

Several of Jujul's people understood the White Man's tongue. They explained what Larson had promised as they watched the dust of the police car disappear toward the jagged horizon. Jujul wasn't surprised. Even without the rocks he would have expected them to return with reinforcements. He looked at his shadow. It was mid-afternoon. He had no idea how quickly the automobile could carry its passengers back to Sells and Papago Agency Head-quarters, but he had a fair idea of how long it would take to gather and organize the necessary men. A little before dawn, he decided. It would take them at least that long and they would favor that hour, being themselves normally unprepared then. It was long enough. He would be ready this time. Not like that spring in 1916 when the soldiers came because of the man named Pancho Villa.

⌐

The screams woke him. For a moment Jujul lay in the half dark and wondered where he was. It was not quite dawn. Magician's Daughter, the morning star, hung where Father Sun would soon begin to burn his way up the sky.

Sleep clouded Jujul's consciousness. He fought it, reaching out for the comforting forms of his wives beside him. They weren't there. He rolled out of his blankets, grabbed his rifle, and scrambled outside. He felt a sense of danger, but he couldn't place it, couldn't even determine whether it was real or only the remnant of some already forgotten dream.

It was very quiet. No breezes stirred the creosote. No birds called from the groves of mesquite and paloverde. The morning was unformed, waiting, breathless for that which would define it.

He heard voices. Not clear, not close. Not the pleasant tones of the Desert People or their kin, not even the liquid flow of Spanish, but harsh, clipped, nasal tones. Gringo voices! Gringos where none should be. He was too numb, too puzzled to comprehend it. Another scream tore him from further analysis, sent him dodging through the underbrush, running headlong toward the dry stream bed below their camp, toward the source of that awful cry.

It was Many Flowers who had cried out, voice full of pain and terror. Behind her wail were Cloud Peak's outraged shouts—denial, anger! Their answer was coarse masculine laughter and a brief exchange in the White Man's grating tongue.

They were upstream. He could hear them clearly now. They were close enough for caution, but he had none. He raced across the sand of the dry arroyo.

A slice of moon and the faint glow of false dawn gave him just enough light to see them. Too much, for the scene seared into his memory the way a glance at Father Sun burns the eye, leaving behind an image that fades only with time. Decades would prove insufficient to cleanse his mind of the agonizing incandescence of that morning.

Many Flowers lay on the sand. Her cotton shift had been torn and casually cast aside. She was pinned beneath the pale bulk of a large, half-naked White Man, his breeches bunched below his knees. Two others knelt beside them, holding her arms and legs while his pallid buttocks pumped at her. Another pair fought with Cloud Peak across the stream bed. She struggled to rake fingernails across their eyes and reach them with her teeth. They were American soldiers. Though he had not seen it often, he recognized their uniform.

He added his own cry to those of his women as he raised his rifle to begin killing them. Only there were more among the trees, not many, but he hadn't noticed them before. One shouted something, probably a warning to his fellows, just as Jujul fired. The old Sharps bucked and threw up a spray of gravel beside the half-naked one, showering him and his companions with stinging debris. Jujul shouldn't have missed at that range, wouldn't have but for the shout. He frantically dug another cartridge from his pouch as the night lit up with muzzle flashes and their thin crackle rolled about him. Bullets swarmed like angry wasps. He found a cartridge, extracted the spent round and rammed the fresh one home.

He should have dived for cover, or maybe charged them, hoping they might panic and run, but he wasn't quite sane then. The big one had climbed off Many Flowers, his erection wilting as he looked down the muzzle of the Sharps. Many Flowers was still partially held, though she swatted at her enemies with a free arm and kicked with a foot. Cloud Peak had broken free. Her captors were too busy reaching for side arms to worry about reclaiming their prize. They drew and aimed as she launched herself toward the men who held Many Flowers. Her breast exploded as the short one's pistol fired, spraying them with her blood as she crumpled to the sand. Jujul swung the Sharps and centered it on the killer's chest, pulled the trigger, then watched him somersault backwards as the huge lead slug propelled his remains into the brush.

Something bit Jujul on the hip. It should have been sharply painful, but the wound went almost unnoticed. He was too consumed with grief and rage. He dug for another cartridge but the Sharps was torn from his grasp as one of the Gringos' bullets struck it and whined away. He found his knife and started toward them. The ones under the trees were too far for their hand guns to be accurate. It was why he still lived. But the big one, the half-naked one, was relatively close. He chose that one, knowing exactly what he would do to him with the knife. He went for the giant until his left leg stopped working and he found himself face down in the sand. He couldn't rise, so he crawled on, dragging the useless leg behind him, unaware of the slug that had torn away so much muscle from his thigh. He would teach the man what it cost to violate his women. He would teach them all, one by one.

Instead, the sun rose. Not in the Eastern sky where he should, but behind Jujul's eyes. Father Sun carried him away, took him to the Spirit World, where he dreamed sad, angry dreams of incalculable loss.

Cavalry to the Rescue

Jesus was driving because he knew the way and because, by the time they'd found Fitzpatrick, he wasn't in the best of shape for it. Tom Edgar poured for his party guests with a heavy hand and J.D. Fitzpatrick was not a man to refuse that particular form of hospitality.

The Ford bucked and complained as they bounced along the desolate trail that led to *Stohta U'uhig*. It echoed the unhappiness J.D. felt at finding himself lurching across the Papago Indian Reservation. He was having one of those bad mornings after. If he'd happened across a temperance meeting about then, he would have signed the pledge and given his undying loyalty to the cause, until chance placed a little hair of the dog in his path.

They snaked up a steep, rounded hill, the Ford moaning in low gear. J.D. only just managed to avoid joining it. The sun was still climbing the empty vault of sky but it was already like an oven, October or not. J.D. should have been grateful for how quickly he was sweating out the poisons, but he wasn't in the mood for grateful.

A miasma of heat waves obscured the horizon and provided a shimmering lake in the southeast that wasn't really there. J.D. watched the road unwind and tried not to think about how his head and stomach felt or how long it would be before he could get some sleep. Heavy is the head that wears the badge, he paraphrased to himself, apropos of nothing. Actually, his Deputy United States Marshal's badge was pinned to the inside of the jacket he'd tossed on the back seat when he gave up trying to use it as a pillow. It lay beside the fedora he usually wore, which, this morning, felt a few sizes smaller than usual.

The Ford finally crested the hill. As they started down its backside, J.D. spotted something ahead. He told Jesus to stop the car and he did, locking all four wheels in a shower of dust and gravel that left them broadside in the so-called road.

It was clear that Deputy Sheriff Jesus Gonzales didn't care for chauffeuring White Men around Pima County. He had developed a simple strategy to avoid the task. Whenever he was placed behind the wheel he drove without restraint. Stop meant foot to the floor, go just put the foot on a different pedal. It probably would have worked on J.D. if he hadn't been too miserable to complain, much less navigate for himself.

The door stuck when J.D. tried to let himself out and he had to shoulder it open. The effort made his head hurt worse but was strangely satisfying just the same. He stepped out onto the road. It was even hotter in the sun, but after hours of rattling and swaying in the confines of the Ford, the parched quiet of the desert was as welcome as a cold drink.

A grey-green forest stretched between jagged volcanic peaks. Up close, it wasn't an impressive forest. Its leafy canopy was sparse and seldom rose above head high, though thick saguaros and the spiked whips of ocotillo branches rose considerably farther. The forest's floor was covered with occasional clumps of grass and a myriad of sharp things, thorned and needled, protruding from a soil that was not much duller. The ground seemed equal parts sand, sharp gravel, broken rock, and dust. Teddy bears peered out of those woods, their soft, cuddly forms just one more desert mirage. These were cholla cactuses and their deceptive fur nothing but a pelt of wicked spines. Not a friendly landscape, J.D. decided. On his better days he appreciated its stark beauty for that very reason.

He tried the field glasses but they didn't help. Too much heat distortion. He was right, though. There were two or three rounded shapes that could be cars at the base of the low range ahead. They didn't match the form of the sharp boulders that dominated this bleak landscape. And they sparkled with what might be sun reflecting off glass or chrome. Few boulders do that.

He got back in the Ford and told Jesus to go ahead, then wished he'd remembered to add a qualifying slow to the instructions. Jesus fishtailed the Ford down the hill and through the valley below.

As they bounced across the desert, Fitzpatrick felt a sudden twisting in his guts that had nothing to do with last night's booze. It took him a few seconds to recognize it because he hadn't felt it since the hospital when he came home from Spain. That had been long enough to let him hope he might never feel it again. He suddenly, desperately, didn't want to go to the foot of that jumble of rocks ahead. The vegetation wasn't the same and the sun hit it from a different angle, but it reminded him of a place just outside a tiny village the maps had called Tres Santos. What happened there had cost him too much.

Their path across the valley was relatively straight, with only an occasional bone-jarring pot hole or dry drainage. Fitzpatrick tried taking a few deep breaths but choked on the dust that rolled in his window. When he could breathe again he was all right. The organism was back under control, panic lost to rationality. There was nothing to be afraid of here. Whatever had happened was over. He and Jesus were just cavalry to the rescue, not prey being lured into a trap. He had a .38 Smith & Wesson in a shoulder holster on the back seat with his jacket and hat. He thought about putting it on, then rejected the idea. He wouldn't need it, not even to reinforce a battered psyche.

They were cars all right. The Buick had gotten well up toward the pass before it went off the road and down among the tumble of broken rocks below. From the look of its roof it had rolled at least once before coming to rest a few yards from a chasm that probably housed an impressive waterfall every other year or so.

Somebody had tried to throw the Chevy off the road in a hurry and hide it behind a boulder that was about the size of a locomotive, but he'd been going too fast and its front end was crumpled up in an attempt to conform to the rock's irregular surface. There was some damp earth under it where the sun hadn't reached yet. They would have to install a new radiator before driving it home, after they pulled out the fenders so the replacement rims and tires it needed had enough room to turn.

By comparison, the Ford truck was almost untouched. Both its headlights and all its glass had been shot out by someone showing off with a rifle that threw slugs the size of artillery rounds. They'd gotten it back on the road, changed the shot-out tires, and were in the process of putting a patch on the one that was only flat because they'd driven over a young barrel cactus.

There were a couple of men being tended to in the shade of the rock behind the Chevy but both of them sat up to look as the Ford drove into view. There wasn't much blood and no covered bodies or suspiciously grave-like piles of stone so Fitzpatrick started relaxing. It was a mistake. He almost put his head through the windshield when Jesus stopped.

Starting a War

"…and when we came around this curve, somebody shot out a front tire on us, Luis lost control and we went off the road and hit something and went over and ended up down there," Larson said, still very excited and talking too fast as he pointed a thick finger at the remains of the Buick. He was keeping a white-knuckled grip on the carbine in his other hand. "The rest pulled over looking for cover, but, shit, Papagos can't drive worth a damn. The Chevy's totaled and we're just lucky there wasn't anything big in the way of the truck.

"All of us in the Buick got battered up some, but aside from a fractured arm and maybe some busted ribs, nobody's hurt bad. We just all of us piled out and hunkered down behind cover while they kept us pinned down from up there in the rocks and some bastard worked over the truck with a fucking cannon. We shot back some, but other than muzzle flashes, we never had any targets. I don't think we did them any harm.

"Then, all of a sudden, about dawn, they just quit. We stayed down for awhile, putting an occasional round up where they'd been, but they never answered. Maybe an hour ago I sent Drum Stomach and Sam Hawk-Bow up to scout it out. They tell me Jujul's men are all gone, but I had enough trouble getting them to even go take a look. No way I could convince them to follow the trail. Bastards could be just another hundred yards or so up the slope for all I know. That's why I'm keeping everybody down and mounting a guard and all."

"Good," J.D. told the overweight little man. He looked to be pushing thirty from one way or the other. If he'd been much older, J.D. would have figured him as a prime candidate for a stroke or heart failure. As it was, if he kept up this exciting lifestyle, he was going to get his weight back under control in spite of himself.

"Say, where are the rest of you?" the fat man asked. "You guys the advance scouts or what?"

J.D. felt like laughing but his head still hurt too much. "Sorry," he said. "Jesus and I are all you're going to get. Nobody else is coming."

"What the hell's going on?" Larson demanded, putting on his offended bureaucrat's heads-are-going-to-roll face. "I called at least a half-dozen agencies in Tucson last night. I told them I was bringing a squad of tribal police and volunteers out after a federal law violator and that I expected trouble and wanted help. Are you trying to tell me you're all they sent?"

"Uh-huh."

"Shit!" he said. "Somebody's going to pay for this." He finally took notice of the man he'd been talking to. J.D. didn't look impressive. He was on the back side of forty, tired, rumpled, and hung over. He was a tall, thin man, sort of a dark-haired Dashiell Hammett gone to seed. He hadn't spent his morning having a grand time playing Cowboys and Indians with real Indians either.

"Just who the hell are you, anyway?"

J.D. dug out his billfold and flashed his ID. "And I assume you must be Larson."

The fat man acknowledged it, though J.D. thought he would have been wiser to come up with an alias.

Larson looked at J.D., then back and forth between Jesus in the Ford down by the truck, and the rocks up above. "Shit," he said again. He should have let it go at that. Instead he launched into an outraged harangue, the gist of which had to do with the sort of incompetents who would send, unaccompanied, an old man and a Mexican to help put down the first Indian uprising in Arizona in a quarter of a century.

J.D. wasn't in the mood to listen. He shouted at Jesus to bring up the car. It slammed to a stop beside them, enveloping both in a cloud of dust that choked off Larson's tirade and didn't do J.D. all that much good either. He held his breath until he could begin to make out Larson's corpulent form through the swirling, sepia gloom.

"Hey, wait a minute," Larson coughed. "What are you doing?"

"The old man and the Mexican are going to take a look up ahead," J.D. said.

"You can't go up there alone. Let me get some men. If Jujul's not still up there he may be back in his village, thinking he's scared us off. We might just surprise the old bastard and bring him in."

"No thanks," J.D. replied. "You've done enough for one day, Mr. Larson. Jesus and I aren't the reinforcements you asked for. If you'd stayed around and waited for somebody to return your calls as you were instructed, you'd already know the government didn't want you out here starting a war. Technically, Jujul is guilty of inciting his people to violate a federal law requiring some of his men to register for possible induction, but there's considerable opposition to the idea of a peace-time draft in this country, or the suggestion one can take from it that we aren't going to be at peace much longer. Nobody wants you creating a *cause célèbre* for those people to rally behind. In other words, Larson, my instructions were to stop you, not help you. That or try to fix any blunders you might have already made."

"Why you...you..." Larson sputtered, rendered uncharacteristically epithetless. With a great effort of will he controlled himself enough to try again. "Listen. That fucking old Papago has broken a federal law, damaged tribal property, resisted arrest, and assaulted myself and other officers acting in the line of duty. This is my reservation and I want him in jail and not you or anybody else is going to stop me."

J.D. considered trying to explain. This being 1940, BIA people couldn't run around arresting whoever caught their fancy. But J.D. was out of patience. He reached over and took the carbine out of Larson's hands, swung it by the barrel, and shattered the stock on a nearby rock. He dropped the remains at the fat man's feet.

"If you annoy me again, Larson, I'm going to take you in on one of the John Doe federal warrants I've got and put you in a cell with some murderers and perverts and then lose the paperwork for a few weeks during which not even J. Edgar Hoover will be able to find you. Now shut your mouth and go help the remains of your posse get started back to Sells. We're going to take a look at the top of this pass and maybe see if we can find anybody in Jujul's village to apologize to. When we're done, we'll come back and pick up whoever won't fit in your truck. I suggest you not be one of them. If I find you here when we get back I just might leave you and let Jujul or the buzzards do what they like with you. I'd be doing the BIA a favor."

He wrenched at the door of the Ford and it stuck again, spoiling the effect of his exit a little, though maybe the violence with which he finally ripped it open made up for it. He got in and purposefully neglected to mention anything about going slow until they'd showered Larson with the dust and gravel of a Jesus-style departure.

The Gospel According to Fitzpatrick

They parked the Ford near the top of the pass and got out to look around. It wasn't hard to see where Jujul's men had waited. They'd gotten comfortable where they had a clear view of the path for a long way and where they'd be impossible to avoid.

"Only eight, ten men," Jesus said. "He left most of them back at the village."

J.D. just grunted. He was still trying to cool back down, suppress the violent urges the chubby little bureaucrat had inspired. At least, he was hardly conscious of his hangover anymore.

"Good spot," Jesus continued. "They'd have seen headlights coming practically forever, or heard the motors for miles, even if the posse tried driving in blind."

J.D. leaned over one of the rocks someone had used for a shooting station and looked down at Larson's crew.

"They weren't trying to kill anybody," he said. "I've got a clear view of at least half the ones who think they're still under cover down there."

He reached down and picked up a shell casing he'd kicked up from the dust and tossed it to Jesus. "What the hell is this?"

The Indians had picked up most of their brass but they'd been in enough of a hurry to miss some in the dark. Jesus examined it and let out a low whistle. "*Hay chingada!* Big mother, huh?" He rolled the casing around in his fingers like a shopper looking for a price tag. I've heard the old man's got a Sharps, an old-time buffalo gun, but I've never seen one of its loads. I don't know for sure if that's what this is, but that'd be my guess." He stuck it in his pocket.

"Jesus!" J.D. said. He pronounced it the English way so the deputy knew he wasn't being addressed. "That pompous ass could have gotten them all killed. He's just lucky nobody up here wanted to bother.

"Come on, Jesus," this time he made it rhyme with stay loose. "Let's go take a look at the village. Bet we won't find anybody home," he added as they got back in the Ford.

"Not at home, maybe," Jesus replied, "but somebody'll be watching. They'll want to see if anybody comes and what happens if they do."

The village was a random collection of crude adobe mud-brick houses with occasional round earth-covered lodges the Papago called *kihs* mixed in. There were also some ocotillo sheds, half a dozen ramadas, and a few ramshackle corrals. It all sat at the base of a low range of hills a couple of miles beyond the pass. A narrow scar of green pointed toward the village from where a water tank uphill leaked a lazy trickle down a thirsty slope. There were a few irregular fields along the primitive irrigation system, but nothing much in them. By October, anything that could survive the brutal heat of summer was long since harvested.

The place was deserted, though the former occupants didn't seem to have departed in a big hurry. At least they hadn't left much behind.

"Anybody else keeping an eye on us," J.D. asked as they got out of the Ford, "other than the one up in the rocks near the tank?"

It was Jesus who was supposed to be good at that sort of thing so he didn't mention that he hadn't noticed that one. "Just the fellow out in the brush beyond the corrals," he said.

"I don't think it'll do any good, but why don't you try talking them in? Maybe we can start working things out right now."

Jesus didn't think it would work either, but he gave it a shot. He was a big man, broad faced, broad shouldered, and broad bellied. He had a big voice too.

"*Chum ach dodolimdag,*" he shouted. "We are wanting peace. We are not wanting trouble. We are not the people who came this morning. We are not of the tribal council or the Bureau of Indian Affairs.

"You may know me. I am Deputy Sheriff Jesus Gonzales. I grew up beside your cousins at the San Xavier Mission. If you know that, you know I can be trusted. This White Man with me is a Federal Marshal, but, even so, he is honorable and also worthy of trust. Come, talk. Let us solve this while it is a fresh bud, before it blooms into something deadly, before the desert flows with the blood of the People."

Jesus went on like that for a while, but all it accomplished was to send both the watchers back into better cover. The only answer was a soft rustling breeze through the paloverdes and the shrill chatter of a nearby cactus wren.

J.D. prowled through the village while Jesus continued spreading the gospel according to Fitzpatrick. It was cool inside the adobes. He wadded up his jacket, tossed it in a corner, and stretched out, just trying to get comfortable for a few minutes. When he woke he felt like a man willing to take a chance on what life might offer again. He walked back out into the blinding daylight, yawning and rubbing his eyes. Jesus had found a shady spot under a mesquite where he could keep an eye on the watchers. He was smoking a cigarette. J.D. smiled sheepishly.

"They still out there?"

The deputy nodded.

"OK," J.D. said. "Let's leave them a gift, say a pack of your cigarettes. I'll see that you get reimbursed out of the federal budget."

J.D. reached into his pocket and pulled out a business card. "And leave this with the cigarettes."

Jesus produced an unopened pack of Lucky's and put it and the card out in plain view, a small stone on top so the breeze wouldn't carry off the latter. He was polite enough not to mention how unlikely it was that any of Jujul's people could read it, nor his opinion that he was the one most likely to be contacted, if either of them were. He was Mexican. The Desert People and the Mexicans had known each other for a lot of generations. They understood what to expect from each other. Both were still getting used to these pale-skinned late arrivals.

The two lawmen climbed back into the Ford while a mockingbird complained about the heat. This time J.D. drove.

Larson had left five volunteers behind at the ambush site. He hadn't exactly overcrowded the truck for the trip back. J.D. grumbled about it, but he jammed the posse in and they made the long, uncomfortable drive to Sells.

It was after sunset when they arrived. They dropped their passengers off at the federal building and went in to report to Reservation Superintendent Bill Fredericks, who, like J.D., had been in Tucson the night before. It was why Larson had been left in charge.

Fredericks was in, but he was busy. Larson was with him. They could tell because Fredericks' voice was sufficiently raised to carry clearly through his office door. They stood and listened for a few minutes, then J.D. grinned and offered to buy the deputy supper down the street.

"We'll come back later and mop up whatever's left of Larson's ego," J.D. said.

The deputy followed him out of the building, smiling with surprise. "Damn!" he exclaimed. "It wasn't what Fredericks was saying so much as how he said it. I never realized before what an expressive language English can be."

Worthy of His Passing

The village at the foot of the hill still smoldered. Sasaki had ordered this insignificant piece of North China burned during the night of October 19. By midmorning, little remained beyond a few piles of glowing cinders and smoking rubble. A cutting wind with the taste of Arctic climes teased the remaining flames and carried smoke and ash and sparks across the rutted road and abandoned fields.

It had rained lightly in the hour before dawn. The resulting puddles were skinning with sheet ice. Sunrise had brought light but not heat. Scudding low clouds maintained a sort of pulsing twilight. Sasaki considered the clouds and wondered if they would provide snow as a backdrop for the drama that would be acted out here.

For a change, it seemed, the Chinese offered him a worthy opponent. From the head of the valley, the hill appeared well fortified. Strands of barbed wire and sharpened stakes blocked the approaches. A pair of machine guns had been placed where they could guard the flanks and still overlap at the center. The defenders seemed securely dug in, occupying a series of trenches that crisscrossed the hilltop.

It was Sergeant Itho's squad that had burned the village. Since dawn they had maintained their position in a convenient ditch at the base of the hill. From there, they kept up a steady fire at the enemy above. Sasaki had expected the assault on the village, and this probe, to draw an angry response. It had not. These troops held their place and their fire, waiting on some greater threat or, as the bodies of several men of Itho's squad attested, good targets.

It was satisfying to be offered the resistance of an opponent with some knowledge of the art of war instead of the confused mob hysterics Sasaki had come to associate with resistance to Japan's conquest of China. It was also depressing to realize how easily he could brush aside even this almost competent defense. He could call in artillery, shell this position until there was no longer a high ground for them to hold. He could go around them, for they had no support on either side, then see if the back of this hill was as well fortified and if they had enough men to defend it from two directions at once. He could call in tanks and let them walk across the stakes and wires and level the earthworks. All these things, Sasaki could do, but simple slaughter was without beauty. It lacked honor and glory.

Captain Kozo Sasaki was a warrior by birth and by choice, not by proclamation. He expected to fulfill his destiny on the battle-field. He considered himself an artist. Conquest was his canvas. War was the text he must shape into poetry, the clay he would mold from confused struggle into magnificent contest. Perhaps, he hoped, fate had delivered this insignificant hill into his hands so that he might make of it a place worthy of his passing.

There was no honor in exploiting the weakness of a weakling. Sasaki determined to avoid the militarily sound approach. He would take on his enemy's strength, and crush it.

His officers had their instructions. He gestured for his orderly and the man ran to his side and bowed. "Now," Sasaki told him. The man bowed again, then fired a single flare across the valley toward the hill. Legs spread, hands folded behind his back, Sasaki stood and watched the battle unfold.

The result was disappointing. Their machine guns chattered only briefly, then lay still. They stood at their posts for a single volley and a few scattered shots before throwing down their weapons and breaking before his charge. After that, only Japanese guns spoke above the wind and blended with the cheers of the victorious and the cries of the dying.

After, as his troops formed in the valley, preparing to load into the trucks that would carry them to the next village, Sasaki walked through the ruins of his enemy's fortifications. From the fabric of desire his mind had woven a more formidable opponent than fact revealed. They had dug in here because they were too cold and tired and hungry to run any further. Like a whipped mongrel they had found a dark corner from which to growl and nip, briefly, before cringing and accepting the inevitable. They had not shown discipline. They held their fire because they had no ammunition to waste. They broke because even their despair could not match their terror. Sasaki felt diminished, and for the first time that day, he felt the cold.

The Chinese dead lay where they had fallen, pitiful rags barely covering gaunt bodies that would feel cold and fatigue and hunger no more. Their officer's beheaded corpse lay among his followers and Sasaki cleaned the man's blood from his sword on a convenient shirt tail. Sasaki would have fought to the end, using hands and teeth if he could find no other weapons. But this man, seeing his troops break, surrendered. The same exposure to European or American tactics that had allowed him to offer the pretense of a fight had led him to see war as a contest where, win or lose, the strategists would later share a snifter of brandy and discuss the battle's highlights. Sasaki could not respect a man who was not prepared to act as an example, and, if need be, die gloriously for the sake of glory. This Chinese officer was not without some shallow worth, or he would have been far from the fighting with his generals, but it was insufficient. This place could have been an homage to the artistry of carnage. It had delivered only shame. The officer had paid the price of Sasaki's disappointment.

Grant me just one worthy enemy, Sasaki begged the souls of his ancestors. If they heard his prayer they gave no answer. There was only the wind tearing at the ragged uniforms of the dead and numbing his mind and body.

Where within this endless nation were its military leaders? Sasaki had not found them, nor encountered evidence of their existence. Could it be that by 1940, China held only peasants and bandits and no warriors? Perhaps the might of Imperial Japan was unstoppable, but other peoples had faced similar odds and fought beautifully. The American Indians never had a chance against the invading European hordes. Those outnumbered and virtually unarmed savages produced countless military geniuses, men who held at bay the irresistible might of their enemy for impossible periods of time. Where were China's Chief Joseph and Red Cloud and Geronimo? Oh, those were men who understood the honor, the glory, of war.

For a brief moment, Sasaki wished he had been born Chinese. It was impossible to demonstrate his genius at his chosen trade against incompetent opponents and inferior troops. A challenge worthy of him would be to organize this infinity of peasants into a guerilla force that struck and ran and fought where it was not expected. To force the ponderous Japanese advance to pause and turn its full attention upon him, then to defeat it anyway. Such an effort would earn him the adoration that was his due, the recognition for which he was born.

Sasaki sheathed his sword and pulled his collar up against the wind. He stalked down the hill and through the smoldering remains of the village to where his orderly rushed to open the door of his staff car. It was time for them to move forward again. Time to find themselves another village. This was China. There would always be another village.

The Grace of a Harlot

The multicolored mosaic dome of the Pima County Courthouse was out of place, even in the heart of Tucson's unusual potpourri, where bland modern structures of brick and stone haphazardly sprouted among more ancient, flat-roofed, squat adobes. The dome fit in with all the grace of a harlot attending a church social, J.D. Fitzpatrick thought. It belonged in North Africa instead of Southern Arizona, though it was impossible to blame even a dome for preferring the latter on this white-hot fall Monday.

Fitzpatrick lurked in the doorway of a restaurant south of the courthouse on Church Street, considering lunch and the inappropriateness of the domed building's presence in the middle of the Upper-Sonoran Desert. No more so, he decided, than the twelve story Pioneer Hotel or the Ionic columned city hall, or, for that matter, J.D. Fitzpatrick.

The restaurant was a middle-aged brick structure. Its deteriorating charm made it a certain target of future urban renewal. Too much deterioration, not enough charm. Again, he decided, not unlike himself.

Fitzpatrick's collar was loose and his tie comfortably askew. The brim of his fedora was pulled low over his eyes. He looked weary, bored, but he was carefully surveying every figure who exited the courthouse onto Church Street.

He was tired and a little hung over. Neither state was unusual so he hardly noticed them. He felt the urge for a cigarette. It was amazing how often that craving still tickled his subconscious, even three years after the doctors convinced him to quit. He was also getting uncomfortably hot. October's sun seared its way across the cloudless sky. He stepped back into the shade of the doorway a little. The howl of an evaporative cooler within nearly drowned out the street sounds. It even wafted an occasional cool breeze through the cafe's screen door which seemed there primarily to keep the flies, buzzing and bumping against its rusty surface, from escaping.

In spite of his mild discomforts he continued to monitor the parade of figures leaving the courthouse until he saw the one he'd been watching for. A dark-skinned man, wearing a suit and carrying a briefcase, walked purposefully out of the building and turned south. From a distance he looked like a Negro. There weren't many Negroes in Tucson, fewer still who walked around downtown in a suit with a briefcase. He drew stares from those he passed as he strode in Fitzpatrick's direction, but he either ignored or was oblivious to them.

As the man drew nearer it became clear he wasn't a Negro. His facial features were all wrong and his black hair was fine and straight, an ebony mane neatly trimmed and parted with tonsorial skill. He wasn't a Mexican either. His face didn't quite match any of the more familiar ethnic categories.

Fitzpatrick waited until he was just in front of the restaurant to step out and intercept him. The dark man tried to both dodge and ignore the tall figure who suddenly blocked his way until J.D. put out a hand and touched him on the shoulder.

"Mr. Parker," J.D. said. "We need to talk."

"I haven't the time," the dark man replied. "I'm really quite busy." He glanced up at Fitzpatrick as if to force this obstacle from his path by sheer will power. Fitzpatrick was accustomed to dealing with people who preferred to avoid him. He used his other hand to pull back his suit coat and reveal the badge pinned just inside the lapel.

"Perhaps you could slip me into your schedule for just a few minutes," Fitzpatrick suggested.

"Well, OK," Parker reluctantly agreed, "a *very* few minutes."

Fitzpatrick gestured toward the restaurant and the two men stepped inside, dodging the rush of flies that took advantage of the open screen to make a dash for freedom. They found an empty table and ordered two coffees. While they waited to be served, the dark man lit up a cigarette. J.D. looked at it longingly.

The coffee arrived and both men sipped it, then wisely used cream and sugar to kill the taste.

"What can I do for you, Marshal?" the dark man asked.

"Well, you could tell me where to find Jujul." J.D. pronounced it right.

A newspaperman from San Francisco, in town to satisfy his wife's annual urge to remind herself why she'd left home in the first place, occupied an adjacent table. He preferred to avoid the gradually building tension at his in-laws' so he had walked downtown to find a place where he could sit quietly and read. He was always curious about the competition. Even competition that really wasn't, like Tucson's two small dailies. That was why he'd been browsing through the morning edition of the *Arizona Daily Star* as he nursed a cup of coffee and a piece of pie with a filling unidentifiable by taste, texture, or color. The lead stories debated England's chances of surviving the Nazi blitz and Willkie's chances of unseating Roosevelt (neither considered likely). There was a more interesting item that began at the bottom of the front page before being passed deep within to compete for attention with ads for console radios and phonographs and a sale on women's nylons. "Papagos Attack Federal Agents!" The story indicated there had been armed resistance to the Selective Service Act on the nearby Papago Indian Reservation. It caught his notice.

So had the tall man waiting in the doorway. His curiosity ratcheted up another notch when he saw the man step out and intercept the dark one. He'd seen the flash of badge. Still, their conversation hadn't meant much to him until he heard the name "Jujul." His mind translated those softened consonants and rolling vowels into the name of the Papago draft resister mentioned in the Star's story. That was when he began to pay close attention. They hadn't noticed him. He liked it that way. He raised the newspaper ever so slightly until his eyes just peered over its top and he could watch the expressions on their faces. Otherwise, he didn't move. Like some urban chameleon, he faded into his surroundings and became invisible.

"Surely you've heard of the attorney-client relationship, Marshal. Its confidentiality is nearly as sacred as the confessional's."

"I assume you have some proof you've been retained as his counsel, then," J.D. countered.

The dark man looked uncomfortable.

"Look, Mr. Parker," J.D. continued. "I'm not interested in playing games here. You want to gain sympathy for yourself, pick up a few more anti-BIA votes in the next tribal election, fine. You did a real nice job of that in the courtroom, all those motions to quash warrants and change venue and what not. But, bottom line, what kept them from being charged with anything more than assault is what I did behind the scenes. Now I don't give a damn who gets credit. All I want is to see that nobody gets killed over something this trivial. Is there one man in Jujul's village who can meet the Selective Service literacy requirement? Ask your client that, Mr. Parker, then tell him what the answer means. Tell him, so far, nobody wants to make a big deal out of this. Nobody's been seriously hurt and if we clear this up quickly, we can make sure no charges get filed by the federal government. But it has to be quick. The longer this goes on, the more likely it is somebody's going to get in the way of some of the lead that's been flying around out there. When that happens this turns into a different ball game. So how about it? Do you know where he is?"

The dark man didn't like being lectured. His backbone straightened against the whiplash of J.D.'s words.

"I have absolutely no intention of answering that. There are other issues here, sir. None of those people are allowed to vote, except in those tribal elections you mentioned. When they have equal representation, then, maybe, Selective Service registration might be appropriate. In the meantime....Well, I will, of course, relay your message to my client, and, if he so chooses, his reply to you."

The reporter's mind was racing. So, there was a militant wing to the Papago tribe, one that supported violence in pursuit of its rights. The noble savage came alive in his mind as he began creating the article he would telegraph back to his paper. He missed the tall man's disappointed grumble.

"That's what I thought. You don't know where he is either."

"Good day, Marshal," the dark man said angrily. He got up and stalked out the screen door, leaving his coffee almost untouched and J.D. with the bill.

The reporter was a master of the provocative half-truth. The article he telegraphed to his newspaper was one of his best. Even so, it didn't cause much of a stir, buried among the avalanche of stories which daily documented a world going mad.

One of those who read the article was the Third Assistant Secretary to the Attaché for Cultural Affairs in the Japanese Consulate in San Francisco. It was his job to look for such items, translate and then forward them in a special diplomatic pouch to an office in Tokyo. The reporter would have been amazed to discover where his story made its biggest impact.

Browsing for Ethnographers

J.D. found out he owed the Papago Tribal Police the price of a carbine when he got back to the office. The United States would take it out of his next pay check. It would wipe out the gas and mileage allowance he was supposed to get for taking his own car out to *Stohta U'uhig*, but he didn't complain. He hadn't realized Larson was just borrowing the gun. Still, the look on the fat little bureaucrat's face had made it worth every cent.

Larson owed them a lot more, repair and towing charges on a tribal Chevrolet, and some extensive glass replacement on the Ford pickup. If Uncle Sam was also taking it out of his pay, Larson was going to wait awhile before he saw another check. The little fat man didn't owe anything to anybody on the Buick, unless it was a finance company. It was his car and his responsibility. Larson was still the number two BIA representative on the reservation, but by a pretty fine thread. If J.D. happened on a pair of scissors he'd know what to do with them.

With amazing speed for a series of bureaucracies, the BIA in Washington consulted with the Reservation Supervisor who consulted, in turn, with his tribal police. They discussed it with state and county authorities, and the Federal Marshal's office put in its two cents. They all left it up to the local draft board, which went through its own agonies before deciding Jujul's band was a bad precedent. If the village could be persuaded to come in and register peacefully, fine, no need to press charges. But if they couldn't be convinced by gentler means, they would have to be brought in by force. That left a chance to keep things calm. Larson remained the fly in the ointment. Despite pressure to the contrary, he'd filed assault charges in federal court against Jujul and a dozen Papago Juan Does. As Deputy U.S. Marshal for Southern Arizona, J.D. was responsible for enforcement of both matters. His reaction was not exactly delight.

That was why he'd had his little chat with the attorney Parker. Jesus Gonzales had suggested he should start with the man. "He probably won't know anything yet, but he may find out."

John Parker, according to Deputy Sheriff Gonzales, was a half-breed. His father had been a missionary to the Papago; his mother, a convert. The Reverend Parker must have chosen his profession out of some confused need to offset the darker side of his nature. He preached the gentle love of a redeemer, whose personal representative he claimed to be, then threatened the fires of hell and eternal damnation on those who refused the salvation he offered. He drank. He beat his wife and child. He sowed his seed in more than one unwilling member of his flock, and left behind a trail of bastard siblings for his only legitimate son. He died, so drunk he choked on his own vomit.

John Parker grew up with a special loathing for his father and the culture that produced him. But his father survived long enough to force him to face that culture and to know it. He sent his son off to far away schools, and made him stay until he came back a lawyer.

Parker would try to get himself involved with Jujul's case, the deputy suggested, because it was a challenge to the BIA and the tribal council. He regularly ran for a seat on that council on a militantly anti-Anglo platform and he just as regularly lost. Any cause that might harm those agencies would draw him "like *caca* draws flies."

Gonzales was right. The moment the court began to consider Larson's charges against Jujul and his band, Parker was there, an endless source of objections and legal technicalities. All of which had only delayed and not halted the issuing of warrants. It would get some publicity though, and that was probably all the attorney ever intended. After their brief interview, J.D. was confident Parker didn't know any more than he did, at least not yet. But he also had the uncomfortable feeling the attorney wouldn't cooperate, even to stop bloodshed. Not unless there were some way for him to profit from it too.

So J.D. began to consider where to look for a bunch of Papagos who've suddenly gone feral. Their reservation was big enough to hold all of Delaware and Rhode Island with room to spare. Some sixty miles of its southern border, hardly marked, was with Mexico. Most of the rest of its boundaries were just as unclear and similarly desolate. Jujul could be almost anywhere.

J.D. spent Tuesday asking everyone, Jesus Gonzales, the Papago Tribal Police, the people (Larson excepted) in Bill Fredericks' office. He asked everyone with an opinion, and he got lots of them, but the bottom line was always the same—Mexico. The Papago had seasonal villages. Many spent half their year south of the border. Jujul would know enough to understand that the BIA and tribal police had no authority in Mexico. They would just head south a little earlier than usual. Probably. He alerted the border patrol. Now, what to do next?

There was something that bothered J.D. about all those opinions. They might have come from people who either were or knew Papagos, but in every instance they were tame Papagos, Americanized Papagos. To find out what sort of folk Jujul and his band were, he was either going to have to go out in the less affected parts of the reservation and ask people who would be reluctant to answer, or find someone else who might already know.

J.D. parked his Ford in a faculty slot, leaving a U.S. Marshal's business card under the wiper blade. It had saved him a lot of parking tickets from the City of Tucson and seemed a good bet to be just as effective at the University of Arizona.

The campus was a verdant oasis of neatly trimmed lawns and palm-lined drives, lying behind low walls of volcanic stone. The library stood just inside the main gate on the left. It was a large red-brick building, light on the ivy. Inside, schools of serious-eyed students circled the card catalogue, darting in to nibble at the contents of its drawers in a continuous learning frenzy. He got out a notebook and cautiously joined them. There were depressingly few listings, and all those proved to be no more than references to passing comments in general texts. No one had seen fit to publish the sort of tome he wanted. There were several eighteenth century Spanish documents in the special collections section, but they were as apt to give him an inaccurate view as a result of their age as he was getting from his modernized informants. He tried the information desk. A frumpy, thin-shouldered woman of indeterminate age hid behind glasses so thick it seemed unlikely she could read anything in her place of employment.

"You might wish to browse through the various ethnographic publications in the library's collections," she offered in a whisper. "I'm sure there have been several valuable articles over the last half century or so."

When he discovered the majority of those publications had yet to be indexed, he decided to go browsing for ethnographers instead.

The Arizona State Museum was directly across the palm-lined drive. Its dim interior was deserted except for an elementary school class which crowded around a distant exhibit while each member shouted questions at their befuddled guide. There was a studious looking woman behind the information desk who could have been a twin to the one across the street. He asked her who could tell him the most about the Papago.

"Spencer," she whispered.

He had trouble hearing her over the kids. "Where do I find this Spencer?" he whispered back.

"What?" she asked, cupping an ear.

He asked again in a normal voice. What the hell, it wasn't going to disturb the kids.

She frowned her disapproval but provided an intricate set of directions. He followed them faithfully and got thoroughly lost. After inquiring of three students arguing the merits of isolationism as they sat beside the campus' centerpiece fountain, he finally found the Department of Anthropology. There was another one there, behind the secretary's desk. Triplets, he thought, or a good argument for environment over heredity. At least this one didn't feel compelled to whisper when she asked what he wanted.

"Spencer," he told her.

"L.J. or M.B.?"

"I don't know," J.D. admitted. I'm looking for the guy who works with the Papago."

"L.J.," she decided for him. She gave him still more intricate directions. This time they worked.

It was a classroom filled with partitions and desks, not students' desks, full-sized ones. There was a sign on the wedged-open door that proclaimed this to be the Department of Anthropology

Graduate Research and Teaching Assistants' Office. It also gave a list of names. J.D. peeked inside. There weren't many people there but L.J. Spencer was one of them.

He looked up with a pleasantly surprised smile and said, "J.D., what are you doing here?"

It took J.D. a moment to put a name with the face but when he noticed the sign on the desk said Larry Spencer, it helped. Tucson wasn't such a big town that, having cracked the social whirl, you could easily miss anyone else who had managed to do the same. He'd met Larry at a party, several parties, actually. If he'd ever known his last name was Spencer, he'd forgotten. J.D. wasn't that good on names and faces from parties, especially the ones he met later in the evening. This face was attached to a big, good looking, athletic lad. J.D. seemed to remember he was some kind of archaeologist, which made him wonder if the third triplet hadn't sent him on yet another wild goose chase. He also remembered that the kid had been very curious about Spain and the Abraham Lincoln Brigade. J.D. didn't like to talk about Spain so he hadn't liked talking to Larry Spencer. All of which had something to do with why he barely recalled him.

J.D. needed information, though, so he was polite and friendly and tried it from the top. When he finished, Larry cleared it up for him.

"I see what's happened," he grinned. "It's Mary you want. Mary's my wife. She's a grad student here too, you probably remember her." J.D. didn't. "She's the Papago expert, has all her preliminary research done and is about to start her field work. Me, I've worked with a lot of Papagos, used them as crew on some of my digs. When you assumed your Papago authority would be a man, that's where the confusion set in."

Actually, what J.D. had assumed was that he was looking for a faculty member and not a student. He put it a little more tactfully, though.

"Strange that an anthropology department right on the edge of the reservation wouldn't have somebody who's a Papago specialist." He was still hoping that might get him the name of a professor who, if not an expert, at lest knew them pretty well.

"That's part of what got Mary interested," Larry confided. "Very few people have spent much effort on studying and describing

Papago culture. The tribe didn't fight any glamorous wars like the Apache or Navajo, don't have picturesque villages like the Hopi and Pueblo, and don't produce any collectable artifacts, aside from some very nice basketry, that anybody is much interested in. Dr. Sherwood is the Southwestern Indian man on the faculty," (J.D.'s hopes rose) "but he's into Navajos. He only started mentioning the Papago in his lectures in more than a passing way when Mary became his teaching assistant and started writing them for him," (and J.D.'s hopes fell). A little of the disappointment must have shown in his face. "Mary may not have lived with them yet, but she knows Papagos as well as any living White. If anybody can tell you what you want to know, she's the one."

It was probably an exaggeration, but having no other hot leads to follow, J.D. decided he might as well talk to the girl. He asked where and when he could see her. Larry decided her schedule was too hectic for the remainder of the day and most of the next. "Why don't you come over for supper tomorrow night," he suggested. "We can chat in comfort and without distractions." J.D. had the sinking feeling the kid wanted to chat about Spain and the Civil War, not the Papago. He tried to think of a reasonable excuse that would still give him a chance to pump the girl for whatever she might know. He couldn't come up with anything convincing off the top of his head. What the hell. Maybe she'd turn out to be a good cook, and if the boy archaeologist was too much of a pest he could always plead urgent business the next day and make a run for it.

"OK," J.D. agreed. "Where do you live and when should I get there?"

"Oh good," Larry said. He jumped up and grabbed J.D.'s hand, sealing the bargain with an overflow of enthusiasm seldom encountered outside a used car lot.

Rita Hayworth on a Good Day

Mary Spencer was late so she slipped quietly in through the classroom's back door. Dr. Sherwood stopped lecturing to give her a cold stare while the rest of the class turned to see who was causing the problem. She found a seat near the door and gave Sherwood a pretty smile, and a flash of tanned thigh. He hurrumphed and bent back over his notes, trying to recall what he'd been saying.

Most of the class probably thought she'd just made a bad impression. They were wrong. She'd done that a long time ago. It was early enough in the semester for most of them to be unaware she was their teaching assistant, and not in danger of flunking on the basis of an occasional tardy arrival.

Dr. Sherwood was a man on whom she could never have made a good impression. For all his education, he was a firm believer in the myth that a woman's place was behind her husband instead of beside him, and there in silent acquiescence to fulfill his every want and need. A woman's day should consist of washing, cooking, sewing, cleaning, and maybe plowing the south forty in her spare time. Having babies and mothering them shouldn't interfere with the smooth running of her husband's household or keep his meals from being on time, his socks from being darned, his shirts from being ironed, or the south forty from getting plowed. Not too surprisingly, Dr. Sherwood was a bachelor, having yet to encounter a woman who could match his ideal.

"Ahem, yes," he was saying. He'd liked that flash of thigh, though he probably thought a proper young woman would show only about that much flesh during the sex act itself, and then demurely.

Mary suddenly realized the poor old dear had completely lost track of where he'd been in his lecture. She knew he couldn't have been very far along, she wasn't that late, but she couldn't help him. He'd stopped talking to give her that cold, disapproving look the moment she came into the room. Finally, one of her fellow graduate students who was auditing the course took pity on the professor.

"You were going to tell us about the Hohokam, sir."

Dr. Sherwood hurrumphed again, took a quick peek over the top of his glasses in Mary's direction in case some thigh was still visible, discovered it wasn't, and said, "Yes, exactly. Yes, that's right. The Hohokam." He'd found it in his notes.

"The name Hohokam is a bastardization," he said, pausing for a round of titters from the young innocents whom college had once again exposed to a term with which they were quite familiar, but felt they shouldn't be, "of the Pima/Papago word *hekihukam*. It means 'an old thing.' It was the closest we Europeans could come to pronouncing the word they gave us when we asked about the impressive ruins that are scattered about their homeland. Though they didn't realize it, it is quite likely that the modern Pima and Papago, who are but two branches of the same tribe, are the descendants of the Hohokam and once possessed a more technically advanced and economically successful adaptation to their environment. There are many theories regarding the disappearance of the Hohokam and the advent of the Pima/Papago peoples. Plague, drought, conquest. Such answers, if they are to be found, are better left to the spade and trowel of our archaeological colleagues. What concerns us in this overview of the peoples of the Southwest is their culture."

Mary leaned forward, opened her notebook, and began jotting down what she wanted to pick up at the market for supper. Dr. Sherwood nervously consulted his notes to see if she'd caught him in a mistake. Mary had pretty much written this lecture for him, all but the pomposity which he'd added by himself. The Papago were her specialty. She knew a lot more about them than he did. In fact, she probably already knew more than anyone else in the department, even though it closely hugged the border of *Papa-gueria*. When she finished her dissertation, she would be *the* expert.

Sugar, she wrote. That was easy enough. They'd run out of sugar with Larry's second cup of coffee that morning and Larry hated coffee that wasn't two or three teaspoons sweet. It was a start, but didn't solve anything. Such as, first and foremost, what she wanted to serve her dinner guest.

Just what sort of food would a man like J.D. Fitzpatrick like? He was mature, he was worldly, what wouldn't he like? It was stupid, she told herself, but she wanted to impress him. Stupid because she was already married, had been for three years, and, even if it wasn't what she'd fantasized, she wasn't unhappy, wasn't looking for an alternative. Stupid, maybe, but fact. The man fascinated her. When she thought about him she found herself wishing America was a polyandrous society. No such luck. In fact, the part of America she occupied contained more than its share of Mormons, some of whom were still living at the opposite extreme. It was high time a woman founded a religion, she thought, and set down laws and customs that favored females for a change. Dr. Sherwood wouldn't like that. Now that she thought about it, neither would Larry. While he would prove downright narrow-minded about sharing her with one or more fellow husbands, she knew he would adjust to a polygynous relationship with hardly a second thought, except, possibly, delight.

Spanish food, she decided. Not Mexican, Spanish. Ruth Gibson said her husband had told her J.D. came to Arizona, in part, to recover from wounds and a severe lung condition after fighting in Spain. She'd told Mary he was a hero there. Of course, she'd also said he was a Communist, but not even F.D.R.'s administration went around appointing active members of that party to Deputy United States Marshal's positions, no matter how heroic they happened to be.

Spanish food was a terrific idea, or an absolutely awful one. If J.D. fought and almost died there it might revive unpleasant memories. In fact, since the Fascists had won, that would be almost inevitable. OK, she decided, no Spanish food. It was a step. Now she only needed to eliminate a few hundred other national cuisines.

J.D. was a bachelor. That meant he probably ate out a lot, or confined himself to simple sorts of home cooking. She supposed he was accustomed to lots of cheap cuts of fried beef and a variety of chicken dishes. She could make a pork roast with all the fixings. That was bound to be a nice change, but what if he was Jewish? With a name like Fitzpatrick? But then his mother could have been Jewish. There was that chance in a thousand he was kosher. So OK, she told herself, no pork.

She knew some good Mexican and Chinese recipes, but those were two types of ethnic foods that abounded in Tucson's restaurants. That let them out.

She could be really original and prepare a Papago meal. She even sort of knew how a few were made, but it was already afternoon and J.D. was coming for supper that night. She'd have to drive clear out to the mission to get the right ingredients. There just wouldn't be enough time.

Well, fuck it, she thought. Larry hated it when she said fuck. Dr. Sherwood would probably have a heart attack on the spot if he even dreamed she knew the word. A tendency to that and a few other salty phrases hadn't damaged her reputation in local society nearly as much as she feared. Anthropologists are allowed an uncommon level of eccentricity, especially when they happen to resemble Rita Hayworth on a good day.

Fuck it! She'd buy the best steaks she could find and let Larry cook them on the grill in the back yard, and she'd make a simple garden salad and a vegetable dish and top everything off with a chocolate rum cake. If it all turned out to be a disaster, she could just eat cake until she got blind.

Below sugar she wrote steaks. It sent Dr. Sherwood running back to his notes. If she timed it right she could keep the professor at a peak of anxiety for the remainder of his class.

At a complex point of the lecture concerning Pima/Papago religion, she wrote down chocolate under steaks, experimentally accompanying it with a faint frown which she aimed in the doctor's direction. He went into a coughing fit while he searched his notes and memory for the error he was sure she'd caught him in. She stopped paying attention.

Ruth had also said she'd heard J.D. had the most awful scars. One, like a knife wound, or maybe a sword, across his left shoulder and down his chest. Ruth was incurably romantic. Hers was the sort of mind to convert the Spanish Civil War into a swashbuckling adventure and J.D. into the Errol Flynn lead, swinging about the countryside from convenient ropes that undoubtedly hung from the Spanish sky, sabre clenched in his teeth, smoking pistols at his belt, bared chest sporting those dramatic scars.

Ruth had told her Maggie Edgar was her source of information about the scars. The Edgars had a swimming pool and apparently J.D. had taken advantage of it. Maggie had thought him a marvelous swimmer, but it was the scars that really grabbed her. There were three other scars, she'd said, along his right side. One was just below his shoulder, one in his side, and one in his thigh. They were small round white scars, pairs, front and back, and she thought they might have been from bullets. Then Ruth had blushed and gotten giggly and said Maggie had told her the scars were spaced in such a way that it seemed quite likely there was a fourth pair where it would be hidden by his bathing suit. Mary had been full of that same dreamy, girlish curiosity too, until she heard about the fourth wound. Then, all of a sudden, it hit her. It would have taken a fully automatic weapon like a machine gun to place four shots in such a neat row. Her imagination immediately showed her J.D. lying torn and bleeding in the dirt and it hadn't seemed romantic anymore. J.D.'s quiet intensity, the way he seemed to watch everyone and everything from a distance, made her wonder if there weren't inner scars as well, wounds to the spirit. She'd felt a sudden urge to take him in her arms and hold him and tell him it was all right. And she'd discovered the urge was not entirely platonic. That was where it got complicated, because she still loved Larry, didn't want to do anything to hurt him. And yet she desired a man she hardly knew.

Fuck it, she thought. She wrote rum under chocolate and underlined it three times. Lots of rum. She didn't even notice what it did to the flow of Dr. Sherwood's lecture.

Who Could Forget

J.D. had spent most of the intervening time back in the library. He'd even found a couple of articles on the Papago. By the time he set out for his dinner engagement he knew the rudiments to the manufacturing process of Papago baskets and the gist of a couple of their songs. He didn't think Sinatra needed to feel threatened.

The Spencers lived in a neighborhood west of the university, most of which hadn't existed half a century before. It was a mixed bag, ranging from expensive to modest middle class. There were lots of grassy yards filled with shade trees and flowering plants, and the houses were of a style that made you think you were only a couple of miles from a Southern California beach. Their home was one of the nice ones. The boat-tailed Auburn roadster sitting in the driveway indicated that academic excellence and scholarships weren't all the Spencers had going for them. Somebody's mommy and daddy had money.

J.D. went up a shady walk between flowering shrubs and climbed the steps to a generous porch. It was an ideal spot for rocking chairs and long summer evenings. He rang the bell. Mary Spencer answered it and he remembered her after all. Who could forget?

She was tall and slender, with all her curves in the right places. If that wasn't enough, she topped it off with a classically beautiful face. Helen of Troy should have looked like Mary Spencer. Maybe she had. J.D. would have launched a ship for her.

She was wearing a pair of slacks and a blouse, both too large, and no make up. She seemed to be trying to hide, rather than accentuate, what nature had given. It didn't work. She was just too spectacular, regardless of disguise.

He'd met her at a party and noticed the ring before anybody got around to making it formal and telling him her name had a Mrs. tacked on the front of it. J.D. hadn't been involved in a serious relationship with a woman since before Spain and he made it a practice not to fool around with other men's wives, even when only physical needs were involved. He didn't let it matter even if they were bored or beautiful, so he'd simply written her off. She was great to look at but he hadn't bothered getting to know her. He didn't remember her in connection with the boy archaeologist, but he certainly hadn't forgotten her. Women who look like that inspire masculine recall. And she was also intelligent enough to be working on a graduate degree. Beauty and brains could be a very dangerous combination.

"Hello, J.D.," she said. "You probably don't remember me. I'm Mary."

"Oh, I remember you all right," he said, then decided he'd done so too enthusiastically. It wouldn't be a good idea to tell her he remembered her because she was easily the most beautiful woman he'd ever met. It would have sounded like a corny line even if she was single, and she wasn't. He didn't want it to sound like a come on.

"At the Gibson's, I think," he said. "Some middle-aged professor of classics decked out in tweeds, bow tie, and an affected accent was pontificating on the situation in Europe. He said something about how, if Hitler was persecuting the Jews, it was because they're so cliquish, so rigidly incapable of blending into the culture where they live. They were bringing most of their troubles on themselves. You straightened him out. Made him realize, probably for the first time, how equally out of place in Tucson's culture he was. I seem to recall a colorful phrase or two that you used."

"Oh fuck!" she said. It came out involuntarily and she blushed.

"That was one of them," J.D. agreed, accelerating the process.

She rolled her eyes. "Time for the cake," she muttered. J.D. heard, but didn't understand. Before he could ask for a clarification she went on. "So much for my sweet and innocent image."

She smiled. It lit up the world. J.D. hadn't realized how dark it had been until then. He stood there and felt foolish and awkward, like he'd suddenly returned to puberty. He expected his face to start breaking out again. He brushed a hand at a cowlick he'd tamed in his mid-teens. Cut it out, he told himself, simultaneously delivering a swift mental kick to the seat of his pants. She's married. You can't have her.

"If being in the presence of a woman with a sailor's fondness for expressive vocabulary won't offend you too much, come in. I promise I'll try to watch my language."

She took his hat, gave it to a maple hall tree, and led him inside. The living room was large and comfortable with more than its share of overfilled bookshelves. Colorful Indian pots stood on the mantel, and blankets and intricate baskets hung where you would have expected to find reproductions of the masters or originals of those who never would be. He followed her, surprised to find his feet still worked and that he could nod and make appropriate, if simple, responses in her presence. He rather expected to fall down and maybe drool a little.

"Larry's out back, burning some otherwise perfectly good steaks on his grill," she explained. J.D. hadn't even started to miss him. "I let him ruin the meat because it makes what I fix seem so much better by comparison. Also, it keeps him out of my way when I'm in the kitchen."

She continued with the casual banter. Somehow, he filled in his parts. She got him a drink, the preference for which he could not remember having expressed, then ushered him back down the hall, across a narrow back porch, and onto a shaded patio where the boy archaeologist was sacrificing something on an altar of flame.

"Hi, J.D.," he said, giving the marshal's hand another enthusiastic workout while the girl disappeared back into the house. J.D. tried to disengage himself and turn the kid's attention back to the steaks. The fire looked ready to spread to a pair of nearby elms.

We, the People

Supper was over, but J.D. couldn't have told you exactly what he'd eaten. He could tell you what color Mary's eyes were though, and had nearly determined just what shade of mahogany most closely matched her hair.

The meal had been accompanied by small talk, most of which involved J.D. trying to avoid Larry's none too subtle probing about Spain. But with dessert finished, and Larry briefly away from the table freshening drinks, J.D. prodded himself out of his sudden return to adolescence and asked her to tell him about the Papago. It wasn't the conversation Larry wanted to rejoin, but he listened quietly while J.D. tried to concentrate on what she was saying and not how she looked, or how strongly he was drawn to her.

"Their culture was outwardly simple, even at the time of Spanish contact and it's not so very different today, for all their forced coexistence with a civilized world. If there's been any significant acculturation, most of it occurred among the river people, not their desert kin."

He'd heard that eyes could glow with excitement, but this was the first time he'd witnessed it. The topic was obviously one she was enthusiastic about and her wide eyes seemed to catch and reflect light from every available source. A man could get lost in those eyes.

"Actually, the Pima and Papago are a single people, split by limited opportunities to exploit river valley environments. In the Southern Arizona and Upper Sonoran Desert there are only so many places where there could be river people. Excess population had no choice.

"Both branches of the tribe call themselves *O'odham* which means 'the people.' You may have noticed that primitive peoples almost always call themselves by words that translate that way, but remember our own Constitution begins with the phrase, 'We, the people....' Each of us may further categorize ourselves, as in the American People or the Mexican People, but in the end, 'the people' is all any of us ever are."

She had these great dimples when she smiled. J.D. had never seen dimples that were quite so cute.

"The Pima called themselves the *A'akimel O'odham* or 'River People' and the Papago were the *Tohono O'odham* or 'Desert People.' We named the Pima because of their habit of answering questions put to them in a language they didn't understand with the natural reply, 'I don't know' which is *pimatc*. We couldn't reproduce the click of the 'tc' sound at the end of the word, so we just called them Pima."

And perfect teeth that gleamed as she demonstrated the alien syllable.

"Papago is about as close as we could come to saying *Papavi O'odham*, or 'Bean People,' which is kind of an insult since it hints that someone on such a diet might fart a lot."

J.D. wasn't really hearing most of what she was saying. He was wondering if Larry might have some mysterious and fatal disease to which he would shortly succumb. He was wondering what her lips would taste like. He was wondering if he shouldn't excuse himself and go home and take a cold shower.

Emotions and logic mix about as well as fire and water and about the only way J.D. would have gotten into a cold shower just then was if Mary accompanied him. He was caught in the magic of her spell, unintentionally cast or not. For a timeless while, she talked and he listened, but her words were only part of what he heard.

It was well past midnight before Larry's rattling of ice cubes and jaw-stretching yawns finally caught his attention and J.D. guiltily said his goodbyes, got in the Ford, and aimed it homeward. His conscience was starting to nag him and he knew he should make himself see as little of Mary as possible. He also knew he wasn't going to do that. Benny Goodman was playing "Somebody Stole My Gal" on the car radio. J.D. reached out, shut it off, and finished the drive in silence.

A Conqueror's Reward

The town lay on the bank of a lethargic river. A hard wind had blown out of the west for days and yellow dust from the Gobi covered this desolate region of Northern China and tinted the sky a pallid green.

Most of the city was on the far bank. If they had defended or destroyed the bridges, Sasaki's advance would have been difficult. But they didn't. There was only token resistance in spite of the strong garrison that had been quartered there. Before his troops entered the place, its defenders streamed out into the hills beyond, followed by most of the citizenry.

Sasaki inherited a town with its population more than halved. Only the old, the infirm, and a few women and children remained—those to whom leaving seemed a greater risk than staying.

It was common policy for the Imperial Japanese Army to allow its soldiers a conqueror's reward, letting them loot and plunder the places they took. Sasaki had refused to let his troops enjoy the practice. Until now. He was becoming desperate, anxious he would never encounter an enemy capable of offering meaningful resistance. Perhaps he could provoke it, incite his foe into magnificent battle. He gave his men their reward and to the Chinese who stayed behind, cause to regret their decision.

By dusk, much of the city was in flames, mixing its sooty cloud with the sickly twilight. A shroud of smoke cloaked the place. The screams of the tortured and brutalized must have carried to the hills where those who had held the place ran. Sasaki ordered no precautions against counterattack. His invitation to the Chinese army was an open one, addressed in the agony of those they'd left behind, printed on the ruin of their homes. He did not understand how anyone could ignore it.

The night passed and they did not come.

It was balmy, as inappropriate to the season as the enemy's lack of response to wanton brutality. Unable to sleep for the sounds of the dying city, confused by a people who tolerated what he allowed, Sasaki wandered the streets alone. They weren't safe for anyone. The streets no longer belonged to humans. Beasts, rabid with blood lust, caught up in an orgy of destruction for its own sake, had claimed them. His men were as drunk on violence as on what they had plundered from the wine merchants.

It was in the Street of Cloth Sellers that Sasaki encountered his first citizen of the place not already dead or dying. He was an old man. His robes were made of good material, but frayed and worn. Fortune had turned against him before the Japanese arrived. He sat in the remains of a ribbon stall at a corner of two avenues. His stall had been casually destroyed, torn apart without purpose. Ribbons were hardly the stuff that soldiers looted. Someone had tried to set fire to the place and some of the wares were charred. The rest had been tossed about, trampled, crumpled into the dust of the street. The merchant sat cross-legged in the center of the ruin, rocking slowly back and forth. His hands were burned, perhaps from extinguishing the flames that consumed his livelihood, but he was oblivious to their state. He picked up the soiled, wrinkled remnants, carefully wound them onto their spools, and restacked them on a broken shelf. Each spool rolled along its canted length and tumbled into the street. Several had unwound their contents as they rolled across the intersection, leaving bright fingers of ruined silk pointing out the tragedy of one man's life.

"Ribbons," he called in soft Mandarin. "All colors," he chanted. "Ribbons, most reasonable."

There was no truly wealthy section to the town, though it had more than its share of slums. There was less to steal than Sasaki's men might have wished, but plenty to burn, plenty to kill. The Street of Rewarded Merits was as close to a prosperous residential avenue as the town contained. Along its length, small broken lions guarded shattered red gates. Patched, crumbling walls and peeling paint revealed that merits here had not been rewarded generously.

As Sasaki passed one of the gates, something caught his attention. He turned in, stepping over one splintered half and around where the remainder hung precariously from broken hinges. The red spirit wall just inside was undamaged. Perhaps it continued to block the passage of evil spirits, whom the Chinese believed able to travel only in a straight line, but it hadn't slowed the Japanese soldiers within. The three pavilions of the house flanked a paved courtyard and were linked by low verandas with blue tiled roofs. There were four soldiers. Three of them sat on the steps of the veranda on the right, passing a wine jar back and forth and making bawdy comments, heavily slurred, on the attempts of their companion to rape the woman who lay on the stones of the courtyard. She was motionless under him, moved only by his clumsy thrusts. But for her ragged sobbing, Sasaki would have thought her dead. The soldier had drunk too much. He stroked at her for a moment, then lay still, as though he had forgotten where he was and what he was doing there, then the jeers of his fellows would rouse him and he would begin again.

In addition to the woman, there were two other Chinese there. On the floor of the yard near the woman and her attacker, a boy, perhaps six, clawed his way up the wall against which he appeared to have been hurled. He had probably lain there, unconscious, for some time. Awake again, he fought back to his feet, clutching a shard of shattered tile to his narrow chest. From the way his left leg twisted, Sasaki was sure it must be broken. The boy made no sounds as he struggled to rise. The soldiers were too drunk to notice.

The piece of tile was an unintentional gift of the adult Chinese male who clung to the roof of the veranda above. Sasaki wondered if he had hidden there while the woman and child were attacked, or had only crawled to the spot moments before, on his way to exact vengeance. Perhaps this was evidence that the behavior he sought was not alien to the Chinese. Sasaki stood in the shadows, unmoving. None of them had seen him.

The man on the roof had something with him. It might be a club or a sword, perhaps even a rifle. From the way he clutched it Sasaki knew it was a weapon. He and the man on the roof watched the child rise and begin a tortured journey to where the woman and soldier lay. Each time the boy put weight on his injured leg he let out a small gasp, but even that was insufficient to attract the attention of the soldiers. If the man on the roof intended to attack, his victims could hardly have been less alert.

At last the boy reached the coupled figures. He raised the jagged tile in tiny fists and brought it down with all his might. He was too young to understand mortality, his own or his enemy's. To the neck and the blow might have caused a serious wound, maybe even a fatal one. To the back and it was only painful, but it succeeded in gaining the soldiers' notice at last.

The rapist jerked with a spasm born of pain instead of pleasure and cried out. He swung out behind him in reflex. The blow tumbled the boy across the stones to where he struggled faintly but did not rise again. The tile protruded from the man's back and he roared and stumbled to his feet and awkwardly tried to reach it. His companions doubled over in drunken merriment, grabbing their sides at the humor of his plight. Two of them actually fell off the veranda and lay on the ground, wheezing besotted laughter into the stones of the courtyard floor. The third clambered unsteadily to his feet and weaved to the woman. He clumsily began to unbutton his trousers so that he might take up where his friend had left off.

The wounded man finally jerked the bloody tile from his back. He turned with a curse and flung it at the boy. His aim was wild and it skittered to Sasaki's feet. The man didn't notice. He wobbled to the small form of his attacker, muttering curses as he felt for the knife that should have been at his belt, if he wore a belt, or any part of his uniform but his socks and cap. The man on the roof would never have a better chance. Two of his enemies lay helpless with wine and mirth. The wounded one had his back to the roof and was naked and unarmed. The last had dropped his pants to his knees and was focusing his attention elsewhere. The man on the roof clutched his weapon and watched, unmoving.

The injured soldier picked up the child and threw him head first against the nearest wall. Once would have been sufficient. The first time obviously broke the boy's neck. After that he was dead, but the man repeated the process several times, then contented himself with kicking the little body around the courtyard.

Sasaki shook his head. Only the child....

He stepped silently from the shadow of the spirit wall and used his sword. He took the wounded one from behind. The man's head seemed to gape at Sasaki in surprise as it rolled across the stones to lie beside the child. His body sprayed the courtyard with crimson and took two steps before it fell. Sasaki was equally quick and efficient with the man's companions.

When it was over, the woman still lay sobbing, staring vacantly at the sky. The man on the roof continued to cling to the tiles. Sasaki stood and looked up at him long enough for it to be clear that they saw each other. The man's eyes watched from the darkness. Only the small stream of urine that flowed down the blue tiles to splash onto the courtyard and mingle with the blood and wine gave Sasaki any indication, other than his eyes, that the man knew he was there.

Sasaki watched until he knew that if he stayed any longer he must go up and kill that one too. It was not something honor required. He turned, instead, deliberately exposing his back, and walked slowly out to the street.

On his way back to headquarters he passed the ribbon seller's stand. Someone had strangled him with his ribbons.

A Renegade Village

After supper Jujul walked through their new village, a place called
Black Caves. His people were already settled in. The transition
was relatively easy for a folk so nearly nomadic.

It was Fair Cold month, the White Man's November. There
were no crops to till, no weeding or planting or harvesting. Only
a little gathering and hunting and a few skinny cattle to herd.
Their evening meal complete, his people relaxed. Some of the
young men were playing kickball behind one of the corrals. Not
far away, another group ran relay races, hiding their shadowy forms
in a cloud of dust turned golden by the setting of Father Sun. A
group of women sat near the coals of a fire and played the game of
the four black and white sticks. One laughed happily as she scored
while her companions complained about their lack of luck and
the gossip they shared was momentarily lost to the demands of
the game.

He walked past them and climbed slowly up to the mouth of
the largest cave. He limped. Winter is hard on an old man's old
wounds. The cave was black with the soot of the fires of countless
generations of *O'odham*. All the caves here were the same. It was
how the place came by its name. He knelt at the mouth and lit the
fire that had been laid there.

They had built only a few houses so far. For the time being,
the shallow caves sufficed. This, the largest, took the place of their
meeting house. The men would see the fire and know there was to
be a council meeting. They would come, but it was tradition that

the chief summon them. Jujul raised his voice and roared his invitation to the evening. Then he sat and smoked while he waited.

They had gone east because it would be expected for them to go south. His band normally spent part of its year below the border with Mexico. Larson and the others who wanted to arrest him and take his young men would probably find that out. They would only have to ask the tribal council. One of the few things Jujul knew about American law was that it did not extend into Mexico. For both reasons, then, it was a logical place to go. That was why he had chosen this direction instead. The Anglo's army would comb the desert along the border, searching for some sign of them, and they would bring powerful weapons to the task. They had automobiles and trucks and far-seeing glasses. They could use their far-talkers to speak across great distances. They could even send winged machines to prowl the winds in search of his people. If the village went south and the Americans looked for them, there was a real chance they might be found.

We are the Desert People, he thought. This is our land. I will not allow the Whites to find us unless I choose to let them. Since the search would concentrate to the south, he had gone in another direction, toward the edge of the Reservation and the White Man's village of Tucson. One cannot find that which is not where one looks.

He had first visited Black Caves with his father. The place became deserted during his childhood, but when they had passed through it on their way to visit relatives at the place where the river sank and the grand white mission of the Catholics stands, the place called San Xavier del Bac, it had been a thriving village. The water in the springs here had turned bitter after the long ago day when the earth moved, and, though it was still plentiful and safe to drink, the People abandoned it. Now Jujul needed it. His band could put up with bitter water for a time.

Jujul liked the place. There were few villages nearby. Ample game roamed the vicinity and they had found plenty of roots and berries and wild seeds. They were near the invisible border of the reservation, close to White ranches where they could trade, so long as they did not let it be known who they were. Close, also, to the San Xavier Reservation where many cousins from his clan would welcome visits from members of his village. There was interaction there. Whites and Mexicans lived and worked alongside the People. News could be gathered, information about how the Anglos intended dealing with his village. And information was what he needed.

He had sent people to the San Xavier and a few other villages already. He had also sent a party of young people to trade at one of the nearby ranches. That group was back. It was what he wanted to speak of at tonight's council.

All the men in camp would come. It was their right and duty, but only the mature ones, those who had lived at least thirty summers, would be allowed to speak. It was a place for wisdom, not passion or intuition.

The men filed in. They nodded greetings as they passed Jujul and took their places in the circle, places won by right of age or a history of sage advice. The young men crowded in behind in no particular order. Most of the women casually wandered up the slope and found comfortable spots to sit and gaze at the place where Father Sun had gone to rest. They could watch as the stars came out of hiding, and, incidentally, overhear whatever might be discussed in the village council. Women had no official place there, no voice in the proceedings, but woe to the man who did not take his women's opinions into careful consideration before he had his say.

Traditionally, a village must be in unanimous agreement over any matter before it could be acted on, but that practice had weakened over the centuries since they came in contact with the Spaniards, then the Mexicans and Anglos. In practice, Jujul always tried to achieve that unanimity, but, if necessary, he held the deciding vote. It was a vote he seldom cast. Wisely so, for he had no wish to be replaced as governor of his village.

Jujul took his place at the head of the circle and they began without ceremony. He talked about the day's events, what hunter had brought in game, which foragers had added to their larder. There were no interruptions, no comments as there might normally have been.

"You all know," he told them, "Fast Walker and his group have returned from trading with the rancher." There was murmured agreement. Fast Walker stiffened his spine with pride. Jujul had sent him because he was a man who needed to be kept busy. Like most of the young men, he'd taken too much pleasure in the rock throwing and been hard to restrain from killing when Larson came back with the others. Like all young people, he did not comprehend the possibility of his own death. All he saw in these events was adventure. He had liked it, and wanted more. But Fast Walker was clever. He could follow instructions when he understood the reasons. The village needed to find out what the Whites were doing about them, but they needed to do so in ways that would cast no suspicion. Jujul sent him with a few cattle to trade for ammunition and tools, and impressed on him the need for secrecy. He had Fast Walker and his men take along their wives, making it less likely they might persuade themselves they were on a raid.

"I hoped the rancher, a man whose name is Burns, would not know about the affair at our village. I thought, perhaps, we shamed Larson and the tribal police sufficiently so they might not talk of this thing. I told Fast Walker and his people that they must be very cautious in asking about the event, but they did not even have to ask. It was the favorite topic of conversation of the rancher and his hands, many of whom are themselves *O'odham*. When our people were asked if they had heard the news, they pretended they had not. They were immediately told several versions, each noteworthy for its elaborate detail, and its inaccuracy. Larson apparently vilified us, claiming we were dangerous, cold-blooded killers who struck without cause or warning. He might have been widely believed but for contrary statements from Deputy Sheriff Gonzales and the White Man with him.

"Now, it seems, the Whites are of mixed council as to how we should be dealt with. Some even side with us and say we, not Larson and his police, were right. Others wish to hunt us down, make us examples, so our tribe will not forget what happens to those who challenge the White Man's rules."

As he spoke, Jujul unconsciously stroked the pouch at his belt in which he kept the paper the federal man who had been with Gonzales left along with the gift of tobacco. It was a puzzling thing. He knew White Men used paper to send messages. Its marks and squiggles were undoubtedly meant to convey some meaning to him, but he had no idea what it might be. It was one of many things he needed to learn about the people who must now be regarded as his enemies.

His was a small band, less than two hundred, even counting those too young or ancient to chew their own food. The Anglos were said to be a mighty people, but Jujul knew almost nothing about them. He had purposefully avoided them for more than twenty years. Few of his people had ever lived among the Whites, and those had only worked at their ranches. Some of the men had been to tribal headquarters at Sells, but Sells was a mixed community with pieces of three cultures. It did not seem a good place on which to base too many assumptions. None of his people had ever visited the Whites in their own villages. Thus, Jujul did not know how they lived or what they wanted. His only clues to how they would fight were based on two encounters and only one of those had been against warriors. He needed knowledge, and, surprisingly, he had been offered a chance to get it.

"The trading of cattle is a new thing for Fast Walker, so I will not blame him for getting too little ammunition and too few tools for our stock." Fast Walker's spine slumped a little. Best to instill some humility to offset his growing pride.

"Perhaps, because he was able to make such a profitable trade, the rancher Burns has offered us a valuable gift. It seems there is a White Woman who seeks to become a sort of elder among her people. Such elders achieve their status through the acquisition of knowledge. Apparently, each elder concentrates on knowledge of a very specific sort. This seems most peculiar, but the Whites are a puzzling people and we need to know more about them. This woman wishes to become an expert among her kind on the *Tohono O'odham*. She desires to gain that knowledge by living with the People and observing us. She does not wish to learn from those who live near and among White Men. She wishes to find a remote village, one which maintains the traditional ways. She will bring many valuable gifts to whoever will accept her—blankets, cloth, tools, and much more. Such things might be considered ample recompense for her support during the time she would live among them, but I am told it is her intention to work alongside the women and, so much as is possible for an outsider, live and contribute as would any member of the village.

"Burns, perhaps because of our ineptitude at the art of trading, thinks we may be the sort of village she would like to study. He has offered to tell her about us and see if she might come to us if we will have her. Our cousins who work for Burns say she has visited with them and, though they found her strange, she seemed kind and sympathetic. She speaks our language. They believe she would be harmless and entertaining to the village that accepts her.

"I believe we should ask her to come live with us." The council immediately erupted with exclamations of amazement and denial. Jujul ignored them and, after regaining their attention, calmly explained it was necessary to learn something of the White Man's ways, and it was unlikely they would find a better opportunity. There seemed little chance this was a ruse. The Anglos put too much value on their women to risk one as part of some wild scheme to catch a renegade village. Her purpose was almost certainly legitimate. And, if she should discover who they were, there was little, other than their location, she might learn which could be a danger. But, oh, what they might learn from her!

Pedro Round-Frog argued that the Whites possessed too much magic. "We cannot take the chance that she may use it to tell her people where to find us," he said. Some of his friends nodded at his wisdom.

"Then we shall be certain she does not know," Jujul told them. "The party we send to bring her here can do so by a long, circuitous path. Our new home lies on the west slope of a range which hides the sacred mountain from view. If we make at least part of her journey on a cloudy night when she can see neither stars nor landmarks she will not know exactly where she has been taken."

That brought Round-Frog and his followers to the Chief's side, but Rat Skin still held out, and he spoke for two others. He rocked back on his bony haunches and grasped his arms around his knees as he spoke. Whether it was done out of emotion or to keep his thin old body warm, Jujul could not tell.

"Their magic is just too powerful," he whined. "She may still have ways to know where she is. She may still have ways to far-talk to her people and bring them down on us." It was a frightening thought. They all knew the Whites were capable of amazing exploits. Jujul noticed a wavering among those who had come to side with him.

"Yes," he agreed. "It is true, the White Men have great powers. But their powers are in the things they make. They have no personal magic. The things they do that seem fabulous to us are always done with the aid of some tool. Perhaps there is magic in their tools, but I do not think so. We use many of these tools—

rifles, knives, skillets, axes. What magic do they have? None. They are only tools. The woman offers gifts as part of the bargain she would make with the village that takes her. If she is a spy, and I doubt that she is, it is among those things she would hide the tools to use against us. We can still take her in and learn from her. On the trail here, the party that escorts her can cache everything she brings. That should render her harmless. They can even supply her with clothing and leave her own behind. Let her come to us with nothing from the outside. We can watch the cache and see if her people come to it. If they do not, we can assume she is not a spy, and we can gain much wealth at some later time, when we have learned what we need from her and sent her back to her people."

The men sat, nodding, talking among themselves. They were reassured. From out of the darkness on the slope below the cave they heard the voice of Cornsilk, Rat Skin's senior wife.

"I cannot imagine being afraid of any single woman, no matter what color her skin, can you my sisters? And I have never seen a White Woman. It would please me to discover in what ways we are different and in what ways the same." It was a casual comment, gossip among women who sat watching the stars, but spoken in a voice that clearly carried into the council cave and cast aspersions on her husband's bravery.

Rat Skin chewed his nearly toothless gums in suppressed fury, but he knew when to give in. "I fear there is great danger here," he said, in a voice as thin as his shanks, "but Jujul is right when he says we must learn about our enemies. I do not like it, but I also say, let her come."

The two who had followed his lead continued to do so.

"Yes," one said.

"Let it be so," agreed the other.

Jujul had won. They would invite this strange White Woman. With luck, she would come.

As the men began to rise and depart from the council he pulled out the bent and frayed paper the stranger named Fitzpatrick had left. There was so much to learn. What message, if any, had been sent him? And, if it was important, why entrust it to so fragile a material? What manner of man was this Fitzpatrick? Could he be reasoned with, or might Jujul have to kill him? So much to learn, so very much. At least now there would be a chance to learn it.

An Immortality Few Earn

Kempeitai Headquarters in Tokyo occupied a modern building of insipid European design only a few blocks from the American Embassy. The army staff car delivered Sasaki there after only one minor accident. The bicyclist they struck wasn't seriously injured, if the tenor of his curses was an indication, but the chauffeur and his escorts didn't stop to find out.

An unusual snow had recently fallen democratically upon the roofs of rich and poor alike, thatching them with the same thin blanket of sooted white. The snow had been shoveled from the streets and lay in melting piles along the sidewalks, dikes to hold back the traffic from the shops and homes behind—a congested flood that moved with the sluggish uncertainty of a serpent caught by an early cold snap.

The car pulled up at the main entrance and Sasaki and his heavily armed attendants spilled into the smoke-tinged air. Sasaki automatically scanned his environment, weighing threats and evaluating opportunities. As usual, these men who had surrounded him from the moment he returned to his headquarters in the ribbon seller's city stationed themselves in a professional manner. He was contained or he was dead. There might come a time to choose the latter option, but not yet.

Guards at the entrance came stiffly to attention in recognition of his rank, or the authority of his companions. Inside, it was warm from the steam heat and concentrated tension of those crowding the building's foyer. Not many people awaited appointments with the military police without trepidation. There would have been nearly as much sweat here had there been no heat.

They took him to a reception desk where a small clerk with thick spectacles shuffled one pile of paper into three, then recombined them into a new order. Sasaki had the feeling he could make the job last a week.

"Captain Kozo Sasaki to see Mr. Renya Kira," the commander of his guards said. Sasaki's name didn't impress the little man, but Kira's did. At his mention the man transformed himself from a bored, impatient clerk into an obsequious instrument of their pleasure. Given the speed and efficiency with which his removal from the Chinese front had been carried out, Sasaki suspected Kira must be an important man. The clerk's reaction confirmed it.

"Allow me please, and I will inform Mr. Kira of your arrival," he said. He bowed so deeply and frequently Sasaki was concerned he might begin banging his head on the desk. It was embarrassing, to see the man humiliate himself so. Under other circumstances, Sasaki might have forcibly stopped it.

The clerk picked up a telephone and held a whispered conversation with the instrument while continuing to favor them with a reassuring smile, easily as genuine as his paper shuffling.

In a remarkably short time a tall young man in a western-style business suit approached the reception desk, nodded at the servile clerk and the escorts, then offered a deep bow.

"Captain Sasaki, I presume?" he inquired, extending his hand for a western handshake. Sasaki accepted without comment. The gesture might or might not be an insult.

"I am Mr. Kira's personal secretary. Mr Kira is anxious to meet you, but you may have some time to freshen up first."

Sasaki had been in his uniform for more than forty hours. It was soiled and wrinkled, quite out of place alongside the secretary's neatly pressed garments. Sasaki liked the contrast. Warrior and bureaucrat, actor and audience. Besides, he was anxious to find out what this was about, to know how seriously his life was threatened by the Kempeitai's interest. He brushed at his great coat and a little dried mud fell on the tiled floor at their feet.

"No, let's get on with it. The Emperor's business cannot wait on niceties."

"Very well," the man agreed. Sasaki was surprised to discover that, though the secretary was put off by his refusal, he lacked the nerve to insist. Perhaps Sasaki was not in as much danger as he had imagined.

They took an elevator, then the secretary led the way down a long corridor. Sasaki's boots, and those of his escort, echoed hollowly while the secretary's shoes hardly whispered. Even the tiles seemed to recognize the difference in their status.

Sasaki detected no signal, but the men who guarded him peeled off at the door to Mr. Kira's office and flanked it, waiting. The door itself was unmarked. Behind it lay a large outer office, richly upholstered with furniture and carpets as western as this secretary's suit and manners. Everything was spotless, immaculate. Sasaki shrugged out of his great coat and tossed it onto a plush couch. For a moment he thought the secretary might throw his body across the sofa to protect its brocade surface. The potential damage to his suit must have deterred him and he merely stood and stared. Sasaki enjoyed his reaction, enjoyed establishing control.

"Mr. Kira?" Sasaki prompted.

"Ah, yes," the man agreed. He went to his desk and picked up the phone. He was returning it to its cradle when the door to an inner office opened. A short, thick man with a grey moustache and goatee advanced into the room like some miniature sumo wrestler.

The newcomer bowed slightly, smiled, and took Sasaki's arm. He led the way toward the inner office.

"My dear Captain Sasaki," he proclaimed. "I am so delighted you could manage to visit me. Come in, come in." The voice sounded genuinely pleased, devoid of irony at Sasaki's lack of choice in the matter. "Please, take a seat, anywhere, make yourself comfortable." The offer was made with the generosity of a man who could delegate the necessity of cleaning up after to someone else.

Kira's office was considerably larger than his secretary's. Its furnishings were likewise western, but less ostentatious. There was only one hint that they were in the heart of Japan. A portrait of Mr. Kira being warmly received by Emperor Hirohito hung on the only wall without a door or a window.

There was a plain wooden chair in front of Kira's desk and Sasaki took it in preference to one of the several easy chairs.

Kira made his way behind the desk. Like his office, it was large, with three telephones, several neat stacks of paper and files, an ornamental clock that doubled as a pen holder, and a jade-handled letter opener with an unusually long, sharp blade. It all hardly began to fill the sweep of the desk's surface. The Venetian blinds at the window behind Kira were open on a stunning scene of a delicate Shinto shrine and the smoke belching factory behind it. Sasaki couldn't blame the man for turning his back on such a modern view, however symbolically appropriate it might be.

Kira sat in a swivel chair, rocked back and stared at his visitor with a wide smile for several moments. It was more disconcerting than the interrogation Sasaki had anticipated.

"They don't think I'm quite sane, you know," Kira said and smiled some more. Sasaki began to understand why "they" might feel that way. "You either, of course," he added. He reached down, picked up a file and opened it.

"Kozo Sasaki," he read aloud. "Born, 1905, Kobe. Parents, Admiral Atsumaro Sasaki and Helen Davidson, daughter of Lawrence Vernon Davidson, Assistant Chargé D'Affaires of the American Legation in Osaka from 1898 to 1905." Except for the continued benevolent smile, this was more the behavior Sasaki had expected.

"Father, the eldest son of an old and important Samurai family. Expected to rise in power and influence following his sweeping successes in the Russo-Japanese War, but hampered by the embarrassment of an Occidental bride and a half-cast son. Retired from service, 1913, entered diplomatic corps and served at the embassy in Washington, D.C., United States, until his death in 1921. Cause of death, suicide due to grief following wife's demise in automobile accident.

"Subject was then raised by maternal grandparents, but after a series of incidents, returned to paternal grandparents and Japan in 1923. Admitted to the Army Academy and graduated with honor in 1928. Subject showed flair, even brilliance, in matters involving personal combat and guerrilla warfare.

"Subject has seen service in Manchuria and North China. Pursues the war with ruthless abandon. Reckless, but successful. Respected and feared by those under his command. Disliked and avoided by fellow officers.

"Subject is believed to have murdered as many as six persons, though, in each instance, no proof exists. These include a schoolmate at the Fenster Hill Academy in Virginia, U.S.A. (the incident that resulted in his return to Japan), a fellow cadet and an instructor at the Army Academy, an American merchant in Osaka, and two superior officers in China."

Kira looked up from his notes for a moment. "And they tell me there was fresh blood on your sword when you received your invitation to join me here." The smile widened briefly before he began to read again.

"Subject appears motivated by a need to erase the shame of his parents' relationship, especially the humiliation of the unmanly form and cause of his father's death. He willingly serves Japan and his Emperor, but, ultimately, the service of his insatiable ego will remain the primary factor by which his future actions will be motivated. Subject is considered useful under certain circumstances, but highly unstable and potentially dangerous.

"Recommendations, in order of preference: One—terminate. Two—utilize with extreme caution in scheme which will feed subject's ego, producing results favorable to Japan, and resulting in subject's death. Three—continue observation and analysis, instituting option one at the first sign subject may be beyond our control."

Sasaki listened impassively, watching Mr. Kira for clues. Though not completely accurate, the Kempeitai obviously knew him better than he'd suspected. One of the bodies they'd attributed to him was not his, though it was offset by more than a dozen others still undiscovered. He was surprised they suspected as much as they did, but he didn't let it frighten him. Mr. Kira wouldn't have wasted so much time and effort if he intended to follow the dossier's first recommendation.

⌒

The Apache sprinted up the hill, ducking through the dogwoods and maples. He was fast, but the enemy had longer legs, was steadily gaining. He could hear the footsteps, even over the voices. Not much farther.

The Apache knew the place. He had been here before. He ducked around a thick stand of young oaks and threw himself into the dense laurels that lined the trail, worming his way to where he could no longer be seen from behind but could watch the trail ahead. He made it, but only just.

The enemy hurtled by. A few steps closer and he would have seen the Apache leave the trail.

The enemy slowed as he realized the Apache was no longer ahead of him. But his momentum was enough. He screeched, a high, almost girlish sound, as he sprung the trap and the noose closed around his leg. The sapling straightened and left him dangling, his head just bouncing on the mossy soil. The Apache of Virginia was surprised. He hadn't thought it would work even that well.

"God damn it, Sasaki," the enemy bawled. "You better come let me down if you know what's good for you."

Sasaki, the Apache, crawled out of the laurels and went to examine his handiwork. He stayed well out of the reach of Todd Walters' flailing hands.

"If I know what's good for me?" he mocked. "You were going to beat the shit out of me. Now I should let you go so we can get on with it?"

"If you don't let me down, you little half-breed Jap bastard, I'm gonna kill you."

Todd Walters, as head bully of Sasaki's class at the Fenster Hill Academy of Arlington, Virginia, had been "killing" Sasaki little by little for years. The Indians—Sasaki was always an Indian because of his eyes and his skin color—had always lost to Todd's Cowboys. Usually, they lost painfully. He and Todd hadn't played Cowboys and Indians for years, until today, though only Sasaki was aware of it so far. There were lots of new games for the always bigger and stronger Todd to beat Sasaki at, and up, in the process.

Sasaki decided the rope would hold. He went over and got the blanket full of tools he'd cached in the hollow trunk of a dead oak nearby.

"What're you doing?" Walters demanded. "My buddies are gonna whale on your scrawny yellow ass as soon as they catch up."

"You don't have any buddies," Sasaki told him. "Not really. And they gave up half a mile ago. They're probably back down in the dorm by now."

Todd didn't argue. He knew he had followers because tougher than anybody else. He didn't really have friends. "W have you got there?"

Sasaki had, among other things, another rope. He tossed it over the limb of a mature maple, made a lasso out of one end, and began trying to secure Todd's other leg. He wasn't very good at roping, but no matter how much the other boy flailed and yelled, it was just a matter of time.

"Listen, Kozo. I'm sorry. I didn't mean all that stuff," Walters pleaded as Sasaki began to haul on the second rope. Strain as he might, he only managed to raise Todd another foot or two in the air.

"Of course you meant it," Kozo Sasaki said as he secured the second rope and went for a third. "But you probably are sorry, at least right now. Of course you'll still whip me again, every time you get the chance, if I let you go."

"No, really I won't." Todd grabbed at the next rope Sasaki threw and succeeded only in getting both his hands caught by this lasso the first time it was thrown.

Sasaki yanked it tight, carried the other end of the rope back down the trail to another limb, and hauled on it until Walters was suspended, face down, some four feet above the forest floor.

"Ahhh! Jeez, Kozo! You don't know how much that hurts," Todd howled. "What are you doing to me?"

Kozo wasn't sure he could explain. He just got the scissors instead and began cutting away Todd's clothing. What with all the thrashing and yelling, it took a while and proved Kozo's theory that Todd's followers, in this case, hadn't.

When Kozo pulled out the razor blade, Todd the bully began to cry. "Kozo! Please! I promise! I'll do anything you want!"

He was right. He died slowly and in agony, just the way Sasaki had imagined.

Kira placed the documents on his desk, picked up the letter opener, and began tapping the point absentmindedly against his incisors. It made a faint ringing noise that grated on Sasaki's nerves and made him wonder how unconsciously it was being done.

He could take the letter opener from Kira and kill him. That was no problem. Nor would the secretary be one. Getting past the professionals who had accompanied him from China, however, was unlikely, and surviving to escape from this building, unimaginable. He wasn't afraid of dying, just dying without purpose, without an appropriately glorious cause to demonstrate his superiority and uniqueness. This wasn't it.

"So, you've decided against killing me," Kira said. It was eerily as if he'd been reading Sasaki's thoughts. Kira put down the letter opener (it would have made an excellent defensive weapon) and leaned back in his chair. "A wise decision, Captain, because I plan to make use of you in a way which I think will satisfy us both."

He picked up Sasaki's file and dropped it in a waste paper basket beside his desk. "Facts, errors, and half-truths, I suspect. You should see my dossier. As I said, they think I am insane. But they are also aware of the brilliance of my espionage capabilities, and my family connections make eliminating me a dangerous undertaking. Still, they've tried twice, and solely because I am only sexually aroused by persons recently dead." He said it as casually as one might confess to a slight social indiscretion, shrugging his shoulders in apology. "Each of us has our little quirks, Captain. You are prepared to embrace death in your way, I in mine."

He *was* insane. For the first time, Sasaki felt uncomfortable. A lunatic was deciding his fate.

"Your dossier mentions that you have a fascination with the American Indians, that you are an expert on their methods of warfare. May I ask why?"

It took Sasaki a moment to adjust to this shift in the conversation. "I spent a great deal of my youth in the United States," he finally responded. "A common children's game there is Cowboys and Indians. When I was invited to participate, I was always cast in the role of the villainous Indian, thanks to the color of my skin and the slant of my eyes. I began to identify with them. I spent much of my spare time reading about them and the abuses they suffered during the centuries of conquest. Considering the widely divergent levels of technology of the combatants, the result was never in doubt. Just the same, I was constantly impressed with the skill they brought to that impossible struggle."

Todd Walters had proved a valuable lesson. It was amazing how easily difficulties might be overcome if only unusual solutions were pursued.

"I've read your papers from the Academy," Kira said. "They imply that the American Indians were among the world's finest warrior peoples, natural guerrilla fighters. Those wars ended half a century ago. Might the descendants of those warriors retain such skills?"

Sasaki had never thought about it. In fact, he'd never seen a live Indian. He had nothing to base an opinion on except what he wanted the answer to be.

"They've been subjugated a long time. The very best were nearly all killed. But I believe a nucleus remains. Given an opportunity, it would seem likely."

Kira leaned his chair back again and examined his fingernails. They were immaculate.

"Are you familiar with a tribe called the Papago?" he asked.

Sasaki thought for a moment but he didn't recognize the name.

"They are inhabitants of Arizona in the American Southwest," Kira prompted. "I am told they are related to the Pima."

"Ah yes," Sasaki said. "The Pima were traditional enemies of the Apache. The American Cavalry used them as scouts and allies."

"Were they capable warriors?"

"They must have been if they fought the Apache and survived. The Apache were probably the finest guerrilla fighters the American Indians ever produced. Though very small in number, they denied control of vast territories to their White enemies. Any group that fought against them successfully must have been fine warriors indeed."

Kira nodded. "It doesn't really matter, but it would certainly make things more interesting if you are correct."

He leaned forward again, putting the letter opener down. He rested his elbows on the desk and steepled his fingers.

"Have you managed to stay abreast of world affairs from your position at the front?"

"In general, I suppose," Sasaki replied. "But news often reaches us late and we lack the time to study it."

"Are you aware that the American government has begun to enlarge its armed forces? That they have instituted a conscription policy again?"

"Yes," Sasaki lied. He had heard something, but thought it was only in the works, not a policy already implemented.

"It's further evidence that the Americans will soon involve themselves in the war in Europe. There are some who argue they only intend to go to the aid of the tottering English and won't risk fighting on more than one front, but those people are fools. They don't understand America any more than America understands us. They don't see that America believes herself to be the champion of world morality, however tempered by the quest for profit. They can't understand why the Americans believe us to be another Fascist nation and do not realize we are only technologically modern. Psychologically, we remain a nation of feudal lords and peasants. America sees our invasion of China as evidence of a policy of world conquest and domination, not the senseless inability of our government to control its commanders or those commanders to control their troops.

"You realize, of course," he confided, "the moment we went beyond the conquest of Manchuria, the moment we entered North China, we lost this war. We should be preparing to fight the Soviets, our true enemy in Asia, and befriend China, our natural ally. We should be preparing to meet the inevitable challenge from America for control of the Pacific. But, alas no, like dead leaves we rush wherever any impetuous breeze may carry us, and it carries us, devoutly screaming banzais, to our doom. So be it. If all that remains for us is death, at least we may occasionally choose a magnificent one."

Quite mad, Sasaki reflected. Such talk was treason. No wonder "they" had tried to kill him. And yet he made sense, this admitted necrophiliac. Sasaki found Kira intriguing.

"Plans for the invasion of the continental United States are already underway. A waste of time, of course, since we must first dislodge the Americans from the Pacific. One of the more exotic approaches has us launching an invasion from the northern end of the Gulf of California, striking across into Arizona and cutting or controlling America's primary sources of supply to Southern California. It's not so foolish as it may first seem, provided only that we have eliminated the American Pacific presence and can build enough aircraft carriers and planes and troop transports and so on. Then we could hit Southern California from the sea, invading in several places. With a pincers movement we might carve out a vast chunk of American real estate on which to build a secure beachhead and amass the men and materials that a drive north and east would require.

"Strategically the concept is not unsound. The absurdity lies in expecting to clear the Americans from the Pacific in the first place. Nevertheless, certain wildly imaginative generals have become aware of an interesting development in Southern Arizona and would like to see it exploited in the hope it will make their subsequent invasion of that area less difficult.

"There has been a small rebellion among some Papagos against the requirement of Selective Service Registration. Actually, there are several small rebellions, but in one case an entire village has apparently taken up arms against the United States and gone into hiding in the desert.

"We want someone to make contact with the renegade village, rendezvous with a submarine which will supply them with modern arms and ammunition, and, by craft, promises, lies, or force, lead them in a guerrilla action against the government and people of the United States. To direct them in such a way that the rebellion spreads among their fellow tribesmen, perhaps even to other tribes in the region. Any time wasted by the United States in coping with an Indian uprising inside their own borders will be beneficial to the Japanese Empire. There is almost no chance it will succeed, of course, but in the short run...." He spread his hands as if to say "who knows?" and leaned back in his chair again, studying Sasaki's reaction.

"It's a suicide mission," he added as an afterthought, "which makes you the ideal candidate."

"What assistance can I expect?" Sasaki asked.

"We'll fly you to San Francisco, smuggle you out of the Consulate there and into mainstream America where your upbringing should suffice to grant you mobility. We'll provide a considerable amount of cash, a submarine filled with weapons and tools of the saboteur's trade, and very little else. Japanese do not move easily or inconspicuously in America, especially now that awareness of the probability of war has begun to reach the average citizen. We have no network of agents in place, no safe houses. In fact, no presence whatsoever in the state of Arizona. We can't even give you the names of sympathetic Japanese Americans. There may be some, but we are so ill prepared that we don't know who they are."

"But you can put me in contact with the dissident Papagos?"

"Not even that," Kira admitted. "As I told you, it's all quite hopeless, quite suicidal. We can give you the name of the most prominent opposition leader among the Papagos, a man who is at odds with their tribal council and its attitude of cooperation with federal authority. It seems likely he may know where to find them, but we don't know that for certain."

"And you seriously expect me to accept this assignment?" Sasaki asked. Not that he would refuse it. He only wondered if Kira understood him.

"Yes. Because there is that chance in a thousand you might succeed. Even in a small way. Because it's a task only a genius, a superman, might accomplish. Because you believe you are such a man. Because you might even be right. You may find them, arm them, train them. You may even blow up a bridge, derail a train, strike an army installation. And, in the process, you may create a legend, bring in more dissatisfied Papago, Pima, maybe even other Indians. There is that chance in a million you could pull it off, regardless of what becomes of Japan. You just might establish a Native American Nation on the face of their own continent. It would assure you an immortality few earn."

Yes, Sasaki thought, he understands me fairly well.

"And, there's the other side of the coin. You've heard the recommendations in your file. If you refuse, those men waiting in the hall won't be escorting you back to the front. I don't know what they have in mind for you, some quiet little assassination, I should guess. I rather think you might enjoy pitting yourself against them, against the Kempeitai, perhaps as much as you would enjoy the other, but in the unlikely event you succeed here you will merely survive. There will be no public glory, no recognition. Yes, I think you'll accept."

Kira was right, except the pudgy little madman didn't really believe Sasaki had a chance.

"When do I begin?" Sasaki inquired.

Kira smiled again. He reached into a new file and handed the Captain some documents. "The first of your new identities," he explained. "Background information, your ticket to fly on a trans-Pacific clipper to San Francisco. You have already begun, Captain Sasaki," Kira said, indicating with a wave of his hand that their interview was concluded, "and I wish you good fortune."

Sasaki accepted the papers, rose, bowed slightly, and turned to leave. At the door he stopped. He was curious.

"What about you?" he asked. "Will you fight them or will you run?"

"Run?" It sounded as if Kira had never considered the option before. "No, certainly not. I'll stay. I'll survive. I'll wait. Were you in Nanking, Captain?"

"I've been there," Sasaki said, "but I wasn't present during the slaughter."

"They tell me it was a charnel house," he said, wistfully. "I missed it too. A sad thing for a man of my proclivities. But before this war is over, Tokyo, all of Japan, will come to make Nanking seem a childish amusement in comparison. I'll stay and survive and, in the end, I'll enjoy my just rewards."

"Yes, I see," Sasaki told him. Quite mad. He pivoted and left Kira's office. The man understood but underestimated him. Sasaki would succeed because he was prepared, without hesitation, to destroy anyone or anything in his way.

Talking About Spain

It was a warm night for a Sunday in mid-November, and the Spencers had dropped by J.D.'s for drinks. It was also supposed to be a short night because J.D. had to work the next morning and both of them had classes, but the conversation had been intriguing and no one seemed in any special hurry to end it. They were on J.D.'s front porch, watching the moonlight play across the rugged Catalina Mountains just north of the city. Mary knew it was late and she was feeling a little tipsy, even though she'd been drinking a lot less than the men. J.D. didn't show any effects, but Larry wasn't doing as well. He had just dozed off in his chair.

"Well," Mary said. It wasn't necessarily meant to be the beginning of an "it's time to go" speech. It was time to go, but she really didn't want to. J.D. had been talking about Spain, nothing very weighty, but he'd been letting Larry and the alcohol loosen his tongue. And then he'd stopped and just stood there with his shoulders slumped and his back to her. She guessed what she was offering him was the beginning of an exit line, if he chose to interpret it that way, or a little gentle sympathy.

J.D. didn't seem to have heard her. He was standing next to the porch railing, leaning against a pillar, looking out at the night. She felt the urge to take him in her arms and say "there, there," and "it's OK," but however that might help what was troubling him it would only make everything else more complicated. She was still wondering what she should do, what she would do, when

J.D. started speaking. He didn't turn around to face her, just spoke softly into the darkness. She had to concentrate to understand.

"That summer the planes were coming nearly every day," J.D. said. "If they thought they saw something they bombed or strafed. It was bad."

She turned and looked at Larry. He was sprawled in a chair beside her with his head slumped forward on his chest. His breathing was deep and regular. She had the feeling that this was what Larry, with his growing case of hero worship, so desperately wanted to hear. She thought about shaking him awake but wasn't sure she wanted to share it, or, for that matter, hear it herself. She thought about interrupting J.D., explaining that it wasn't really necessary for him to tell her those things, but she knew that wasn't true. J.D. badly needed to tell someone. She, apparently, was it.

⌒

They lived like animals, burrowed into the hillsides in shallow dens or under the cover of dense thickets. They regularly patrolled the front, or their little section of it. The front stretched the length of Aragon. Occasionally they exchanged shots with a dimly seen enemy, then both forces would melt back into the forest, neither being inclined to press the action toward what might prove an unacceptable conclusion.

Thanks to the Collectivists, they ate well enough, but they had little ammunition and their uniforms were in tatters. Even though it was summer, there were never enough blankets for the nights. J.D. wasn't the only one who had started to cough.

They were constantly besieged by rumors. The Nationalists' strength was steadily increasing and it was expected that they would soon push forward in a major offensive. The way their planes kept coming seemed to prove it. That was bad enough, but then they heard there was feuding between the Communists and the Anarchists, two of the most important factions in the Republican Army. J.D.'s was just a small band. Half of them were politically unaligned beyond being ardent Anti-Fascists. The rest were local Trade Unionists and militant peasants.

As the rumors became more persistent, they started losing men. Then they learned that Lister's Shock Battalion, who were supposed to be on their side, had started breaking up Republican Collectives in the rear. It was too much. The last of the locals packed up and marched off to stop him. They'd been the contacts with the nearby peasants and food all but stopped coming in.

Saturnino Martinez was the commander. He was a short, bulky man. He had a disconcerting way of looking out of the corner of his eyes when someone talked to him. He'd been too close when a grenade exploded. It cost him the hearing in his right ear, so he always cocked the left toward whoever was speaking.

Soon after the last of the locals left to join the civil war within a civil war behind them, Martinez gathered those who remained. It was obvious they couldn't hold their section of the line much longer. A peasant from Tarragona, a small village in Nationalist hands, had come in the night before. The man claimed the Fascists were building an aerodrome in the valley below his village. While he still had men and ammunition, Martinez wanted to go and do something about it.

They set out before dawn. The peasant claimed the road was clear all the way to Orduna. Martinez decided to chance it. That way they could make the journey in a single day, hit the airfield that night, scatter and head back for Angüés to regroup and find someone in authority to ask how they were expected to hold the line with so few men and no supplies. It would also give them a chance to find out what was really happening in what remained of Republican Aragon.

It was a trap.

They went through a little village called Tres Santos about midmorning. It was deserted. Nothing surprising in that, it was close to the front. The track that passed for a road rose out of the village into a low, jagged range of hills. They hiked up it silently, slowly. They were all tired and undernourished. They were saving their breath because they needed it for the climb and to listen for the motors of the airplanes. They could usually hear them coming long enough to dive off the road and hide.

It was quiet, except for the wind sighing in the trees and the irregular tramp of their boots, until the machine guns opened up and the grenades started falling. Half of them were dead before the rest knew what was happening.

The trail narrowed as they climbed into the pass. There were Nationalist troops above them in the rocks and brush. Martinez had led them into a place without cover, impossible to defend.

J.D. was walking steadily, concentrating on not coughing because he thought if he started he probably wouldn't be able to stop. When he heard the first explosion he looked up from the feet of Fuentes, the man he was following, and saw Carlos Grijalva just beyond, stitched from crotch to clavicle, his body almost ripped in two by machine gun bullets. Fuentes turned to scream at him to take cover but his skull came apart in J.D.'s face. A grenade exploded and Pablo's hand grabbed him on the shoulder. J.D. turned to see if he was hit or what he wanted, but Pablo wasn't there, just the bloody stump of his wrist and the hand with the signet ring he'd said was the only thing he had that was his father's. J.D. took the hand from his shoulder and held it, not sure what to do with it.

Medina came running back down the road, drawing fire. His gun was gone and he was wounded. He was screaming hysterically, mad with terror. He wasn't even looking for cover, just running, responding to a desperate need to be elsewhere that J.D. felt just as keenly. Saturnino Martinez reached after Medina as he went past, then fell like a stone, the back of his head missing. J.D. dropped Pablo's hand and tried to swing his rifle up to find a target but Medina ran headlong into him and both of them cartwheeled into the dirt. J.D. started to get up but the shooting stopped. It was quiet except for Medina's mad howling. J.D. watched him scramble to his feet, then a machine gun opened up again. What was left of Medina tumbled against the rocks at the side of the road. J.D. lay still and tried not to breathe.

They came down out of the brush and boulders, grinning, joking, well fed men with fine modern weapons and neat uniforms. They began systematically looting the dead. Occasionally they kicked a body they thought might be faking, or stuck it with a bayonet. J.D. must have looked convincing. He'd been close to Fuentes and was covered with his gore, and there was the blood from Pablo's hand.

J.D. was lying on his back. He kept his eyes open, just narrow slits, and a hand near the knife at his belt. Not that it would matter. If they found him, he was dead.

One of them wanted J.D.'s pack. It was under him, the strap across his shoulder. The man pulled at it and when it didn't come easily, sawed through the strap with his bayonet. He cut J.D. from shoulder to mid-chest in the process but J.D. was so terrified he hardly felt it. He didn't make a sound. He didn't move. Somehow he managed not to cough.

And then they found Questas. Like J.D., he was only wounded, pretending to be dead. He must have made a less convincing corpse. One of them prodded Questas in the ass with a bayonet and Questas jumped and yelled. He also tried to get at his rifle, but they kicked it away and suddenly he was surrounded.

They grabbed and held him and one of their officers began to ask questions. When Questas wouldn't answer, the man got out a knife. J.D. couldn't see it except for the crowd of uniformed backs. But he could hear when Questas cried out and when, eventually, he begged them to stop. It didn't matter. They no longer cared whether he told them anything or not. They were getting too much pleasure out of the knife. Then Questas started screaming. They were agonized, blood-chilling cries. In between screams he pleaded and sobbed while they told him how they'd cut him next. Then they'd do it and Questas would scream again.

⌒

Mary couldn't remember getting to her feet. She was almost to J.D., reaching out for him. It was either the moment when she most needed or least wanted her husband to interfere. Larry did, though hardly in an orthodox fashion. There was no query of what was going on here, no sudden jealous rage, just a thump followed by an "Ooof!" and a muffled "Ouch," as he fell head first out of his chair.

They both turned to help him up and see how badly he was hurt, which wasn't much since they couldn't find a cut, just a sore spot above the hairline that wouldn't even leave a visible bump. But Larry, it was obvious, needed to be taken home and put to bed and whatever had been about to happen there in the moonlight would have to be put off until another time.

J.D. helped her get Larry out to the Auburn, which she both adored and despised for its ostentation, then stood awkwardly at the curb while Larry mumbled complaints into the leather upholstery.

Neither she nor J.D. could think of anything appropriate to say except goodnight. He was still standing there, watching, when she turned at the corner and headed south. The Auburn's straight eight growled a throaty challenge from its exhaust, just loud enough to keep J.D. from hearing the expletive she suddenly couldn't contain.

Zigzag

SCREAMING!

Someone was screaming. J.D. bolted upright surrounded by the dying echo. Something imprisoned his arms and feet. He strained and tore free. They were only sweat-soaked sheets.

He stood beside his bed, confused, not yet sure where he was or what, if anything, he'd heard. His breath was short and ragged and his heart slammed in his chest.

There was another sound, hammering. Fists against a door. His door. And a voice.

"J.D., you all right? J.D.? Open up!"

"Yeah. Right. I'm OK. I'm coming." His voice croaked, was hardly recognizable. He cleared his throat and tried again.

He was starting to wake up, the dream was losing its stranglehold. He had an uncomfortable idea that he knew who had been screaming, screaming along with Questas. He had done it before, but not for a long time. He had thought, hoped, it was over.

He found his way to the light switch, grabbed a robe, and went to the door. Jesus Gonzales was standing there, looking worried. He had his gun out of his holster and J.D. thought maybe he'd been close to kicking his way in.

"You OK?" he asked. J.D. didn't look so good. He still didn't feel that great either. Too many shreds of the nightmare clung to the corners of his mind.

"Yeah, fine," he lied. "Put your gun away and come in."

It was bright morning outside. A cheerful place, very different from the one he'd just left. He went around the living room opening shades and curtains, letting sunshine in and ghosts out.

"Want some coffee?" J.D. asked. Jesus stood in the doorway. He'd put the gun away but he still looked worried, uncomfortable, like a mother who's just begun to wonder if her child might somehow turn out to be abnormal.

J.D. found his way to the kitchen. Sure enough, it was right where he'd left it. The way he was feeling, that was reassuring. He hadn't quite been confident it would be there.

He searched for the percolator and found it under the stack of dirty dishes in his sink. He substituted a clean sauce pan and started boiling water while he set out cups on the table in the breakfast nook. When the water started rolling he poured in some coffee grounds. What he really wanted was a good stiff drink, but Jesus was already too worried about him, and the deputy might not think morning drinkers were appropriate material for the law enforcement field.

J.D. also wanted a cigarette and spent close to a minute prowling around the living room looking for one before he remembered that he hadn't smoked since Spain. After the pneumonia the doctors recommended against it, and he'd taken so long getting back his strength that he'd started doing what they asked. He turned on his radio instead, twirling past a couple of soap operas and a gruesome account of what Hitler's blitz was doing to London until he found a station that was playing Mozart. It was just the thing to coax his soul away from the realm of the dead and back to that of the living. He picked up his notebook and carried it back into the kitchen, tossing it beside his cup so Jesus wouldn't realize how confused he still was. As he wandered around he muttered a half-hearted explanation about a bad dream as a result of an over spiced supper.

Jesus didn't look convinced. "Come in, sit," J.D. told him. The deputy obeyed, but he moved slowly, softly, with exaggerated care as though he was afraid any sudden sound or movement might shatter his host. J.D. had to admit that he felt a little fragile.

"How you want your coffee? Cream? Sugar?"

"Just black." The wooden bench of the nook groaned beneath Jesus' weight as he lowered himself onto it. He was a big man and the fit was tight. J.D. refrained from a sympathetic groan of his own. He pulled the boiling coffee off the stove, found an egg, and broke it into the mix. It was a trick he'd learned in Spain. He'd learned a lot there.

J.D. filled the cups. His hands didn't shake nearly as much as he expected when he carried the coffee to the table. He put the saucepan back over a low flame and sat down across from the deputy.

"So, what brings you out at this ungodly hour? Just drop by to interrupt my sweet dreams?" The clock over the stove said that it was 10:30. It was pretty weak humor, but the best he could manage.

"I called your office. They said you hadn't been in yet. I thought you might still be here. They said you work pretty late sometimes."

J.D. wondered if they hadn't meant drink late instead, then he realized Jesus' tone had been a little distant, maybe faintly hurt. The big man was genuinely concerned and he'd been trying to laugh the whole thing off.

"Whatever, I'm glad you came," J.D. said, trying to sound conciliatory. "That dream needed interrupting."

"What was it about?"

"You know," he lied, "I can't remember already. Just something big with fangs and claws that had me confused with a Baby Ruth.

"But then, unless you've taken up psychoanalysis as a hobby, I'd guess you didn't drive over here just to talk about my dreams. Aren't you on night shift? Didn't you just get off? Shouldn't you be working on dreams of your own about now?"

There was room for more than one motherly act in that kitchen. Jesus grinned and nodded. "Yeah, long night. They've had me working downtown on that Hollywood-style premiere of *Arizona*, you know, the movie made at that town they built as a set on the other side of the Tucson Mountains. Big crowds, big stars, big deal in a small town like Tucson—even a fake Indian village on Congress Street. Lots of foolishness, but folks were pretty well behaved.

"After I freed up last night, I did some prowling around out among the real Indians on the San Xavier. I've been looking up people I know and keeping the word out that I was interested in getting in touch with Jujul and his village. I ran into a couple of kids I grew up with. They'd had too much to drink and I drove them home. On the way we talked some old times until they decided they could still trust me. They tell me one of Jujul's people was visiting some of his relatives out on the west edge of the San Xavier Reservation. Neither of them saw this fellow, but pretty much everybody out there knew he'd come in. It's a hard place to keep secrets, even though they're all real worried about how this thing's going to turn out.

"Jujul must have sent that one in to try to get a feel from his civilized kin about what's going on. What the tribe and the BIA and the rest of us are up to and how hard we're looking for them, not to mention where.

"I asked if maybe they could set up a meet. Just me and him and whatever friends he wanted to bring along so's he could feel safe. Me, I'd be there unofficially. My word not to try to arrest him. Just talk. I'd tell him what we wanted and he could tell me what they wanted. We'd look for the easiest way for all of us to get out of this without anybody getting hurt. But the boys tell me they think he's gone already. They promised to get word to his people though. They'll set it up if he's available and willing, or leave word in case he or somebody else comes back."

J.D. sipped his coffee. It was pretty awful. There were lots of loose grounds the egg had missed. Not surprising, the trick hadn't worked that well in Spain either.

"You think they were in good enough shape to remember to do it?"

Jesus tasted his coffee. He scowled and put the cup back down. "They'd had a lot," he admitted, "but by the time we talked about that stuff they'd sobered up some. They'll do what they promised."

"Did you expect one of Jujul's bunch to show up this soon?" J.D. asked.

"Yeah. It's been a month. He's had time to move his people quite a ways and set up his winter village. Course, he could have sent one out while they were still moving. Still, I guess I've been expecting somebody any time.

"What interested me most, though, and brought me over to interrupt your beauty sleep, was that when I asked my friends if Jujul and his people were in Mexico they said they didn't know. Apparently, this one was keeping real quiet about where they are. He just wouldn't say. It makes me think maybe Jujul didn't go to Mexico after all. If they were safely across the border, I think this guy would have bragged about it. Said something about how they were where we couldn't touch them instead of keeping his mouth shut."

"Zigzag," J.D. said. It didn't sound like an appropriate comment and Jesus looked at him curiously. "It's how his name translates into English. Mary Spencer told me that just the other night. She said it was traditional for the Papago to have two names. The practice is becoming less common, but Jujul's is a fairly primitive bunch. She said they get one name from a medicine man. That name is secret. It wouldn't get shared, except maybe with people they were really close to. So they called each other by nicknames or relationships. Jujul's old enough to have been named in the traditional way and have picked up a nickname that stuck. Nicknames usually reflect some physical aspect or the sort of character a person is. Zigzag. Don't you see? He could be called that because he's a perverse bastard with a tendency to do the unexpected."

J.D. realized he'd almost been babbling with excitement. He shut up and looked at Jesus expectantly. "What do you think?" he asked. "You know the Papago a lot better than I do."

"When you've got a name like mine, you tend not to think too much about other people's, except as something handy to call them by. I never thought about how his name translates, but you could be right. The old man's certainly proved contrary enough so far. Somebody said they had trouble with him during the census. He didn't want his people and cattle counted, but whatever started this probably goes back a lot further than that."

"So, if we're right, Jesus, where do you think he might be? If he didn't take his people to Mexico, where would he take them?"

Jesus contemplated his coffee but prudently refrained from drinking more. "Big desert out there," he said. "He could be anywhere. He could have chosen almost any of it for almost any reason. Could have even headed right back to his old village, except that I've had the tribal police keeping an eye on it. Maybe somewhere along the north part of the reservation, if he's expecting us to think he went south. Just knowing he's contrary doesn't tell us what he's contrary to. Hell, J.D., I don't know. If it was me, I'd have gone to Mexico."

"Me too," J.D. agreed. "But all of a sudden I've got this gut feeling he's come closer to Tucson. You sure they couldn't be somewhere on the San Xavier?"

"No, they could be. Not likely, but they could. But if they are, I'll hear about it. I've got too many contacts out there with too many people who like to gossip."

"You're right, of course, but wouldn't it be a colossal joke on us for him to move his people right under our noses. It strikes me as the sort of thing that would appeal to a man with a zigzag in his personality."

Jesus absently toyed with the badge on the front of his uniform. "Yeah, Papagos have a sense of humor all right." He confirmed it with a laugh.

They batted ideas back and forth and Jesus refused J.D.'s offer to warm his coffee. They finally agreed the San Xavier Reservation was almost certainly out, as was the area right around Sells. Both were too crowded with people willing to cooperate with the tribal police or friends, like Jesus, in other agencies. But there was a lot of area along the eastern border of the Reservation, not too far from Tucson, that was still pretty remote. Places where it would be relatively easy for Jujul to avoid contact, not only with the various agencies searching for him, but even with other Papago if he wanted. J.D. suggested asking some pilots to fly over the area and see what they could find, but Jesus pointed out that Papagos move around a lot and there probably wasn't any way of telling one bunch from another from the air. They settled on putting out fresh feelers to the Papago villages they knew of along the border and asking the ranchers in the same area to let them know if they encountered any strange Papagos looking for trade or work.

J.D. offered Jesus a fresh cup of coffee but he politely refused, made some excuses, and began his retreat. He was almost out the door when he turned back and smiled apologetically.

"Speaking of names, J.D.?" he asked. "It occurs to me I don't know yours, just the initials."

"With good reason," J.D. replied. "For what it's worth, though, I'll tell you what Fitzpatrick means."

Jesus managed to look interested, even if it wasn't what he'd asked.

"It means some English or Irish noble once had his way with a peasant girl. Put her in the family way, as my father liked to explain it, without putting her in his family. Though he didn't marry her, he was at least kind enough to acknowledge her child. Fitzpatrick means Patrick's son, or more exactly, in the idiom of the time in which such names originated, Patrick's bastard."

Jesus laughed. "That explains a lot about your character," he said. He went down the walk and waved as he climbed into the patrol car. Out of habit, he left the neighborhood with his foot to the floor.

J.D. was feeling better, almost human. He had a sudden urge to talk to Mary. See if the likelihood Jujul hadn't gone to Mexico gave her any ideas. He'd forced himself to stay away from her for three whole days. This was a good excuse to see her again. Any excuse was a good one.

Kiva on a Shoestring

Larry had a pencil in his mouth and a sheaf of papers in his hand when he answered the bell He opened the door wide and stepped aside so J.D. could enter.

"Come in, come in," he said around a delighted grin. "I've been working on an article for *The Kiva*, trying to trim two thousand words down to the three hundred they've allotted me. Having some publications is going to be important when I get my degree and start job hunting.

"I think if I cut out everything but verbs, the length will come out about right. It won't detract much from what I say either. You can't do much theorizing about Hohokam culture in three hundred words, or if you do, offer any evidence to support it. On the other hand, I can't blame the Arizona Archaeological and Historical Society. They publish *The Kiva* on a shoestring. If your entire journal can only be about ten pages long, you can't offer most of it to the first graduate student who happens along.

"I haven't gotten very far. I was still wondering whether they'll count the words in the title against me when you rang the bell. Come on in and let me get you some coffee."

J.D. followed Larry out to the kitchen, depositing his hat on the hall tree as they passed.

"Sorry to bother you," J.D. apologized. "It's just that something's come up and I wanted to get Mary's point of view on it."

"I've been meaning to call you," Larry began.

J.D. waved off the apology before it could get started. "You were just tired. I should have sent you home at a reasonable hour. Not your fault, mine."

Larry still looked embarrassed and not entirely convinced, but he didn't argue.

J.D.'s opinion of Larry was more than a little confused. He never would have put up with the lad if doing so hadn't provided an excuse to be near Mary. Still, it was hard to dislike someone who seemed to think you were the prototype for the hero of Hemingway's new best-seller, however absurd the comparison. Under other circumstances he might have learned to like Larry Spencer, maybe even tolerate the insatiable curiosity that prompted the archaeologist to pry into J.D.'s life with the same enthusiasm he brought to opening ancient graves. Larry was oblivious to the horrors he might find, or the fact that anyone's sensibilities might be offended. He just couldn't pass up a chance to expose himself to that which was previously unknown.

J.D. sipped his coffee. "Actually, that wasn't why I was going to call," Larry told him, stirring cream and sugar into his. "Mary wanted to call you herself, but things just moved too fast and there was too much to do."

J.D. raised his eyebrows and peered across the table letting his impatience show. Larry wasn't slow. He caught on and got to the point.

"She's in the field," he said. "Left first thing this morning. She got word from a rancher that a fairly primitive Papago band had come in to trade, and it was one of the places she'd put out feelers. Anyway, the village talked it over and agreed to take her. She got the call night before last and she's been frantically making arrangements ever since. Old Doc Sherwood nearly had a conniption, having to change teaching assistants in the middle of the semester like this, but he'd known it might happen so there wasn't much he could do other than grump about it. Still, we had to get formal permission for her to take incompletes on this semester's course work, and she had lots to explain to the guy who's going to take her place with Sherwood. She already had her trade goods packed, and couldn't take much personal stuff, but we went out and bought her an old pickup truck so she could get it all out to this fellow's ranch and so she can get back whenever she wants. After all, we've got no idea how long she'll be away, so I wanted her to have some sort of transportation as handy as possible."

"She's gone?" J.D. asked. He suddenly felt a lot older.

"Yeah. Don't worry, though. She'll be OK. She knows these people and she knows the desert. She'll get along just fine.

"Listen, if what you've come across is really important, maybe I can help. A little of what she's learned has rubbed off on me. Or maybe I can find somebody who can get you an answer. If it's not too urgent, we should be able to get word to her in a few weeks, probably get a reply back in less than a month."

"No, no, it wasn't really that important," J.D. said, climbing out of his chair. "just an excuse to drink somebody else's coffee. Sorry I bothered you, Larry. I shouldn't have."

Larry followed him back down the hall, telling him he hadn't interrupted anything and was welcome to stay for as much coffee as he liked. J.D. thanked him but kept going. As J.D. climbed into his Ford, Larry called out something about getting together soon. J.D. didn't seem to hear.

When Larry went back in the house he discovered J.D.'s hat was still on the hall tree. It confirmed the gravity of what he thought the marshal was involved in, and made a three-hundred word article on Hohokam archaeology seem awfully insignificant by comparison.

Participant Observer

It was mid-morning before Mary got to Burns' ranch, not because it was so far, but because the road from the highway barely qualified for the definition. It was distinguishable from the desert because its surface wasn't as smooth and it contained marginally less cactus and brush.

She was already worn out. Between her frantic preparations and the excited anticipation of finally achieving the goal she'd been working toward, she'd barely found time to sleep since she got the call. Remnants of euphoria saw her through the long drive and remained, as limited reserves, when she guided the truck into Burns' front yard.

There were about a dozen young Indian men and women lounging around the ranch's outbuildings, waiting for her. Bill Burns hurried out to introduce her to the group that had come to escort her to their village. They were all very quiet and shy. She could feel their eyes on her as they unloaded the pickup, but whenever she glanced up, they'd be looking elsewhere, busy distributing the load and packing it for the trail.

Mary declined Bill and Edith Burns' offer to spend the night. It might have been the sensible thing to do so she could start out fresh, but the *O'odham*, though they didn't say so, seemed anxious to leave and Mary felt the same way. She thanked Bill and Edith for helping her make contact and gave them the packages she'd brought by way of thanks, a new straw hat for Bill and a silk scarf for Edith. She wrote a quick note to Larry, telling him she'd arrived, was OK, and would be in touch as soon as she got established and the next party from her village went somewhere to trade. She tried to find out when that might be from the leader of the group but he couldn't provide a specific answer, just when the need arose. She thought about sending along a note to J.D., then decided it wasn't wise. Instead, she just asked Larry to tell him hello, and that, when she came out, she could be a lot more help with his Papago problem, if it hadn't solved itself by then.

Aside from her natural pleasure at beginning her field work, she realized this was a good time for her to get away. There had never been a man in her life but Larry, and even if his occasional digressions into the arms of other women were humiliating, she hadn't considered paying him back in kind—at least not until J.D. The marshal was really getting to her, and it was obvious he felt something as well. What they'd been headed for had begun to seem almost inevitable, and Larry had been unwittingly encouraging them every step of the way.

She needed time to think. To get her head on straight, or, if straight wasn't where it was going to end up, be sure she was satisfied with its new direction. She didn't want to see J.D. again until she was sure how much she wanted him, and how much she was willing to sacrifice in the process. Maybe it would have been best for her to go into the field with Larry for a few months. Then, his good qualities could have their daily, uninterrupted chance to win a reconfirmation of her feelings for him. It might work, at least until she saw J.D. again.

Oh, fuck it, she told herself. She slung her pack on her shoulders. She wasn't going to solve in one afternoon what she hadn't been able to solve for weeks. The further she got from the people involved, especially J.D., the more rational she could be about how she felt and what was important.

Mary was a little surprised that the Indians hadn't brought any horses, but Bill Burns had told her the first group that came trading herded their cattle in on foot, so she'd come prepared. She fell into line and the little group hiked up out of the valley where the ranch buildings lay clustered in a grove of mesquite and cottonwood, out into a wilderness of desert broom and creosote and cactus. Abbreviated peaks of volcanic stone rose intermittently, sentinels to warn the desert of this miniature invasion. Broken clouds produced a fitful November sun that gave the day only a sort of half-hearted warmth. It didn't matter, she was sweating from exertion before they went a hundred yards.

Within half an hour they had twisted and turned so much she wouldn't have had any idea where she was if it weren't for the peaks of the Baboquivari Range playing hide and seek with the clouds rolling lethargically in from the west. She wasn't sure she could find her way back to the ranch. It gave her a little twinge of panic, realizing she was trusting her life to people she didn't know, whose ways and thoughts were alien. But it passed. In fact, she reassured herself, she did know them, and she could hardly have chosen a gentler people. She would be safer in the middle of the desert in the company of these strangers than in some parts of civilized Tucson, even with her husband.

They moved quietly, in an unhurried fashion that devoured the miles. The *O'odham* didn't talk among themselves and Mary took her cue from them, matching their pace and keeping her mouth shut except to breathe. They were working her hard, especially since she hadn't slept much in the last few days, but she was determined to keep up and not be a burden at such an early stage. She was making her first impression, and she very badly wanted it to be a favorable one. It could make a big difference in how quickly they began to accept her and how soon she could start collecting the information she needed.

They flushed a covey of quail once, and several times rabbits broke from cover beside their line of march. Birds watched them pass from the safety of the scrub brush or a perch among the spines of a cactus. Occasionally they passed a giant saguaro, arms raised in surprise at encountering anything as unlikely as an anthropologist in this endless landscape.

It was the season for occasional, gentle, weeping rains, and it could become quite cold, especially at night, but Mary was prepared for whatever they encountered. What she wasn't prepared for was continuing their forced march straight through the day and beyond. When twilight gave way to full dark and they kept moving, Mary started to worry. There was a limit to how long she could last.

It was after midnight when they finally stopped at the mouth of a rugged little canyon that wandered down from a low range she hadn't even noticed until then. She hadn't noticed much of anything for the last few hours. It had taken all her will just to keep lifting each foot in turn and putting it back down again without putting the rest of her down beside it for a brief nap on the desert floor.

The Desert People started a fire using safety matches instead of twirled sticks or even flint and steel. Mary was too tired to be disappointed. They dug out utensils and food and Mary thought she should be helping or at least taking notes, but she must have drifted off because the next thing she remembered was a dark, leathery face above her, gently shaking her awake and offering a plate of beans, fry bread, and some jerked beef. The woman apologized for disturbing her guest, but insisted it was important that Mary eat a good meal because she must have strength for the trail in the morning. Mary wasn't hungry and started to tell her so, but she was too weary to think of the right words in *O'odham*. She just took the plate because it was easier and ate a little to be polite until the plate was empty and they filled it for her again and she ate that too. Then she rolled over and went back to sleep while they sat and talked quietly around the fire. When they woke her in the morning to offer her breakfast, she discovered someone had covered her with one of their blankets.

They followed the same routine for three days. Though Mary managed to stay awake a few minutes longer each night, long enough to help unload and set up their trail camp, she remained too weary to dig out her notebook and record more than a few cryptic sentences.

The third day was cold and they walked through an intermittent mist that brought the normally distant horizons almost to within touching distance and soaked their clothing. Mary would have dug out her rain poncho, but none of her companions had one and it embarrassed her to be the only one who kept dry. She left it in her pack and shared the misery.

That night they stopped at a rock shelter. It was as though the Papago were so in tune with their environment that their march was planned with the expectation of a wet day occurring when it did so that they could finish their march in such a place. She might have gotten mystical about it, but she was too wet and tired and cold.

They had a much larger fire than usual that night. It wasn't easy because everything was soaked, but they found some tinder that was dry enough to get things started and piled up wet wood close to the blaze where it could dry before it was added to the flames. They had a fresh stew of some sort. One of the men brought in a small animal and cleaned it and chopped it up into the communal pot. It looked like it might be a large rodent. She knew the Papago occasionally ate rat, so she just didn't ask. It tasted fine. The fire warmed and dried them and Mary slept again.

When she woke there was an old man with white hair and a thin white beard kneeling over her. He hadn't been with them the night before. In fact, Mary suddenly noticed, only a few of her traveling companions, all of them women, remained around the dying embers of the fire. Except for the newcomer, all the men were gone.

The old man bid her good morning in a polite, formal fashion, and introduced himself. "I am *Siwani Mahkai*," he told her. It was his title, Chief Medicine Man, rather than a name, but she knew it was possible no one in his village ever called him anything else.

"And you are Marie?" He gave her name a Spanish pronunciation without turning it into Maria. She didn't correct him. She knew she was mutilating plenty of *O'odham* words, and no one had been discourteous enough to mention it. Marie was fine with her.

"You are the woman who would become an elder before her time, a sort of *Mahkai* to your people?"

"Yes, *Siwani Mahkai*," she agreed. Of all the people in his village, this man would be the most important. His title indicated that he was both their headman and their shaman. It was the later role that made him truly important. Papago society offered no higher niche to which one can aspire than maker of magics. If she got along well with the *Siwani Mahkai* she was virtually assured of success. If she didn't, she might as well pack up and go home. Her time in his village would be wasted.

"We are near our village," he said. "There is no longer much physical distance to travel, but if you would come to us as a member of our people, and it is my understanding that such is your wish, then there is still a long journey before you."

Mary was puzzled, not quite awake enough to comprehend. Whatever game they were playing, it was his. He knew the rules.

She would have to learn as they went along. It was what she had come for, though, so she nodded politely, noncommittally, and waited for him to proceed.

"I am told you already know much about the ways of our people?"

"I have learned what I could, but there are many gaps in my knowledge," Mary answered.

"Are you aware of the things which happen when a woman comes of age among the People?"

"I know there is a sort of purification ceremony and then a great celebration."

He smiled. "You are correct. I have thought on it at some length, and decided, since you wish to become one of us, to live among us as a Person and not a guest, we must initiate you as we would a girl child of our own. We have built a woman's hut for you. You will go to it for four days. There, you will fast and be taught and purified. We have built the hut here because you are not yet one of us. You carry strong magics of which you are unaware and which could harm our people unless they are removed. When you have been cleansed and you are a Person, we shall take you home. If you do not agree to these things, you may still come as our guest, but there will always remain a distance between yourself and the People, things you will not be allowed to see or participate in. The decision is yours. Will you become one of us?"

Mary was stunned, but delighted. This would be participant observation at its best. They were giving her a chance to experience some of their ceremonies first hand. The sorts of things a people were normally reluctant to even discuss with an outsider, and they would let her live them. She tried to keep from sounding too eager as she agreed, but some of it must have shown because the old man grinned at her. He had an impressive set of teeth for a man his age who had never seen a dentist.

"Good," he said. He turned and gestured for one of the women. She was as old as he, and she hadn't been part of the group that escorted Mary either. "This is Grey Leaves," he said. "You must go with her and do as she instructs. She will take you to the women's hut. It will be she who spends most of the purification time with you, teaching you a woman's knowledge and preparing you to become *O'odham*. While you fast and are cleansed, I too will fast, and dream for you your secret name."

He rose and turned and walked away without another word. He was a tall, strong man, in spite of his obvious age, but he had a pronounced limp. She wondered whether it was the result of arthritis or an injury.

"Come with me, child," the old woman gently commanded. Mary scrambled out of her blankets and started gathering up her pack.

"No, leave those things," the woman said. Mary badly wanted take along a notebook at least, but, she reminded herself, their game, their rules. Besides, she had a good memory. She could write it all down as soon as the ceremonies were over. She followed the old woman and the younger ones trailed along behind. They walked a short distance into the desert to a low round, earth covered hut. Mary was impressed that they'd built something so substantial in such a short time. She started to bend down to enter but the old woman stopped her.

"You must remove your clothing, child." Mary had thought she was ready for anything, but she wasn't ready for that. Modesty aside, it was very cold under the low, grey sky. There was a dusting of snow on the peaks behind them and frost clung to the surrounding brush. "It must be done," the old woman prompted.

Mary looked around. There were only the other women, waiting patiently with their burdens of pots and baskets. The men had all disappeared. Maybe being a participant observer wasn't all it was cracked up to be. She started working at the buttons and buckles, feeling like an idiot.

She half expected Larry and her fellow graduate students to jump out from behind the surrounding brush and start laughing and pointing. Or maybe all the Papago men would suddenly leap out and shout surprise and have a good laugh at the expense of the gullible anthropologist.

In a couple of minutes she stood there like a desert version of *September Morn*. She felt so foolish she might have started giggling if the old woman hadn't taken a pot from one of the others and dumped the icy water it contained over her head. She gave a small cry of surprise as she became one giant goose bump. Any inclination she'd felt to laugh was gone.

"I wash from you all that is impure," the old woman chanted. "I wash from you all that is unclean. All that is dangerous to yourself and others, I wash it from you."

There were at least a half-dozen pots filled with water. Mary wondered, fleetingly, if it was too late to change careers.

Mirage Talker

The sign read, John Parker, Attorney at Law. It hung outside the weathered frame shack that had originally been built to house his father's church. Sells never had much of a population to draw a congregation from so the building wasn't oversized in its new capacity. Both sign and building needed fresh paint. The sign had become hard to read, not that it mattered, since not many people here could read at all. Few of them had need of his services either, or could understand or afford them when they did. Parker didn't care. He was here to create a political following and make an impression, not money. His crazy evangelical father had left him a small inheritance, as well as the building. It wasn't much, but Sells was a cheap place to live.

Occasionally he even lured in a client. It was a cool November morning on the way to a warm day. Parker heard the bell on his front door ring and got up to see who'd come in. The bell was cheaper than a receptionist. It was a young, wiry guy with a pinched-in face, rodent-like, Parker thought.

"Can I help you?" he asked, doubting it. The guy's denims were worn and dirty and his boots were run down at the heel. No money in this kid's pockets.

"I'm looking for John Parker, the attorney." he said. He spoke pretty good English at least.

"You're in luck then."

"I need your help," the rat-faced man said.

"For?"

"It's a long story. I'd rather not tell it out here where somebody might interrupt us."

Parker thought the man was seriously overestimating the potential for his office to draw walk-in traffic, but he did have his desk and his law books in the back room. It helped keep up appearances.

He would have preferred to send the little guy packing. It was hard to imagine how he could profit from whatever time this took, but everyone was a potential voter and he intended to run for tribal council again. And, you just never knew when something useful might walk through that door, or how it would be packaged. Parker mentally consulted the day's schedule of appointments. It was, as usual, empty. "All right," he said. "Come on back."

The little man looked around the office nervously, then took the chair he was offered. He started talking before Parker could get behind his desk, as if he expected to be billed by the minute and couldn't take a chance on wasting any.

"My name is Pete, but they also call me Mirage Talker," he said. "I guess I was always going on about the things I would have some day—White Man's things. My family lived near here. My mother, she kept house for Dr. Saunders who used to work over at the clinic. She took me with her sometimes, when she cleaned his place, so I got to see more of the wonderful stuff the White Men have than most. My father would laugh at the absurdity of owning more than you could carry, but I was fascinated by the marvels I saw there. I wanted lights that burned without flames and the box that made music and voices. I wanted a car to carry them in, and a great house, big enough to hold all the people from my village.

"As soon as I could, I left home and went to work on a ranch. I'm very good with horses, so I soon learned about money and how it was earned and traded and I began acquiring some of the things I had dreamed about."

"So far, you don't need a lawyer," Parker observed in an effort to hustle the little man along. He might have all day, but he didn't want to take it.

"Maybe I desired those things too much. I learned to save. I didn't drink, didn't waste it on short-lived dreams like so many other hands at the ranch. When I had enough to buy a car, I was going to drive it home and show them it wasn't mirages I had talked about.

"There was a regular poker game in the bunkhouse on Sunday nights. I watched it for a long time before I let them persuade me to join. At first, I was very careful, but I was also very lucky. I saw that car and my return home becoming grander. I would fill it with presents for everyone in the village. I began risking more of my savings. I lost it all. More. I owed the one they called Big Jack Lang several month's wages.

"Three days later I overheard him bragging about how he'd suckered a stupid little Papago out of all his savings at the poker table. I decided I would get it back.

"They called him Big Jack for obvious reasons. He was very large, even for a White Man. I wanted my money, but I knew I couldn't make him give it back. I considered going to the foreman or the owner but I thought they would believe another White Man and not me. So, one Saturday night when Jack and his friends had gone to Sasabe after drinks and women, I slipped into his bunkhouse and went through his belongings. He must have carried most of his money on him, or hidden it elsewhere. I was checking under the mattress when Big Jack came in.

"I had been very quiet. There were two other men sleeping in the same room. If they woke and caught me they would beat me, perhaps send me to the White Man's jail. I had heard about that place and didn't want to see it first hand. I just wanted my money. Then I would leave and find another ranch, far away, where I could earn more and never see Big Jack again.

"But Big Jack came home way early. He shouted when he saw me. I broke for the back door but he caught me and slammed me against a bunk in the corner. I went over it backwards. Hit my head against the stacked crates beside it that made do as shelves. Jack came around the bunk after me. His face was ruddy from the drinking and he was grinning. He was enjoying what he was doing. I had seen him fight before. He liked giving pain. I kicked him in his crotch and the smile went away. So did the ruddy. He backed out in the aisle, holding himself. I jumped over the bunk and sprinted toward the front door but one of the men who had been asleep blocked the way. He was more my size, but he had picked up an ax handle.

"I went back toward Big Jack. My boots weren't hard enough for what I'd done to him. He was recovering, and he was angry. I tried to duck around him but he caught me and threw me against the nearest wall. He grabbed hold of my hair with one hand and began pounding my head against it. I don't remember doing it, but the next I knew Jack had stopped smiling again. He was sitting on the bunk across the aisle, holding his stomach and bleeding from where I had put the knife in him.

"The other two White Men started toward me, but they came slowly because of the blade. I went over to Jack and put it against his throat and told them to stay away. I pushed the big man back on the bed and rolled him to where I could pull out his wallet and take his money.

"It wasn't even close to what he stole from me. I went out the back door. They came looking for me but none of the Papago hands who might have tracked me had any reasons to like Big Jack either.

"I headed back to the reservation. I used the money to buy a horse and some provisions at the first village I came to. Then I kept running. Eventually, I began to wonder where I was running to. I don't want to live here. I want the White Man's world, but I don't want to go to their jail for what I did to Big Jack. I thought about it and decided you would help me. You have a reputation. You fight the authorities for our people. Maybe Big Jack isn't dead. Maybe he is. You can find out. You can find out if I can go back because no one cares what happened, or help keep me out of jail if they do."

Parker looked at him for a minute and wondered whether the story was true or if it just put Talker in the best light. "You spent the money."

"Yes."

"Then how do you plan to pay?"

Parker kept a .44 in his desk drawer just in case, not that he thought pissing the kid off would make him a threat. This Talker guy didn't have any options other than him just now.

"Nothing is free," Parker said. "That's why I won't turn you in for it either. Not likely there's a reward out for you."

The little man got up and started for the door.

"Hold on," Parker said. "I didn't say I wouldn't help, did I?"

"But I have nothing to pay with. Maybe, after, I could send you some of my earnings."

Parker laughed. "No, I prefer to collect up front, and I've got something else in mind. Look, you need a place to hide, right? Well, somewhere out there a whole village of Papagos is hiding. You've heard of Jujul."

"Everyone has."

"OK. Nobody can find him, so far. But I figure that's because the wrong people are looking. Clever man like you could probably find him. And, think about it. If the authorities can't find a whole village, how they going to find one lone Papago thief and assassin, especially if he was to hide in the same place.

"Pete, my friend, you find me Jujul, locate his village for me and I'll not only take your case, I'll get you off scot-free and find you a good job on a ranch where there aren't any Big Jacks and you can start earning those mirages again."

The attorney could see the wheels turn behind the boy's eyes. He didn't like the idea of betraying another Papago, especially not a hero like Jujul. But, even more, he didn't like the idea of being a nobody, hiding out on the reservations for the rest of his life. He had dreams, and they had dollar signs on them.

"OK," he said. "I'll find him for you."

Parker doubted it, but who knew. Sooner or later somebody was going to find Jujul. If it was John Parker, maybe he could find a way to make some of that hero stuff rub off, just in time for the next election.

So That He Might Dream

He had been standing in the darkness above the rock shelter, watching when she came in with the others. Jujul had kept riders near them from the beginning so he could track their wanderings and watch their trail to be sure no one followed. He had hoped clouds, and maybe rain, would come quickly, and they did. Best not to walk her about for weeks. There would be enough reasons for her to become suspicious. The longer it could be avoided, the more they would learn from her.

She was tall and slender, too skinny to be attractive, even with her woman's hips and upright breasts. She looked very young, but he had no practice in judging the age of Anglos. It might be fashionable among Whites for their women to make themselves look artificially young, just as it was once fashionable for *O'odham* women to tattoo their faces with geometrical designs. The modern custom held that a woman should be large and heavy to be beautiful. It conferred prestige on her husband or father for his ability to feed her well.

They had worked the White Woman hard on her journey, but she arrived with a willing step, carrying her share of the burden. It impressed him because the few Whites he had known were not accustomed to much physical effort. When the group stopped, she helped unload, then joined the women in preparing the evening meal.

She showed good qualities: strength, curiosity, and a willingness to help as she learned. Jujul felt uncomfortable about the tricks they planned for her, but her people had sent Larson to attack his village. He did not wish to go to prison nor see his young men taken away to fight a war they could not understand. He did not want them exposed to the White Man's ways. He had seen the effect on other villages. The White Man's path was an inviting one. It gleamed and beckoned, but was not truly open to the People. The only reward he had witnessed for those who pursued it was frustration.

The first test came in the morning. While the girl slept, the men stealthily packed the goods she brought, and set out in silence. They would leave them in a cache, two days south, in case Rat Skin and his friends were right. The cache would be watched, as had the trail, to be sure it drew no police or soldiers. Jujul was sure there would be none, at least not soon.

He kept only one of the men with him. After the girl woke and they took her to the women's hut, someone had to carry the last of her belongings to the cache. Otherwise, only Grey Leaves and the women remained. He had chosen Grey Leaves to assist him because she was an old friend and a medicine woman of some power in her own right, and because she agreed with his plan.

At dawn, he gathered the women and reviewed what was expected of them. Grey Leaves added her own instructions, then Jujul went to wake the girl.

Up close, sleeping, she seemed even younger. For a moment he was reminded of Many Flowers, his child bride, dead so long ago. It took his breath away and briefly, he was able only to kneel and watch her and wonder at the improbability of such a similarity. Their faces were very different. Marie's hair was the color of polished ironwood, dark brown with a hint of rich red. The People's hair was always black until age lightened it. Even the texture of her hair was different. But there was a smoothness to the line of this face that indicated youth and innocence, and there were little wrinkles about her mouth and eyes, tiny remnants of past joys and laughter. Many Flowers' face had been like that, only she had also been pretty, not so pasty and scrawny as this one.

He reached out and woke her. He had let his beard grow since the village moved to Black Caves but it did not change his face greatly. How vividly had the Whites been able to describe him? If she knew about him, would she know what he looked like? If she recognized him they might learn nothing from her, but he could not hide and leave the questions to someone else. He must be there to ask and to judge her answers himself. These were his people. He was responsible for them.

The girl woke easily. It must have been a surprise to find a strange face above her, but if she was startled, she hid it well. She peered up at him and smiled a greeting. Yes, she impressed him, this young woman of his enemy.

He told her who he was and it was true, though he did not give her the name she might know him by. His people had been instructed to call him only by his titles while she was with them. There was a good chance that even the children might remember to do so for a time. He became sure, as he talked, that she did not know him, that she did not suspect he was the outlaw Papago whom her people hunted. She listened quietly and answered correctly when it was required. She seemed genuinely honored at what he proposed to her. It made him feel ashamed that it was an elaborate trick designed to separate her from the last of her belongings and further confuse her sense of where she was. He was glad he had insisted, along with Grey Leaves, that if the ceremony was to be done, it must be done correctly. She would be a fine addition to the People.

When he finished he turned and walked away, leaving things to Grey Leaves. He climbed to another rock shelter where he performed his own rituals, and began fasting and consulting his crystals, so that he might dream her true name. When the dream came it did not surprise him. From the moment before he woke her he knew what he wanted to call her. Many Flowers. It had been too long since the name lived in his village. His dreams confirmed it. Most of them were pleasant, but not all.

—

The sun was high and hot and there was sand in his mouth. For a long time he lay, unable to move, comforted only because he knew he must be dreaming. Pain such as this could not be real. It had to be a nightmare.

But the nightmare would not end. He fought it, trying to free his mind and body from its bindings. He pushed at it with his thoughts, then tried his arms and legs. It only made the pain infinitely worse and carried him away to the realm of real nightmares again.

It was probably the flies that saved him. They were feasting at his wounds, exploring his face and drinking from his eyes. They crawled in and out of his mouth and nostrils. The pain was bad enough. The flies were unbearable. He murmured a protest and brushed a heavy hand at them, one that required tremendous will and concentration to move at all. The flies sensed the lack of any real danger and stayed, tearing at his raw flesh. It felt as if they meant to rip away a piece of his leg as big as a fist. Finally, he could stand it no more. He swatted at them and half struggled to a sitting position.

The world spun madly, the way he remembered it doing at the beginning of the *O'odham* Year in Saguaro Fruit Month after he drank too much of the fermented juice of the great cactus, or anytime he had sipped the potent beverages of the White Men. He grabbed hold of the sand until, gradually, things ceased their wild whirling and the sky slowed and stayed above and the earth beneath, and he knew where he was, and the terrible things that had happened there. He knew where the flies had gone.

Cloud Peak was dead. He had seen a bullet steal her life. Many Flowers had been alive, kicking, screaming, clawing at the soldiers when he last remembered. But the flies were feeding on two bodies, each frighteningly still. He was afraid of who the second must be. He tried to get up, to go to her, but the world spun again.

He settled on crawling, dragging his useless leg behind. Several times he found his face in the sand again and had to remind himself of what he was doing and why. Eventually he reached her. A few flies came to feed on him again. He hardly noticed. Many Flowers was more to their liking. She lay still, uncomplaining of their appetites. The soldiers had slit her throat from ear to ear and she had bled a great deal, enough even, to satisfy the flies. He turned his head away and sank back on the sand. For a time he did not care if he lived or died.

It was because of Many Flowers that they were there. The village had just begun its move back to *Stohta U'uhig* from their other home in the mountains of Mexico when she became ill. It was not a serious sickness, but he knew she would be more comfortable if she could rest until it passed. He sent the remainder of the village on. He planned to build a small arrow brush shelter above the arroyo and stay with her until she was well. She was very young and precious to him. She had only come of age during the winter and they had been married just a short time.

It surprised him when Cloud Peak decided to stay as well. She was his first wife, and while she was proud that her husband was rich and important enough to have a second, she was also a little jealous of the child. When she asked to stay, Jujul agreed. He was pleased to have her aid, and keep her with them.

With the resilience of the young, Many Flowers passed the sickness off quickly. She had been ready to travel for several days, but he insisted they stay. It was a pleasant place and he was enjoying this brief taste of freedom. The constant worries of leadership, the village's daily crises could wait a little. What harm could there be in his taking time to himself and his wives. And there, for the first time, Cloud Peak began to accept Many Flowers, to cherish her also. The three rejoiced in each other and shared pleasures.

That must have been why the women were in the arroyo. He had spent the night coupling with them like young healthy animals in their season. While he slept the sleep of exhaustion and satiation, the women must have woken early and felt a need to wash themselves. There was a deep pool nearby, a place where there was water in all but the driest of seasons. They had often used it as their bathing place. It was where the Americans had come to water their horses.

Jujul would never know most of what happened. He could not understand why they slaughtered Many Flowers, then left him alive. Perhaps they thought him dead. Perhaps they thought he could not survive and would suffer more, left as he was. Perhaps, unmoving, unconscious, he was simply no longer a threat and so went unnoticed in their haste to leave. They had wasted no time once he was stopped. They only killed his second wife, took their dead comrade, and left. Had they thought the rest of his people nearby? Had they believed Many Flowers' screams would bring more warriors? Surely the noise they made trying to kill him would have been enough for that. He supposed it was only that killing her was a quick, easy way to remove an annoyance. Alive, she would have continued to fight those who had harmed the people she loved. He would never know for sure.

He had few clear memories of the days that followed. He must have dragged himself away from the bodies of his wives, down to the pool and washed his wounds. He remembered bandaging himself with strips from a torn shift.

He crawled back to the shelter and fed himself and rested. When he could, he made a crutch and went back and buried his wives. He was too weak to do it well. He only managed to pile stones and sand over them where they lay. By that time the animals and birds had already been at them. He did the best he could, then burned the hut in which they had stayed and cut off his hair in mourning.

He found his rifle. The stock was shattered, but the gun, though scarred, was undamaged. He could carve a new stock. He had plans for the weapon.

After the sixteen days of purification required for one who has killed a man, he packed his rifle, some food and water, and started following the trail the rest of his village had taken. He was still too weak to go after the Americans. His people found him a few days later. He was delirious and near death. They took him back to *Stohta U'uhig* and nursed him.

It was a long time before he was fit enough to look for the soldiers. By the time he returned to the arroyo their trail was gone. Their kind had also gone elsewhere. He did not know where to look for them. The village remained his responsibility. He went back to it reluctantly, but with ample reason to hate the White Man.

The Guest of Honor

She had grown up on a successful Ohio farm where the kitchen never produced meals that were less than bountiful. She owed her figure to genetic predisposition, youth, and metabolism, not a succession of diets. Nothing she'd ever done prepared her for those four days. Giving up cookies for Lent as a little girl just wasn't the same thing. Even then, she'd thought of nothing but cookies from the moment she gave them up. It was like that for the first three days in the hut. Grey Leaves, or occasionally one of the younger women, sat with her and droned on and on about a woman's place in the tribe, her duties and expectations. They showed her how to weave cloth and baskets, how to throw a pot, how a house should be laid out—all of it invaluable to an ethnographer—but she couldn't concentrate. All she could think of was food, and they made it worse by giving her recipes and explaining how to identify edible roots and berries.

Actually, the first part of the first morning she was more cold than hungry. She'd wondered when she would get a chance to take her next bath. She hadn't anticipated it would be a shower nor so public and so soon. When they ran out of ice water they bundled her in robes and blankets and dried her. They gave her a cotton shift like those of the People. Grey Leaves had made it for her. They led her into the low, rounded hut where a mesquite fire smoldered behind a shield of rocks so that Mary could not see it. A woman being purified should not look on fire. It was comfortable in the hut and she soon stopped shivering and began feeling hungry.

The fourth day was different. She wasn't hungry anymore. That was the day Grey Leaves told her how Earthmaker made the world out of a ball of dirt. How he danced on it, flattening it till it reached the edges of the sky. Then, with a great noise, another being who was *Itoi*, sprang out, and together, they shaped the world. Coyote, who had been in the world from the beginning, helped them. There were people in the world also, but they were evil and *Itoi* and Coyote agreed to destroy them with a flood. They wagered that whichever of them first returned from his hiding place after the flood should be Elder Brother and make the new people. *Itoi* won the honor. He shaped the new people from clay and taught them how to live. Earthmaker grew jealous and sank back into the ground because *Itoi* and Coyote had supplanted him. But perhaps Earthmaker, or Coyote, had their revenge, because *Itoi's* people quarreled with him and tried to kill him. So *Itoi* went into the earth also, and found there the *O'odham*. He led them out onto the surface where they drove away the ancient ones who left behind only their ruins. Then Elder Brother taught them how to bring rain and how to keep happiness in the world.

The old woman continued her hypnotic recitation, telling Mary of the great magicians who live at the corners of the world and have houses along Father Sun's path. And there was much more. At some point it all began to make sense, to take on special meaning. Mary began to understand, to see that beneath the words lay a great truth of immense magnitude. If only she could clearly grasp it, carry it back to her people and do justice in its explanation, she would do all mankind a tremendous service. She listened and puzzled and then she did understand and a marvelous peace came to her. And then it was over.

They led her out of the hut into a frosty dawn. A melting drop hung at the tip of a mesquite thorn and the sun shone through it, exploding into a rainbow of hues. The air was filled with its own prism of scents—damp earth, creosote, wood smoke, people, horses. It was all clearer, brighter, sharper than she'd ever sensed before.

When the old man walked her into the desert, she continued to see small details she would normally have missed, heard as the crunch of their footsteps divided into the sound of each bit of earth and gravel displacing itself against its fellows.

"Your true name shall be Many Flowers," he told her when they were away from the others and he could not be overheard. "It is your secret name. You must not reveal it to anyone whom you do not absolutely trust."

"Many Flowers," she said, trying it. She smiled. "It is a beautiful name. Thank you." She knew he was right. Many Flowers was, indeed, who she was and always had been.

They gave her a thin broth and some jerked beef, and, when she was done, loaded themselves and their belongings on horses and rode across the desert beneath a stunted range of dark peaks. She was very weak. She sat behind the *Siwani Mahkai*. She had to concentrate in order to remember to hold on.

The village lay among a collection of sooty caves. They arrived about noon and the old man led her to a cave where the mouth had been partially walled shut with mud and brush. He showed her a sleeping mat, and she lay down. The next thing she knew, it was night, and a grand celebration was beginning. Her presence was required, Grey Leaves explained. She was the guest of honor.

Neither Wondrous nor True

In the morning she rose with the women, helped them prepare breakfast, and begin the day's many tasks. As soon as it was fitting for her to do so, she sought out the *Siwani Mahkai*. Already, the wondrous truth she'd beheld from the vantage of her semi-starved state was gone. Intellectually, she realized that, explained to her now, she would likely find it neither wondrous nor true, but it had certainly seemed so at the time. She regretted not having found some way to set it down, to have recorded it for later analysis. And there were so many other things she had learned. She needed her notebooks. She needed to start recording facts, details, impressions. She wanted to start the job she'd come for.

She had expected to find her personal belongings in the cave she shared with the *Siwani Mahkai's* extended family, but none of her things were there when she woke and no one seemed to know where they might be found. So she went looking for the old man.

He had climbed a ridge above the camp and was sitting with his back to the mountain. He was gazing toward where distant snaggle-toothed peaks had taken a bite of a freshly rinsed sky, across a rolling desert several shades greener than before the rain. His people went about their business, work and play, at his feet.

Despite the feast and a good night's sleep, she was still weak from her fast. She was struggling for air by the time she reached him.

He waved his hand at the sweep of endless cactus and stone and creosote. "We shall pass and be no more," he told her, "but our land shall remain and change not."

Profound, she thought, but familiar.

"The priests of my people tell us something similar," she said. Her tongue felt as stiff and uncomfortable, fitting itself to the People's language, as her feet would in a new pair of shoes. "I don't think I can translate it to *O'odham*. Do you speak Spanish?"

"A little."

She tried it. "One generation passeth away, and another generation cometh, but the earth abideth for ever." Ecclesiastes. She had memorized it once for Sunday School.

His eyes twinkled. "So, maybe I heard it at the Mission." Was he teasing her?

"May I ask something of the Chief Medicine Man?" she ventured hesitantly.

"I have been expecting you," he replied, his expression serious now. "You are wondering where your belongings have gotten to, and what has become of the gifts you brought us."

She hadn't noticed that the gifts weren't about, hadn't even thought about them, just her notebooks. Not too observant for a trained observer. She nodded agreement.

He waved his arm at the village below. "As you see, as you have seen, we are an old-fashioned village. Many of the ways and tools of the Americans and the Mexicans have intruded here and been adopted by us, but more have not. We avoid them. We try to remain true to the teachings of Elder Brother and in harmony with our desert. As Chief Medicine Man of my village, it is my duty to guide my people. It is a difficult task, often complex and unpleasant, but it is my responsibility. I must seek out the proper direction for us to follow and then I must persuade and cajole an often reluctant people to accept it. That requires a good deal of gentle nagging and some heavy-handed flattery. Those are my tools.

"We have largely followed the old ways during my lifetime. We have stayed away from the White Man and his wonders because such things are not natural to our world. But is it clear yours is a young and energetic race. Perhaps Elder Brother has brought you from the bowels of the earth to replace us, just as he once brought us to replace the *Hekihukam*.

"Perhaps, too, the old myths are just stories. The world may be a much wider place than we have dreamed. If that is so, we must learn to adapt to it or be shoved aside and destroyed. These are things I do not know, things I need to know. There are matters I must decide. And on my decisions will rest the fate of my people.

"As your people have touched us more and more through the years, we have retreated from you. There remain few places into which we can retreat. Soon you will touch us anywhere in our desert that you choose. Casually, thoughtlessly, you may brush us aside if we stand in your way.

"I have decided that we must understand your people better. When I learned that you wished to come and live with us, I decided it would be an opportunity for us to exchange information. You may live among us, see how we exist and what we hold important, on what our lives are centered. And I, too, can question you about your people's ways and learn who you are and what makes you so.

"But we have resisted your ways for a long time. It was not easy for me to persuade my people to take you in. To do so, I had to promise them we would accept only you and none of your gifts, not even your personal possessions. This may seem foolish to you, for you will see that some of us wear articles of American clothing and we use many of your tools. Still, there was concern that your coming could be dangerous to us, and that the danger was compounded by the things you brought.

"Your gifts and belongings are cached several days' journey from here. They are safe, but they must remain there, at least for the time being. As my people come to know you, to trust you, I think I can arrange for some of your things to be brought in. Then you may have access to the items you need, but for now you must be patient.

"You may feel you have been tricked, but I hope you will accept what has been done and stay with us a while. If you feel you cannot, I will personally escort you back to the ranch from which you came. But I hope that will not be necessary. I hope you will stay with us for a time and let us learn to understand each other. I believe we both have much to gain."

Quite a soliloquy, Mary thought. When it ended, he sat, watching her, waiting for an answer. She didn't know what to say. What kind of ethnographer just ethnos and doesn't graph? The rest of her stuff didn't matter, at least for now, but how could she make records, keep straight all she was being exposed to without her notebooks? The presents were theirs. They could do what they wanted with them. But she needed her notebooks.

"I must make a history of my time with you," she told him, wondering if there was room to bargain. It was clear he almost desperately wanted her to stay. Still, it could be an all or nothing proposition. "Without that ability I would have to live with you for most of my lifetime in order to know and understand everything I need to take away with me. It is like your calendar sticks. If you did not have them to key your memory, how could you recall the long, complicated history of your people? Without my notebooks there will be too much I cannot remember."

He nodded. "I will argue with the men that you be allowed to have them, but I will not overrule them. I do not honestly believe I can persuade all of them until you have been with us long enough for them to learn to trust you. I could tell you it may be very soon, but that would be false. I doubt it will be before the arrival of the Lean Month."

Jesus! That wasn't until January. What a choice. Pack it in and start all over somewhere else or try to commit an alien culture to memory. Well, she'd planned to spend as much as a year with them, but she'd hoped it would be off and on, with plenty of time back in the comfort of Tucson, transcribing notes and digging through the literature in search of contradictory conclusions and evidence that needed double checking. She had an awfully good feeling about the ceremonies that had initiated her into the village. She didn't think it likely that another village would allow her to take part in such intimacies. And she felt good about the *Siwani Mahkai*. If she could give him the kind of information he wanted, he could prove to be an incredibly valuable informant to her as well.

"All right," she agreed, reluctantly. "Let's give it a try. I should have some sort of feel for how I'm going to get along with the rest of the village in a week or so, and whether I'm going to be able to win their trust in a reasonable amount of time. If it doesn't feel right by then, I'll take you up on your offer. In the meantime, I'll tell you what I can about my people and you can tell me about yours."

"Good," he said. "Let us begin now."

He started asking questions and she began wondering who was the anthropologist and who was the informant. But she did her best to answer.

A Dang Waste of Time

Bill Burns was five years younger than J.D. and looked ten years older. The sun had exacted a toll on his face, and prematurely grey hair that protruded, thatch-like, from under his straw hat, added to the impression of age. The land he had chosen to conquer was a harsh and unforgiving one. His face was evidence of the price demanded from those who would wrest a living here.

He was a big man with sun-darkened arms of sinewy muscle and ropey veins, visible to where he wore his work shirt rolled up above his elbows. His fingers were stained with nicotine from the incessant stream of cigarettes he smoked down to minute stubs.

J.D. had visited him once before, shortly after Mary went into the field. Jesus agreed they needed to put out the word to ranchers in the neighborhood, and when he got over the lost feeling that swept through him when Mary left without a word, he'd started to wonder if she might have somehow managed to put herself into Jujul's band. It was a pretty silly thing to worry about. There wasn't likely to be a band less desirous of having an outsider in its midst than one on the run from federal and tribal authorities. Still, he'd decided Jujul might have brought his people in this general direction and even though Mary shouldn't have been his primary concern, Burns' ranch was one of the first places J.D. stopped. Besides, there was that name, Jujul—Zigzag—and the unpredictable nature he'd begun to suspect belonged to the man behind it.

This being his second visit, J.D. was able to impress Jesus with the expertise by which he navigated the unmarked track that led there. He only took a couple of wrong turns this time and caught them before he got lost. If there'd been a proper road, he could have driven from his office to Burns' front door in less than an hour. The first time it took him over four to find it. This time he made it in two. His Ford sat in the middle of the ranch yard and made occasional wheezing noises by way of complaint, as if it would have preferred a less adventurous lifestyle.

J.D.'s first visit hadn't been very productive, and, worse, it hadn't relieved his anxiety either. Bill Burns had never seen those Papagos before November. They'd impressed him as a particularly remote and primitive folk because they hadn't been skilled traders and he'd gotten an especially good deal on the cattle they herded in—that, and the fact they hadn't known about the excitement on the reservation at *Stohta U'uhig*. Right away he'd thought theirs might be just the sort of village Mary was looking for. The very next time he'd come within range of a phone, Burns called Mary to tell her about them and how he'd put her offer to them and they'd agreed to think it over.

Burns' Papago hired hands all seemed to know the strangers, but when J.D. tried to pin down where their village was, he didn't have much luck. Either they moved around a lot, which was possible, or Burns' people didn't know or weren't saying. But Burns hadn't been worried, even when J.D. spelled it out. He thought there was no way Jujul would take in Mary in the first place. Besides, Papagos were about the safest, most peaceful folks around. Then he got started on the absurdity of making them register to begin with.

"What the heck's the government doing, registering Papagos for the draft for anyway? Just a dang waste of time and money. They's a dang literacy requirement for anybody's drafted. Now how the heck's somebody who can't hardly speak English, let alone read none, gonna pass something like that?"

They were good questions, and once J.D. convinced the rancher he agreed that the whole idea was absurd, Burns calmed down and started being friendly. Burns' arguments were similar to those J.D. hoped to use to convince Jujul of the harmlessness of the registration process. There was no way any of his people were going to be required to serve in the armed forces as long as that literacy requirement remained. He didn't plan to mention the possibility of its being eliminated in the face of a real national emergency. White Men speaking with forked tongues was traditional. Besides, it might never happen and the important thing was to defuse this situation before it got somebody killed.

Burns and his mousey little wife Edith were helpful, but entirely unconcerned about Mary. Before J.D. left, however, they promised to let him know as soon as they heard anything from her or of anything that might suggest he was right about Jujul's band moving into the area. J.D. hadn't felt reassured on the drive back to town.

He'd been in his office when Burns called, even though it was a Sunday. The paperwork he'd promised himself would be done before Christmas still wasn't, and it had to be in before the end of the year, only two days away. Burns wasn't unconcerned anymore. Three Papagos from the village Mary had gone to study had come to his place that morning to do more trading. They claimed Mary had only sent word, and not letters, until Burns insisted there was just no way she wouldn't have written after all this time, what with the holidays and all. Then they admitted she'd sent a pouch that contained letters, but it must have fallen out of the pack they'd carried them in because they'd lost it somewhere along the trail and were ashamed and hadn't wanted to admit it. Bill Burns couldn't imagine a Papago, especially a traditional one, being that careless with messages. There was too much pride and responsibility associated with being entrusted with something so powerful and important.

These three claimed Mary was well and doing fine in their village, that she had no needs of which they knew. She'd only sent greetings to her husband and friends, they assured him, so they asked that such greetings be passed along. They would return with new letters as soon as they were able to make the long journey to Burns' ranch to trade again. And then they'd spread out a collection of pelts and baskets and started dickering. One of the things they wanted to trade for was some unusual ammunition—Sharps, .50 caliber.

There might be another of those old buffalo guns on the reservation, but the chances were awfully slim. J.D. was willing to bet money and offer odds they'd found Jujul, or at least narrowed down his location by a few hundred square miles, and that the old man had Mary.

Bill Burns' certainty about Mary's safety evaporated along with his opinion that J.D. was foolish to worry about her. It took awhile because he seemed to enjoy his guilt, having arranged for Mary to be where she was, but he finally calmed down when J.D. persuaded him she should still be safe. The only reason J.D. could imagine for Jujul wanting Mary was as a hostage. If that was the case, she would be no good to him dead or seriously harmed.

As soon as J.D. reassured Burns, he instructed him to call Larry and tell him the story the Indians had told, to tell it straight, as if he believed it and fully expected a second pack of letters from Mary in a couple of weeks, then get ready to do some hunting— manhunting. Burns agreed, and he must have kept the anxiety out of his voice because Larry called J.D. a few minutes later to pass along the happy news. J.D. tossed in his own casual acceptance of the missing letters. When he hung up he walked over to the map of the Papago Reservation he'd tacked up on his wall. It hadn't suddenly sprouted a big X conveniently marked "Mary is here."

J.D. had put in a call to the Pima County Sheriff's office right after hearing from Burns. He needed help, preferably Jesus. They promised to locate the deputy and have him return the call. J.D. wasn't happy about the delay. He wanted out of his office and into the desert. Waiting for the phone to ring made him feel about as comfortable as a cat in a sack. He buckled on his .38 in its shoulder holster and chewed his way through most of a pencil while he studied the map, paced, and waited for the phone to ring.

When it did, of course, Jesus turned out to be halfway across the county and unable to just walk away from what he was doing. J.D. thought about getting himself a Papago tribal policeman instead, then decided to wait. The tribe might take even longer. Jujul had been there for a couple of months. He wasn't likely to go hide somewhere else in the next few hours. Jesus had been in it from the beginning. He deserved a shot at the finish as well.

Jesus came in a little before dawn. They loaded up and got J.D.'s Ford on the road in minutes, J.D. hastily refusing Jesus' offer to drive. The deputy was tired and tried to catch a nap along the way, but J.D. was keyed up, talking almost nonstop, trying to convince himself Mary was all right and arguing over Jujul's possible motives for wanting her.

"Hey," Jesus finally interrupted. "What's Mary doing out there in the first place?"

J.D. thought the question was an implied criticism, a "what business has a woman got working with primitives in the wilderness anyway?" sort of comment. He was feeling especially protective about then.

"What do you think," he snapped. "She's an anthropologist. She's out there studying them, learning how they live, and what makes them tick."

"Well," Jesus said, "maybe she's not the only one being an anthropologist out there."

It shut J.D. up for a minute. It made more sense than his hostage theory. At least half the problem they had with Jujul was because of Larson's indifference to Papago attitudes and Jujul's lack of understanding of how Anglo culture worked. The old man had shown himself to be a clever, competent leader. What any leader needed in circumstances such as his was intelligence. Not the smarts kind, he already had that, but the knowledge of your enemy kind. What better way to get it than to swap information with an ethnographer, especially if he could keep her from realizing what he was doing? All of a sudden J.D. was sure that was exactly what was happening. Otherwise he wouldn't have made the mistake about the Sharps. If he'd been torturing Mary for information he would have had plenty of time to get everything she knew, and she knew about the Sharps. Larry's favorite part of the story had been what the Sharps did to terrorize Larson and his merry men. J.D. felt his panic drain away a little, though he was still damned worried. Just because Jujul hadn't taken her for a hostage didn't mean he wouldn't be prepared to use her as one.

He started in on that subject until Jesus told him, in a very nice way, to shut up and let him try to sleep. From then on J.D. kept quiet, but he also made sure he hit every bump in the road with enough force to keep the deputy awake. Jesus glared at him a time or two, but they had legitimate reason to hurry, and he was being treated to the sort of chauffeuring he normally dished out. He pulled the brim of his hat down low over his eyes, held on tight, and bore his punishment in silence.

This Way to Jujul's

The Papagos had come to Burns' to trade on Sunday morning and left the same afternoon. As soon as they were gone, Burns rushed to a phone and called J.D. The marshal and the deputy sheriff arrived about an hour after dawn the next day. That gave the Indians a big head start, but the weather was perfect, nothing more than a light dew overnight to interfere with the trackers. J.D. just wished he knew what he and Jesus would do when they caught up with the trading party.

J.D. thought it would be nice to arrive in Jujul's village with an army to insure Mary's safety, but an army moving across the desert was sure to catch Jujul's attention and would probably put her in more danger. That was why he'd only brought Jesus. With Burns and a couple of his most trusted Papago hands they might be able to find the village and remain unnoticed until he worked out how they could grab Mary and make a getaway. If they were spotted, they wouldn't be too threatening, and they still might have a chance of talking her, and themselves, out. Jujul might be willing to trade—Mary for the time he would need to make another run for it. Hell, J.D. didn't know. This was play-it-by-ear time.

Burns was ready for them. He had two Papagos—men he swore could track an ant from Sells to Tucson, even if it never left the road—and horses harnessed and waiting. He found them a couple of saddle holsters for Jesus' twelve gauge and J.D.'s thirty-ought-six, and they strapped them on, tying their packs behind the saddles.

J.D. was hot to hit the trail, but Jesus made him wait while he talked with the scouts and a few of the other hands. J.D. began to think he should have let the deputy get some sleep on the way out. His own eyes were starting to feel a little gravelly, but Mary was out there somewhere. He wondered if the delay was just a way to get even, then realized he knew better.

In a few minutes Jesus was back. He swung up easily into the saddle and they rode out of the valley, up into the desert beyond. After a quarter mile, one of the Papago trackers dropped off his horse and left the reins to his fellow as he trotted along the trail on foot. J.D. watched with interest, despite his impatience at their slow pace. A sabers-drawn, pennants-fluttering cavalry charge was more what he had in mind.

Jesus sidled his mount over beside J.D.'s and kind of swung them off to the side, a little behind the rest of the makeshift posse and out of their hearing.

"I don't know how far we're going to get with this," he said. It wasn't the sort of optimism J.D. wanted to hear. "I'm pretty sure these guys knew, or suspected, Mary's wild Papagos were Jujul's bunch all along. If they'd wanted to play it straight, they would have said something before Mary went off with them."

"Shit! Then they aren't going to follow the trail are they? Not unless this is some kind of trap."

"Damned if I know what they're going to do," Jesus admitted. "We'll just have to go along and see. I don't think they'll put us in danger. They seem genuinely fond of their boss. If they decide to lose the trail, well, I've done some hunting out here, big game and men, and they just may find it harder to lose than they think."

Jesus was right. They rode along for about five miles, weaving through scrub and cactus, before the scouts came to their first problem. They stopped, conferred with Burns for a minute, and he called the lawmen over.

"Trail splits here," he explained. "Goes off in three directions. Whatcha wanna do? Split up and take a couple, or all of us stick with just one?"

"Let's take the middle," Jesus said.

About three miles further the scouts lost it altogether. Burns was embarrassed but his trackers were stoic at their failure.

"She just up and ends right here," Burns announced. "Must've doubled back somewheres, but neither of the boys seen any indication of it."

"Take a break," Jesus suggested. "Let me look."

He rode back down the trail, then called from about a hundred yards away. The others joined him and he gestured off to the south as if he were pointing out a paved highway complete with road signs saying this way to Jujul's. All J.D. could see was desert that looked exactly like what they'd been riding through. Jesus showed them and explained what the man they were following had done. He'd broken off a piece of desert broom and wiped out his tracks behind him, then walked backwards to this spot where he could take advantage of a stony patch to head south without leaving an obvious fork in his trail. J.D. couldn't see any of it except where the branch had been broken. It made him feel pretty useless.

While J.D. was feeling sorry for himself, deciding the average Boy Scout would have been a more valuable member of their party, Jesus and the Papago scouts had a few words. They had them in Papago, and Jesus made the language ring. He sounded like a fire-and-brimstone preacher given the opportunity to address the Society for Creative Deviation of the City of Sodom. The scouts looked embarrassed and their answers were short and sullen, but they answered. Burns looked confused and angry, and more than a little hurt.

"They knew," Jesus said. "They knew from the beginning these were Jujul's people. Not because they recognized them or because the strangers admitted it. Just that their story didn't hold up. They didn't know anybody from the part of the reservation they claimed to come from, and they seemed too curious about what happened at *Stohta U'uhig*. It was kind of a big joke for both groups, I guess, knowing but not saying anything.

"They say they were surprised about the White Woman, but they never worried about her. This one says his cousin promised she would be safe, and he believes it, even though he never met that particular cousin before. Hell, everybody's related to everybody out here. You just got to figure out through which clan.

"They say they'll follow the trail now, if we still want them to, and they won't do anything to warn anyone we're coming. But they also say we'd be better off just leaving things alone and going home. Jujul won't hurt anybody, not Mary or anyone else, if we'll only leave him be. They say the government has counted enough Papago warriors. Let these go."

J.D. couldn't, of course. They went on. The scouts led the way with Jesus keeping a close eye on them and Bill Burns riding alongside J.D., trying to apologize. J.D. ignored him until the rancher gave it up and went away.

Burns' trackers turned out to be good after all. Within a couple of hours they found and solved three more tricks that Jesus had to point out to J.D. After that, the three trails merged again, and, from that spot on, they stopped trying to hide where they'd gone. Occasionally, even J.D. spotted evidence that someone had recently passed that way.

The Papagos had circled around and doubled back along their previous line of march. Their path led up a low volcanic outcrop to a clear, flat space near the top where they'd spent the night. It offered a marvelous view of the route both parties had followed from Burns' ranch, including the spots where the trail had been split and disguised.

"They waited around and watched us this morning, didn't they?" J.D. asked Jesus.

"Grandstand seats. Maybe they caught on that Mr. Burns was suspicious. Maybe they're just naturally cautious. But they sure as hell had a fine view from up here while we followed their trail."

"How long do you think?" J.D. asked.

"About three hours head start," Jesus estimated. "They'd know we were pretty sure to keep on coming after we worked things out back where they split and made their first try to lose anybody following them. Not much point sticking around to watch us after that."

"Then we can catch them," J.D. said, excited. "We're mounted and they're on foot. We'll catch them easy."

"You'd think so, wouldn't you," Jesus agreed. "But don't make book on it."

The trail was easy to follow from then on. They'd just trotted along, not making any effort to throw anyone off. There were places where the little posse actually galloped the horses, making up time. Once, J.D. rode ahead to a high spot and unsheathed his rifle. He used the scope to scan the horizon and a lot of desert in between. The path they were following was so straight he'd felt sure he would spot them, but there was nothing out there except scrub and cactus, and nothing moved in it but heat shimmer. There was plenty of that, even if it was the end of December.

Then they found what the Papagos had been hurrying toward. Their trail joined a wide path regularly used by lots of feet. They were near a village.

They rode on more carefully, Jesus and the scouts watching in case the ones they were following might have pulled some trick and split off again. J.D. searched for any indication they were riding into an ambush. He hoped this would be the village Mary was in, but he wasn't all that happy with what they might run into if it was.

It wasn't. They came around a rocky outcrop and there it stood, a little cluster of adobe and brush buildings, corrals, and lots of sun darkened people tending their daily chores. Burns recognized the place at once. He'd been there before to hire hands and trade cattle. It was a place called *Shongam* after the spring-fed pool that provided it with an excuse to exist. Bill Burns took one look and declared flat out that Jujul and his people hadn't moved in.

"Place would've had to double in size and it ain't. Fact, looks some smaller, like maybe they had some hard times."

Still, it was where the three they'd been trailing had gone. The posse followed them in.

"I wondered how they planned to lose us," Jesus commented. "My guess is they traded sandals with some of their cousins here or picked up some horses and then set out for home. Maybe they split up again. Hell, maybe they're even still here, but that'll only be if they're sure Burns can't recognize them or they figure to stay out of sight while we're here. Whichever, looks like they win this one."

J.D. felt like the stuff in the corrals that was drawing flies. All of a sudden the hours without sleep caught up with him. It was all he could do not to just climb down off his horse and give up for a while. Instead, he rode in with the others while Burns' Papagos circled the village, looking for some sign of the threesome. They didn't find any.

Burns introduced them to the local head man. He was called Fat Wolf, the cause for part of his name being obvious. He preferred to talk about what presents they might have brought him and how many cattle Burns wanted to buy, instead of whether three Papagos had been through his village an hour or two ahead of them. Jesus finally got him onto the subject, but you'd have thought he'd never seen another Papago in his entire life. What did he know about Jujul? Why, he'd never heard of him, and what was a Jujul anyway? Were they sure it was a Papago name? He couldn't recall having heard it. Hadn't they brought any presents, and, as long as they were there, wouldn't Bill Burns like to come look at some cattle and pick out a few head to take home?

J.D. gave them the spiel anyway, Jesus translating. He told them he only wanted to talk to Jujul and wouldn't arrest him or any of his people without trying to work out a peaceful settlement first. He told them about Mary and how concerned her family and government were about her, and how Jujul should send her out to prove she wasn't being held against her will. That keeping her only made things worse. He suggested, in case anyone should happen to remember what or who a Jujul was, they pass along his messages. He left Fat Wolf one of his business cards and a pack of cigarettes which he again appropriated from Jesus. Bill Burns promised to come back for a look at their cattle real soon, and they left.

They got back to Burns' place a little before midnight. J.D. was in favor of getting right back in the Ford and heading for town. He wanted to check with the Army Air Corps and see if they had any aerial reconnaissance photographs of the area and make arrangements to fly over a good deal of it himself. Tuesday, the next day, was the last of 1940. Wednesday, he would play hell finding any help. On the ride back to the ranch he'd started getting keyed and worried again. He didn't want to lose those two days.

Jesus objected. He'd missed the same forty or more hours of sleep and he wasn't convinced they'd created any new threat to Mary's safety. He couldn't see the danger to her of their getting a night's sleep every other day or so. He also threatened to shoot out the tires on the Ford if J.D. tried to go back before morning. J.D. thought he might be serious.

Edith Burns stuffed them full of something warm and wholesome and herded them into a guest bedroom with twin beds and fresh sheets under hand-made quilts to keep them snug and warm. J.D. was dead tired too, but he couldn't help wanting to get back. He started trying to frame a calm, logical explanation that would persuade Jesus to forfeit another night's sleep. Before he got the words properly organized, Jesus was shaking him and telling him it was time for breakfast.

Complete With a Rumble Seat

Three strangers rode into Fat Wolf's village near the end of December. They kept mostly to themselves and that was not like the People. After one night, they left their horses, loaded their belongings on their backs, and set out to go trade with a nearby rancher. That was really peculiar. A horse could carry more trade goods than a man.

"Who are these strangers that they act so secretively?" the kid with the rodent-like face asked. He got the answer he wanted. Jujul's people.

In the middle of the first night they were gone he sneaked into the corral and marked a hoof on each of their horses. Someone would have to look very closely to notice it, but Talker, who had shaped the marks, would be able to pick out their tracks at a glance.

The three came back at a trot shortly after noon two days later. He watched as they sought out Fat Wolf for a hurried council. The three saddled and loaded their horses, then took separate trails out of *Shongam*. That scared him. Someone was chasing them. Whoever was after them might be after him as well.

Talker had started at his home village. After watching it for a day to be sure no one was there looking for him, he had taken the chance. It proved safe, but it was hard going back without anything to show for the time he'd been away. He endured the humiliation of being Mirage Talker again so he could speak to his grandfather. One of the old man's daughters, his aunt, had married a man from Jujul's village.

Grandfather wouldn't tell him where to look, but the old man pointed him in a direction. "Jujul is a man who runs toward his enemies, not away from them."

So Talker headed toward Tucson and the eastern edge of the reservation. He asked at the villages he visited and the answers were usually silence. Occasionally, though, someone would admit they thought Jujul was nearby. Talker knew, if that was true, Jujul's people would have to establish contact with the villages close to him. They would need to trade and get word to friends and relatives that they were well, that babies had been born, that young people needed brides and grooms. Talker decided he was more likely to succeed if he stopped hunting and waited for his prey to come to him.

He chose Fat Wolf's village of *Shongam* because it was a poor place that needed hunters and laborers badly enough to take in a stranger without asking too many questions. He chose it because the rumors he'd collected put it in the right area and because something about the place felt right to him. It didn't take long to find that he'd chosen well. Gossip wasn't always shared with an inquisitive stranger, but a fellow citizen was different. Jujul and his people were, indeed, nearby. No one knew just where, but they passed through *Shongam* often enough and sometimes came for news and trade.

After that, the waiting was hard. The village offered no opportunities for the mirages he dreamed of, but it offered the possibility he might pay Parker. After that....

The posse arrived, too quick for him to slip away. There were five of them, two White Men, a Mexican, and two Papagos. He tried to be inconspicuous, brushing down his mount as if he'd just come back from somewhere instead of having been ready to run.

In the end it was fine. No one paid him any attention. The White policeman spoke and the Mexican translated. No one admitted knowing anything about Jujul, though Fat Wolf was so clumsy about it that Talker was sure they knew he was lying.

They watered their horses and rode back the way they had come. They never gave any sign they were also looking for a Papago thief who'd murdered a man named Big Jack. If they were after him too, their minds weren't on it. Not with a whole village in need of capture.

When he was sure the posse was really gone, Talker resaddled his horse and rode out of *Shongam* along the northernmost of the trails taken by the men from Jujul's band. Since the posse had come from the south he thought that was the most likely direction. He took his time, and where the horse with the marked hoof left the trail, he rode on for more than a mile until he was out of sight of the man who watched from the cliff and there would be no reason to think that Talker followed him.

He called on the lessons his grandfather had taught. He came back to the cliff from the other side. By then, of course, the man was gone. After that, Talker was even more cautious. He found a place with water, hobbled his horse, and followed the trail on foot.

The horse with the marked hoof rejoined the other two at the mouth of an insignificant wash. It was almost dark before Talker found the place. They could be far ahead of him, but he wasn't worried. He could tell by their trail that they were satisfied they'd lost their pursuers. No reason for him to hurry. Their pace was leisurely now. They didn't have far to go.

Talker guessed they were home before dark. It took him longer, but no one knew when he found them and, he took care that no one ever would know. He didn't get too close and he stayed down wind so the dogs couldn't scent him.

They had chosen a good place. The village was well off the regularly traveled paths. And, it was the right village. He recognized the horses, and he recognized one of the men as he treated a cactus wound on his pie-bald mare by the light of a fire.

This would satisfy Parker, then Parker would satisfy him. The lawyer had promised. Talker spent the time it took him to get back to his horse dreaming about the automobile he would drive into his home village the next time he went there. It was a beautiful mirage, complete with a rumble seat.

New Year's Dubious Promise

Tom and Maggie Edgar had a tradition of throwing big, raucous New Year's Eve parties. J.D. wasn't really in the mood for it, but he was less in the mood to sit at home and suffer his own company. By way of excuse, it occurred to him that Hank Lewis might be there. Hank Lewis owned an airplane.

The Edgars lived in a fashionable neighborhood on the east side out past the University at the edge of the desert. El Encanto was filled with immense, ostentatious houses with plenty of room for boisterous celebrations of wealth. J.D. liked the Edgars in spite of their showy lifestyle. They had earned it and they damn well meant to spend it. At least they seemed to be having a good time doing so, and they enjoyed dragging a few friends along with them.

Hank Lewis wasn't there. By the time J.D. established that, he'd had enough drinks not to care so much anymore. Jujul was going to know they were on to him, but he was also going to know that, so far, they hadn't been able to locate him exactly. There wasn't any reason to think Mary should be in greater danger yet. That was going to happen when J.D. got the ball rolling and the real search began.

J.D. stood around and contributed meaningless pleasantries to conversations without significance. And he drank too much. He couldn't get his mind off Mary. It didn't help that Larry was there and wanted to talk to him about hearing from Mary and the letters getting lost and all. The man was a constant reminder of the inappropriateness of J.D.'s level of concern. He ducked out of the conversation at the first opportunity and spent the rest of the evening avoiding its resumption.

An hour and a half after the new year began most of the more conservative guests had gone home. Tom and Maggie were still serving and it was beginning to look like they'd end up with a number of overnight guests, unconscious testimonials to the success of their party. J.D. was looking for the kitchen with the intent of procuring ice cubes for a drink he didn't need. He got lost, which was some indication of how badly he didn't need it, and found himself in a dark hallway at the rear of the house. He opened a door. It led out onto the patio. It was cool and quiet out there. The horns and guns and fireworks that had ushered in 1941 were silent now. Most of Tucson was greeting the new year's dubious promise sensibly, in deep and oblivious slumber.

An eerie mist shrouded the Edgars' pool, shifting and undulating gently as an occasional breeze found its way over the six-foot wall that surrounded their artificial oasis. The crisp air helped clear a similar mist from J.D.'s brain and he suddenly realized he'd drunk too much. He poured the contents of his glass onto the base of a magnificent bougainvillea and wished it a silent Happy New Year. He was ready to go home, but not sure he was in any shape to make the drive. It struck him that a brisk walk across the Edgars' backyard might do him a world of good and provide an accurate measure of the level at which his navigational faculties were functioning. If he could successfully manage a round trip to the rear gate without falling down or getting lost again, he would trust himself at the wheel of the Ford and take himself home.

He made it there all right, but on the way back encountered some shrubbery that wasn't where it was supposed to be. There was no moon and it was pretty dark so he had some trouble finding a way through it. When he did, he discovered that the pool had also been moved to block his path. He decided he needed another practice lap or two around the yard. He was about to look for a way back through the bushes when he realized he wasn't alone.

There was a figure on the other side of the pool, man size, but massively bulky and misshapen. It sobered him more than the cold air and walk had done. The figure moved and separated and became two, and J.D. realized it had only been a man and woman embracing. They were dimly backlit from the house but it was obvious they were naked. The small heaps beside them were probably their clothes. They giggled and whispered and weren't too steady on their feet.

"Come on," she urged. She had him by the hand and was pulling him toward the mists that hid the pool. She had a silhouette that was pretty spectacular. He seemed reluctant to join her, but she went back into his arms for a moment and did some things that helped persuade him. They slipped into the cloud and descended into the warm water. Gentle waves began to slap at the sides of the pool and the woman crooned with evident pleasure.

It seemed like a good time to leave. They didn't need company. Fighting back through the shrubs would be too noisy, so J.D. decided to skirt the pool instead, using the fog and their preoccupation for cover. He set off on tiptoe, his destination the dim light from an open door into the house. He would have made it if he hadn't been watching the mist so closely in order to insure they hadn't seen him. He tripped over a lounge chair. The empty glass he'd been dutifully carrying flew from his hand and crashed onto the patio tiles. It made quite a racket.

"What the.... Who's there?" A masculine voice from the pool. The man half raised himself and J.D. could see the outline of his head in the fog, swiveling, searching for the source of the sounds. It was a voice J.D. recognized. It was Larry Spencer.

J.D. scrambled to his feet and headed for the back of the house, no longer slowed by any need for stealth.

"Who is that?" Larry demanded of the retreating shadow.

J.D. decided Larry didn't really want to know. He went through the door and left Larry something to wonder about.

J.D. found his hosts and said his goodbyes. He drove cautiously home. He had something to wonder about too. If Larry Spencer was being unfaithful to his wife, why should J.D. let an antiquated sense of propriety get in the way of desire? Why shouldn't he go after the half of the union he wanted?

Maybe by the time he found her he'd have an answer.

J.D. never noticed when the patrol car fell in behind him. He was driving with exaggerated care, slower than the speed limit, traffic, or conditions, except possibly those of the driver, warranted. He was lucky it was Jesus who had drawn the short straw and was assisting the City of Tucson in its New Year's eve drunk patrol.

They drove west on Speedway, right on Fifth, then J.D. swung left on Helen. Jesus slowed and stopped at the corner as he watched J.D. make a u-turn in front of his house that went a little wide and left the Ford with a front tire up on the curb, looking as if it was delicately checking to see what it might have stepped in.

J.D. emerged with the same exaggerated care he'd used driving. He had a prodigious capacity for alcohol, the kind only years of practice and a troubled soul can produce, but with it came rigid control. He went up his walk and through his door without the slightest hint of a stagger.

The Plague of Plumbers

At a few minutes before six on New Year's morning there was a break in the plumbing of the Imperial Japanese Consulate in San Francisco. Due to the holiday and the early hour, lots of plumbers were called and offered substantial bonuses to respond to the emergency. Most of them did. Eventually, nine plumbers got in each other's way while combining to fix broken pipes beneath a kitchen sink. All the plumbers were paid in full for the repairs and each was additionally rewarded with a healthy bonus. They departed together, universally pleased by the easy addition to their income, certain it must be a good omen of a prosperous year to come. The staff of the Consulate bowed them out apologetically, locking up behind them. None of the nine noticed that their number had swollen to ten as they left.

Fog hung in the street like wet lace. Sasaki smiled and nodded and exchanged New Year's greetings with his fellows as he toted his tool box from the Consulate to the battered Studebaker van that had arrived, more or less simultaneously, with the plague of plumbers. The man who had brought it should already be in Oakland.

The legitimate plumbers carried wrenches, calks, and torches in their tool boxes. Sasaki had a change of clothes, paperwork for four separate identities, something in excess of $2000 in non-sequential American bills, and a .45 caliber Colt semiautomatic pistol with enough ammunition to establish a respectable beachhead on his own. There was also a shoulder holster for the .45.

Everything but the pistol was acceptable. The local Kempeitai officers had taken forever to arrange his exit, and then argued with him about what he needed and how it should be done. Mr. Kira's plan must proceed, but Kira apparently had no friends in San Francisco to see that it was done properly.

The pistol was a perfect example. They had decided it should be American and in no way traceable to the Japanese government. It wasn't that the .45 was a poor quality weapon or unreliable. Quite the contrary. The problem was its size. A Colt 1911A1 was eight and a half inches long and weighed two and a half pounds. It took a big man to wear a concealed .45 without being obvious. Sasaki was taller than the average Japanese, but more slender. Strapped anywhere on his person, the gun's presence would be obvious to even the most naive. The only place where a conspicuous bulge would go studiously avoided by the sight of most upright American citizens was his crotch—not an ideal place to store a lump of cold metal to say nothing of its inaccessibility in the event of any but the most unlikely of emergencies. For the time being, Sasaki had relegated it to his tool box.

Within a couple of blocks it was clear that a black Packard was following him. So much for the local Kempeitai's assurance that those who watched the consulate would be easy to fool. Sasaki pulled over on a quiet side street and the vehicle coasted silently up behind him. Two men got out. One opened his suit coat as he approached the Studebaker. The other casually brushed a hand against his left armpit, reassuring himself that his pistol was where it should be.

Sasaki climbed out of the car. He left the tool box with the pistol in the van. At the consulate, they had done what they could to make him look like a White Man from a distance. Up close, there was no way he would pass.

"Good morning," he said, disarmingly, a picture of innocence. There was not the least trace of accent in his voice.

"Keep your hands where we can see them," one said.

"Let's see some ID, bub," the other contradicted.

Sasaki shrugged helplessly. "Hey," he said, "who are you guys? What's this all about?" They were close now, one on either side of him.

"FBI," one said, reaching for his badge. Sasaki put the heel of his hand into the man's nose, driving cartilage and bone up into his brain and killing him instantly. He caught the other with a hard elbow just below his sternum, then pivoted and chopped down on his exposed neck as the man doubled over desperately seeking his breath. The second man didn't die until Sasaki was back in the Studebaker, pulling calmly away.

He took a circuitous route after that, designed to reveal or lose anyone else who might be back there. When he was absolutely certain he was not being followed, he drove down to the harbor. A grey Hudson waited for him in a deserted parking lot.

Sasaki shed his coveralls in the Studebaker and emerged in a business suit that was too expensively cut for his taste and circumstances. There was no one in the empty lot to notice. He checked the trunk of the Hudson. It contained two suitcases filled with clothing, no doubt as perfectly tailored as this suit, more papers, even more cash, and a Webley-Mars .38 automatic. It was an even worse choice than the Colt. He left both weapons in the Studebaker. It would be reported back to the consulate. Perhaps the officer responsible for this fiasco might be reprimanded, or more. Or he might be able to find a way to blame it on Sasaki, have it put on his record. Sasaki didn't care. He was on his own. From now on, whether he followed instructions or chose his own path was up to him. If he ever went home again, it would be in such glory that any blemishes on his record would be neutralized. Otherwise, he would be dead. The shame would fall on his family, and they had never expected less.

He took the Hudson down the coastal highway to Los Angeles. Traffic was light because of the holiday. He abandoned the car in downtown LA in the unlikely event it was known or could be traced. He left it unlocked with the keys in the ignition so that anyone trying to locate it would soon encounter a complicated trail. He filled one suitcase with cash and papers and abandoned the other. He walked inland until he found a cheap hotel and took a room. In the morning he went to a department store and replaced his wardrobe with a few off-the-rack selections. Then he found a used car lot and made the salesman's day by purchasing an overpriced DeSoto with a minimum of argument and a chunk of cash.

On his way out of the City of Angels, he made one last stop. He bought a snub nosed .38 from a pawn shop. He preferred to kill with his hands or a sword, but people didn't carry swords here and a pistol he could hide might come in handy. It was convenient that he was in the United States. There were few places in the world where he could have armed himself so easily.

A Key to The Soul

When she realized her period had started, she informed the women
of her family and took her things to the women's hut again.
Counting her initiation, which hadn't corresponded with her cycle,
it would be her third visit.

The *O'odham* had an immense respect for everything to do
with childbirth and reproduction. They believed an awesome magic
surrounded the process, and that this magic took hold of a woman
during menses. At this time, she could be unintentionally dangerous to those around her. She must absent herself from the village
and go live in a women's hut until she was safe again. During
menstruation she must not touch food for people other than herself
or she might poison it for them. She must not touch tools or
weapons, or even look at a fire. What she must do was separate
herself from her village and repeat, though less formally, the four
days of ritual purification she underwent on becoming a woman.

Grey Leaves escorted Mary to her family's hut. The old woman
went inside and lit the fire, hidden behind its shielding mud wall.
She or one of the other women of the family would come back
regularly to see to the fire and bring meals.

It would have been a great time for Mary to catch up on writing
her notes, but she still didn't have any notebooks. She would have
been thoroughly discouraged if she hadn't been listening to the
men's nightly meetings. Some of the younger people seemed to
resent her. Maybe because it was their generation that might get
drafted. But they were too young to vote in the council and only

two of the older men were still holding out against the *Siwani Mahkai*. They were beginning to face a good deal of scorn from their fellows. It seemed likely they would soon capitulate and she could begin making a proper record of her stay. After a month and a half in the village, there was an incredible amount of data she needed to record.

By her fourth morning in the hut, Mary was bored out of her skull. After breakfast she practiced making baskets, a skill that was eluding her. Her baskets tended to look like the ones the little girls sometimes made in imitation of their elders. She had a sound mental image of the technique, but she couldn't translate it to her fingers. She was considering cheating, looking around the mud wall at the fire which warmed her just long enough to watch her latest spastic effort transform itself from error to ash, when she heard her name called softly from outside the hut. It was the *Siwani Mahkai*. For a moment she felt almost as shocked as if she were Papago. Men should have nothing to do with women during this time. It was highly improper.

"Yes?" she answered.

"Come out, Marie. I must talk with you," he said.

She scrambled out into late morning sunshine. The edges between light and shadow seemed as sharp as a cactus spine after three days in the hut. The unexpected visit broke the monotony, but at the same time made her feel uneasy. What momentous event might cause the *Siwani Mahkai* to break such a powerful taboo?

"You shouldn't be here," she told him, then to cover how foolish she felt at trying to explain the proprieties of his own culture to him, asked, "Is everything all right?"

He grinned at her embarrassment. "There is no cause for you to be alarmed, Marie. Nor need you concern yourself with my safety in your presence. I am *Mahkai*. I can handle the danger of a woman in her time. Besides, have you not told me that among your people men are regularly exposed to menstruating women without harm?

"No, there are simply things occurring which make it necessary for us to speak, however inappropriate the timing. And perhaps, when we have finished, we may make a small journey together."

For the first time she noticed the pair of horses nearby, packs and provisions rolled behind their saddles. He seated himself cross-legged in the sand beside the hut and gestured for her to join him. She looked around, half afraid someone would see them together. Women's huts were built some distance from the village to minimize the chances of a man accidentally coming on one, and she was not due to be fed again until sunset. There was nothing there but the horses and the desert. She sat beside him.

"This is difficult," he said, running his fingers through his thin beard, as if he might find the right words in that unlikely spot. "I will explain some things to you. As I do, others will become clear.

"In the little time you have been with us, most of our people have come to like you. Only some impetuous children and the most timid adults still have doubts about you. Soon you will understand and, I hope, forgive them.

"You have been an American all your life. The time you have spent with us cannot replace that, but perhaps it is possible to be both American and *O'odham*.

"Before I continue, I feel it is important to impress on you the level of trust I have come to feel for you. There is only one way I can see by which I might do that. To an American it would have no significance. To a member of the People it would be clear.

"Our people call you Marie. As the *Siwani Mahkai* of our village I know that your secret name is Many Flowers. Have you told anyone else this name?"

"No," she assured him. She'd felt so proud of it she'd been tempted, but she understood the concept of its importance and hadn't wanted to diminish the honor he'd done her.

"When you leave us, who will you tell?"

She wasn't really sure. It depended on whether she went back to Larry or not. The month and a half of separation she'd expected to help clear her mind on that issue had only succeeded in providing it with time for a few dozen changes, back and forth.

"I don't know," she answered honestly. "I may tell my husband. I may tell a close friend. Certainly not anyone else. I haven't decided yet."

"Good," he exclaimed. "You have some understanding of a name's power and importance. For myself, there is no longer any living person who knows my true name. My parents knew it. The *Mahkai* who chose it for me gave it to them when I was very young. When I was grown, I shared it with my wives. But all those people are dead now. My mother was named Two Flowers.

One of my wives was called Many Flowers. Those were their true names, not the names the People called them. They are special names. My mother was a Pima. To me, her true name symbolizes the *O'odham*. You see, the Desert People and the River People are like two flowers which share a single stalk. Over the years, I have come to know there are other blossoms on that stem. For a long time I did not think the Mexicans or the Anglos were actually people. Now I know that they are. It was why, I think, that though I dreamed of the same plant that represented my mother when I long ago named my wife, and again now for your name, each time I have seen that stalk it bears more blooms than it did before. Now I think you do us honor by bringing this special name back among us again."

She was deeply touched, but also confused. She understood her secret name's significance. Why would he break the menstrual taboo to lecture her about it?

"Not even my sons and daughters know my own true name. It is not that I lack trust in them, but it is an almost sacred thing to an old man, and I have shared it with so few.

He paused, leaned forward and looked into her eyes. "My true name is Coyote Among Thistles."

She was amazed. If he'd told her the Tucson Chapter of the Daughters of the American Revolution would be joining them for a picnic lunch she would have been less surprised. To an *O'odham*, giving your true name unlocks a key to the soul. It was like handing her a loaded revolver and leaving himself defenseless. Well, she amended, not quite defenseless. He was the *Siwani Mahkai* after all, and he knew her secret name as well. Still, it was incredible he would tell her. It confused her even more. Why do it? What was he planning to say that required him to overwhelm her so? If he had previously only shared it with his wives, could he be hoping she would become the next? She hadn't been aware of any particular sexual interest from him, but between learning a new culture and her own confused emotions, it was possible she could have missed some clues. They had been spending lots of time together.

While she was frantically trying to guess what was coming next, he reached into his pouch and pulled out two slips of paper and surprised her again. One was very dog-eared, the other relatively fresh. He handed them to her. They were a pair of J.D.'s business cards, each giving his name, title, office address in the federal building at Broadway and Scott, and business and home telephone numbers. Did all this have something to do with J.D.?

"Where did you get these? Is he here?"

"I will answer you in a moment, child, but first, please, tell me what they are. You ask if he is here. Do they signify that someone should be here?"

She struggled to contain herself. "They are a formal means of identification among our people," she explained. "The marks on them are words which tell me who their owner is and where to find him, like the marks on your calendar sticks tell you when an event occurred. A person might present one of these when he called on another as a means of introduction, or, if the person he wished to visit was away from home, he might leave one behind to show that he had been there."

He nodded. "I have looked at these," he said, "and to me their marks seem identical. Do they identify the same person then, and who is he?"

"Yes. He is J.D. Fitzpatrick."

"And you know him?"

"Yes, I know him."

"Among our people, names have meaning. Is it so among yours? Marie I know to be a variation of Maria, whom the Catholic priests claim was the mother of their God. From that I can infer some meaning. From his name I understand nothing. Is there meaning, something which might give me a clue to the man?"

She shook her head. "Our names have less significance than yours. I am not directly named for the mother of Jesus. I was named in honor of a favorite aunt of my mother's. My second name, Spencer, means I am married to a man of that patrinominal descent group. It is something like your clans, but less formal and not so extensive.

"It's funny, you know, but I just realized that J.D., in a way, is like your people. He keeps his name secret and shares it with few, if any. J.D. is only a sort of nickname. Fitzpatrick is his patrilineal clan name. J.D. has never shared his secret name with me, even so, I think I know him fairly well. Now, please, has he been here? Is he all right?"

"No, he is not here, and yes, he is well, or was only days ago when he visited a neighboring village. He left one of these with them and they passed it along to me."

Suddenly she thought she understood. J.D. was still looking for Jujul and something had brought him to this part of the reservation. She wondered if the search would bring him here, and, if it did, how she would react.

"He's still looking for Zigzag, isn't he?" she asked. "Do you know something about him? Are you trying to decide if J.D. can be trusted? Whether you should talk to him?"

"Yes," the old man said. "Yes to all your questions."

"J.D. can be trusted," she told him. "I'll vouch for him. He talked to me often about Jujul and his band. He's very sympathetic. All he wants is to arrange a way out of this situation without bloodshed, a chance to talk to Jujul and convince him that the draft registration law is no threat to his people. Will you talk to him? Can you arrange for him to meet Jujul"

"Child, among my people I am called Jujul. I am the Zigzag for whom your J.D. Fitzpatrick is searching."

"Oh fuck!" she said in English.

"What?" he asked.

"Ah, I have just used an expression from my language indicating surprise and delight," she told him.

"Strange," he observed. "The BIA man, Larson, used a similar term with some regularity on the morning we ambushed him as he came to attack our village. I can understand his surprise, but not his delight."

The Ritual Exchange of Tobacco

Parker was on the phone when the man entered. The Pima County Sheriff's Office knew all about Big Jack Lang. He'd stayed with them so often they'd thought about painting his name next to his cell. But about an attack on him, any injuries a Papago might have inflicted, or the theft of his possessions, they were unaware. The big guy wasn't the kind to bring them his problems, they said. He usually took care of them himself. In other words, they weren't looking for the kid known as Talker.

"Be right with you," Parker told the man. "I'm on long distance." The Sheriff's Office didn't even have a file on the rat-faced Talker. The kid didn't need Parker.

The stranger took off a hat with a band of silver conchos, star bright against the midnight felt, and sat on an oak chair with neatly spaced scars that indicated it might once have sported an upholstered seat pad. Now it sported a couple of cigarette burns and part of someone's initials.

A fine layer of dust covered every surface not in regular use. It matched the fading, water stained paint on the walls. The secretary's desk was as dusty as any part of the office. Parker obviously wasn't making enough to pay his help, or to hire someone to clean the place.

Parker thanked the phone before returning it to its cradle. "Come on in," he called through his office door.

The man with the conchos was about average height but whipcord slender. He was also surprisingly fair skinned for a

Navajo, if that's what he was. Parker was guessing that because of the silver he wore around his neck and wrists and the conchos that circled his hat. The costume was right, even if the build and coloring weren't. Parker gave it a shot anyway.

"*Ya ta hay,*" he said. "Are you of the *Dine?*" he asked, also in Navajo.

Sasaki looked up, startled.

"Hi. You Navajo?" Parker repeated, this time in English.

"Do you speak Navajo, Mr. Parker?" Sasaki inquired.

"Just what you heard and maybe three of four other phrases," the lawyer admitted. "Did I butcher it really badly?"

"No." He could tell Parker was surprised by his initial lack of comprehension. "I just didn't expect to hear it spoken in this part of the state."

He took the stuffed chair across from the attorney, carefully avoiding the stain that could have been blood or wine or any transmogrification in between. Parker reached into a pocket and pulled out a crumpled pack of Chesterfields. Sasaki accepted one, as well as a light from Parker's Zippo.

"The ritual exchange of tobacco," Parker explained. "A modernized version of the peace pipe. May our peoples refrain from making war, at least on each other, or, at least for today. What can I do for you, Mr.—?"

Sasaki smiled at the witticism, but he was faintly puzzled. John Parker was not what he had expected.

"Begay," he said, "Juan Begay." Juan Begay was the Navajo equivalent of John Smith.

"Bet you have trouble with hotel clerks," Parker offered, obviously aware he was being given an alias.

This time Sasaki didn't smile. He took a deep drag on the cigarette and leaned back in the chair. "Mostly with the ones who refuse me occupancy," he replied. "How about you?"

Touché.

"Yeah," Parker agreed. "You're lucky though. You take all that jewelry off and put on a suit and you could at least pass for Oriental. Me, I've got my momma's coloring. I put on my Sunday best and try to pass and they just think I'm a Negro."

"Good," Sasaki said, which didn't sound particularly polite, but he'd finally gotten past the twisted sense of humor to the anger underneath. "I was told you're a man with no particular fondness for the Whites. That's the way it should be with those of us who aren't White. Especially we Indians, Mr. Parker. That's why I'm here."

"You don't say," the lawyer commented. "You hoping I'll help you overthrow the United States Government, Mr. Begay? Maybe replace it with some multi-tribal federation? Hey, sign me up."

He made an exaggerated attempt to peer around his guest into the outer office. "Am I speaking clearly enough for whoever's out there taking this down? You, J. Edgar, and the rest of the G-Men out here rounding up us traitors?"

"Very funny," Sasaki said, looking not the least amused. "You have a delightful wit, but we'll make more progress if you hold it in check for a little while.

"I am not with the FBI or any other law enforcement agency. Neither am I here in an effort to solicit your aid in overthrowing the federal government. I'm here as an unofficial representative of an Indian group that would like to see some massive changes in the level of control the BIA exercises over our people. We're hoping you can help us, Mr. Parker."

"OK, *kimosabe*. I'm listening."

"You've run for the Papago Tribal Council in the last several elections on an anti-BIA platform, Mr. Parker, and you've lost each of them badly."

He could see that the comment had scored. Even Parker didn't find his personal failings amusing.

"It's a matter of public record," the attorney said, coolly.

"Since Jujul took his band out in more or less open revolt against the government's attempt to register Papagos for conscription, the tribe's attitude has shifted, come more in line with your own, hasn't it? If one of those elections were held today you might make a race of it. You wouldn't win, not yet, but you wouldn't be embarrassed."

Parker leaned forward on his desk. The conversation was beginning to interest him.

"I understand you're representing other members of your people who somewhat less dramatically refused to register. I also understand you've contested the warrants against Jujul's band. Commendable, Mr. Parker, and astute. But, in the final analysis, the longer Jujul remains at large, the longer there are hostilities of some sort between the federal government and his village, the stronger your position becomes. I ask you to consider what's going to happen when troops are eventually sent in to find him? What's going to happen when they begin a systematic search of the reservation, interfering in the daily lives of hundreds of peaceful villages in the process?"

Parker knew the answer. He was going to get elected. The only trouble with this scenario was that it wouldn't happen.

"They won't hold out that long, Mr. Begay. Rumor has it the Feds already know more or less where he is. And, so far, they're taking a real low-key attitude on this. My guess is they'll make contact and work out some sort of face-saving deal for everybody before too long. Then I start losing votes again."

"Perhaps that needn't happen," Sasaki said. "Are you aware that there has been resistance to the conscription law on the Navajo Reservation? Also among the Apache, Hopi, Zuni, and Pueblo? In fact, it has been the rule, not the exception, among Indians across the country."

Parker had heard there'd been a little trouble with the Navajo, but not about the rest.

"The federal government has been quietly suppressing that information, Mr. Parker, suggesting the nation's press play it down in these troubled times. The news media have been very cooperative. Only a few stories have been published nationally, but they prompted awareness among our widespread Native American brothers that they weren't alone in feeling the need for legitimate representation within the government before their peoples should be expected to risk their lives in its defense. Jujul and his atavistic return to the warpath represents our best opportunity to draw more attention to our cause. That's why I'm here. It's my purpose to provide aid and counsel to Jujul and his people and keep them out there, resisting, as long as possible, so we may raise America's consciousness and improve our bargaining position with the BIA."

"Yes," Parker breathed, intrigued. "But what's this got to do with me?"

Sasaki hoped he already knew. He reached into his Levis, pulled out a thick roll of bills, and peeled off $100. It didn't make much of a dent.

"We would like to support your efforts in Jujul's behalf," Sasaki said, placing the bills on the desk. "Shall we call this a contribution to his defense fund?"

"We can call it whatever you want as long as I don't have to kill anyone to keep it."

"We also believe you know, or can learn, Jujul's whereabouts. We believe you can put me in contact with him, smuggle me into his camp. If you can do that, Mr. Parker, we would also like to make a contribution to your campaign fund, anonymously of course. The amount we had in mind was $500. Additionally, once I'm in place, I shall likely contribute to your campaign's success in other, even more concrete ways. What do you say, Mr. Parker, are you interested in assisting us in these matters?"

Six hundred dollars came close to equalling John Parker's total earnings for 1940. He reached out and made the hundred disappear.

"Your timing is impeccable, Mr. Begay. I assume you don't need a receipt. Honor among thieves, or should that be Indians? Just when would you like to begin your scenic vacation?"

"Now would be fine, Mr. Parker."

The lawyer smiled, appreciating his client's sense of humor, until he realized the man didn't have one.

"I'll have to make some arrangements."

"Then make them, Mr. Parker. The moment you and I set foot in Jujul's village your campaign fund will become richer."

"I didn't realize you expected my company," Parker observed, "but there are good reasons, your cash included, to spend a few days among my future constituents.

"You really aren't with the government, are you?" He stared hard at Sasaki for a moment. "Nah! The Feds couldn't afford to pay bribes so large for potatoes so small, especially not when they're already close. Besides, I guess it doesn't really matter, not as long as your cash is good and I get to keep it."

"I assure you, Mr. Parker, it is good and you will keep it."

"All right, Mr. Begay," Parker said. "Meet me here at the office first thing in the morning and we'll go find our guide."

"I'll be here, Mr. Parker," Sasaki replied, "then we'll see to your future."

Humming About the Desert Sky

The Army Air Corps didn't have aerial photographs of the Papago Reservation, but they told J.D. they'd be happy to take some if his office would authorize the necessary funds. He checked petty cash and decided he could maybe afford to send someone with a borrowed Kodak Brownie out to a high spot on the reservation. There was enough for a roll of film, but he wasn't sure they could manage the price of developing. Scratch one great idea.

Great idea number two held up all the way to Friday when Hank Lewis came back to town. Lewis was thrilled at the excuse to fire up his biplane and go humming about the desert sky in pursuit of the forces opposed to law and order. J.D. promised to pay for the gas, then started worrying just how much an airplane might use. Whatever wasn't in the petty cash drawer would come out of his pocket.

They took off from Davis-Monthan Airfield about mid-morning and headed west. Things didn't look the same from the front seat of an open cockpit biplane and it took J.D. longer than he'd expected to locate Bill Burns' ranch. Hank didn't care. He was having a ball, buzzing any landmark that might help his passenger decide which way they should be going. Hank's goal in flying seemed to be to create abject terror in his passengers, reducing them to quivering blobs of jelly who, on landing, must be removed from their seat with a small spoon and a damp cloth. He made a habit of avoiding, by the narrowest of margins, ripping the wings off on occasional peaks or tall saguaros. J.D. gave strong consideration to turning in his seat and vomiting his breakfast in Lewis' general direction. When he discovered the effort would require him to loosen his seat belt in order to achieve a proper launch angle, he abandoned the idea.

J.D. tried suggesting Lewis maintain a steadier course a few times, but he couldn't be heard over the roar of the engine. So, Hank shut it off. He had so much trouble getting it started again that J.D. avoided further verbal requests and thereafter made do with pointing. When they found Burns' ranch, Hank took them down between the buildings, close enough that J.D. could have spit on any of them if his mouth hadn't been so dry. Bill, Edith, and their hands ran outside and watched the plane make a repeat pass while Hank waved grandly as J.D. hung on for dear life. Lewis pulled out of the farm yard and put the plane into a giant loop which must have impressed the hell out of the audience. J.D. almost took a blind shot with breakfast. When they were flying level and he could force himself to let go for just a moment, he pointed again—more or less straight up and with only his middle finger. He thought he heard Hank laughing, even over the howling wind and exhaust.

Even having been there, J.D. had a tough time finding Fat Wolf's village, but then losing his map somewhere in the middle of a barrel roll didn't help. They buzzed about the desert in the vicinity of where the place should have been for almost an hour before they found it. They located two other villages as well, and Hank gave each a thrill by roaring through about head high. It didn't do much for their popularity with the Papagos who then had to retrieve scattered livestock. One of the villages even took a couple of pot shots at them. In another, the children waved happily while their parents stood around looking sullen, or wisely scattered so as to be out of the way of any wreckage.

Finally they were low on gas and Hank took them home. When they landed J.D. thanked him, insincerely, and left to compare the position of the two villages they'd found with that of known villages on reservation maps. He'd considered spreading Hank's nose as broadly across his face as the pilot's grin, but when he climbed out of the plane he felt so weak that it was all he could do to walk, rather than crawl, in the direction of his Ford. He decided to save any revenge until he could catch Lewis off guard, and he was certain he would never again have to go up in that fragile framework of cloth and wires.

Great idea number two lost most of the attributes of greatness when he got back to the office and checked the locations of the villages they'd found against those on the BIA map. Nothing matched. He'd known Fat Wolf's village wouldn't because he'd checked it after their visit. It wasn't because they'd moved either. Bill Burns had been visiting them in that location for years. The BIA showed Fat Wolf about twelve miles further southwest. They listed eight villages in the immediate vicinity of where he and Hank had been flying, none in the places they'd discovered from the air. It was nice to know the tradition of carefully avoided infallibility extended to other divisions of the federal bureaucracy, but it made his results doubly negative. First, he had no accurate maps. Second, if they only found three of eight, he'd also proved they couldn't locate villages from the air with any reliability.

As a sort of double check, he called Jesus and asked him how many villages were probably within twenty miles of Fat Wolf's. J.D. felt a little better at his guess of six, but that still put him at only about fifty percent. He explained how he'd spent the morning and Jesus made one sound suggestion.

"If you want to go village hunting, try it just after dawn on a cold, still morning when wood smoke will hang in the air and give you an easier target."

J.D. promised to keep it in mind, but if they couldn't tell which villages belonged where they were and which didn't, he wasn't sure he cared how many he could find. Especially not if it had to be done from the cockpit of Hank Lewis' biplane.

Jesus had heard further confirmation from his contacts on the reservation. Jujul's band was almost certainly within a day's ride of Fat Wolf's village. His people had been using it for trade and as a listening post recently. The same word came from several other villages in the immediate area.

And there was one other thing. "Have you gotten any inquiries about a possible Japanese spy?" Jesus asked. "We got a call from the FBI that makes me think they've lost track of some potentially dangerous Oriental on the west coast. Nothing real concrete. You know those guys, they want to know what you know, but not if they have to tell you what's going on first."

"Not a thing," J.D. replied. "All I hear are the rumors. Half of Tucson thinks every Jap who's here is working for the Emperor and secretly preparing to kill their White neighbors as soon as the invasion begins. If the Bureau knows about a real spy, they haven't seen fit to tell the U.S. Marshal's Office about it. But then cooperation between our agencies isn't what it should be. Why? You get some indication they thought he might be coming our way?"

"State doesn't talk much to us county boys either," Jesus confided. "No, I don't think the Bureau has the foggiest idea where he's going or why. He might not even exist. I just think they were fishing for leads. No reason the FBI can't be as paranoid about the Japanese as the rest of the country. Just can't remember them ever contacting us about anything like this before. Made me curious so I thought I'd ask."

J.D. promised he'd let the deputy know if he did hear anything, thanked him and hung up. It was time for great idea number three. Only problem was he didn't have one. At least not beyond walking down to the end of the hall to see if Tucson's resident G-man was in the FBI's office. When he wasn't, J.D. went back and paced around his office for a few hours, chewed some pencils to death and, finally, gave up.

It was Friday night. Short of declaring some sort of national emergency, he wasn't going to get any assistance from the other agencies involved in the hunt until after the weekend. Maybe by then he'd have come up with a way to tackle the problem. It didn't comfort him to realize that combining Jesus' idea and Hank Lewis' tortuous form of aviation was the only potentially useful approach he had. He could produce a map of his own. Then he and Jesus could start a tour of those villages. It would give Jujul plenty of warning they were coming and time to arrange not to be found. If he was the sort, he might also arrange to eliminate a couple of the more persistent folks who were looking for him. One of those villages on the new map would probably be Jujul's. Keeping the operation small gave J.D. a better chance to meet the man without the complications of tribal policemen, federal troops, or bumbling representatives of the BIA. It would likely keep Mary safer and avoid a big, violent confrontation, but it could also put his life, and Jesus', on the line. His plans were full of little flaws like that. He was willing to take the risk, but he'd have to talk to the deputy sheriff before taking that idea any further. Maybe he'd think of something he liked better in the meantime.

He bit through another pencil and decided it was time to go eat something more wholesome. A concentrated effort to relax and stop worrying for the evening was in order. He let himself out of the office and went across the corner to the Santa Rita Hotel. A couple of drinks, an expensive dinner, and maybe a movie would fill his prescription. With luck he might wake up in the morning with a happy solution firmly in mind. If not, there were plenty of pencils left in the office.

The best steak in the house wasn't exactly in his budget, but then Hank Lewis had been so delighted at his condition when they landed he'd forgotten to collect the promised gas money.

J.D. had almost finished his meal when Larry Spencer and a spectacular redhead were ushered to a nearby table. When he noticed J.D., Larry turned a few shades brighter than her hair. If he was planning to make a habit of cheating on Mary, he was going to have to learn to be a lot more casual about it.

Larry brought the girl over and introduced her. She was also an archaeology student. They'd just finished reconstructing a delicate Hohokam pot so he was going to buy her supper by way of celebrating. He went on babbling away like that for so long J.D. thought he or the redhead would have to use force to shut Larry up.

J.D. didn't recognize her. Maybe, if she'd take her clothes off and stand in a light that silhouetted her obviously excellent figure, he could be sure. Maybe not. But her throaty voice was definitely familiar. The last time he'd heard one like it, it had wanted to go swimming.

This time it just said, "Hello, J.D., pleased to meet you." Her eyes suggested she might enjoy swimming with him too, if only he'd ask nicely. He had the feeling she'd done more than her share of "swimming." J.D. preferred her in Larry's company. It improved his chances with Mary, whose mind interested him as much as her body, which interested him a great deal. The redhead probably had a good mind too, but it was pretty clearly focused on self-gratification. J.D. hoped that self would want to continue to gratify on Larry long enough to help him take Mary away.

He suddenly neither liked nor respected Larry Spencer very much. That helped him shed some of the guilt he'd been carrying around.

They went back to their table where Larry continued to look sheepish. J.D. couldn't take it any more. He denied himself the dessert he'd intended and left. He bought a copy of the evening *Citizen* in the lobby and looked for a suitably innocuous movie. The fare at the nearby Fox looked like it would fill the bill. He decided to make do with some hot buttered popcorn and a soda for his dessert. Larry's would be tastier, but much more dangerous.

Running Out of Time

Mary felt like an idiot. Not inappropriate, since she'd just proved she was, at least in her own eyes. J.D. had spent hours discussing Jujul and his people with her before she began her field work and she'd walked right into his camp without even the ghost of a suspicion. Jujul was an old man, white-haired, very tall and slender for a Papago. He walked with a limp and had a scar on his temple. He was a *Siwani Mahkai*. There weren't so very many men of that rank among the *O'odham*. So he'd grown a sparse beard, big deal. He still fit the description in every other respect, and she'd never even dreamed he might be the man J.D. was looking for.

She should have worked it out, she told herself. Nobody ever visited them. She knew the Papago were a friendly, gregarious people. She'd been mildly surprised that no relatives drifted in and out of the village, but she'd been so involved in what she was learning she dismissed it. It was something to puzzle over later, when she was established and keeping accurate notes.

Idiot, she decided, was too mild a word.

And yet, she couldn't help feeling sympathy for Jujul, in spite of his having made a fool of her. It had been a clever way to find out what he was up against. Thanks to her, he was better able to make decisions now.

She still felt like a moron. It helped a little when Jujul explained that the initiation ceremony, though it was used to put her off guard and intrigue her enough to stay around while he picked her brain, had still been real. They hadn't invented games and rituals to keep her amused. The things she'd been shown and involved in were legitimate parts of *O'odham* culture.

He explained again how a village should be united in its decisions, and how difficult it had been to persuade them to take her in at all. That depriving her of any Anglo artifacts had been their way of assuring themselves she had no means to communicate with the outside world in case she was a spy, or if she began to suspect.

He told her how J.D. had come to their village the first time and left a card and tobacco behind. How J.D. was apparently closing in on them, having worked out that she was with their band. How he and Bill Burns and others had trailed the men Jujul sent to Burns' ranch a few days before. She'd been begging him to let her send out some sort of message, knowing Larry and J.D. and her friends and family were apt to be concerned, especially when they didn't even get word from her over the holidays. He told her about the failed ruse of the lost letters.

He had good reasons to mistrust the Anglos, he explained, though he avoided spelling them out. In spite of that, he was coming to believe he had no real choice. He did trust her, and though the village was not yet in agreement with what he was doing, they were running out of time. He felt he had to act.

"I want to talk to this J.D. Fitzpatrick, face to face," he said. "Can you take me to him? Will he talk to me as one free man to another? If I need to carry his words away with me to weigh them, will he let me go?"

"Yes," Mary said. She guaranteed it. She hoped she was right.

Jujul removed a pack from one of the horses and unrolled it. It contained the clothing she'd worn to hike into the desert so long ago, as well as the notebooks and personal items she'd carried in her knapsack.

"I thought you might have difficulty moving freely among your people without arousing curiosity if you had to wear *O'odham* clothing. We shall probably cause enough consternation because of me, but I am an old man, too set in my ways to try to hide them."

"If we're lucky, nobody but J.D. will see us," she told him, "but, just in case."

Mary changed behind some rocks. Her retrieved wardrobe felt strange, alien and confining. When she was ready Jujul produced a packet of letters his men had brought back from Burns' ranch.

She thumbed through them. There were several from Larry, some official communications from the Department of Anthropology, a few from her family, but none from J.D. That disappointed her. She wondered if she'd misjudged his interest. Was she spending half her time wrestling with her conscience over something she'd only imagined? Of course she hadn't told him goodbye, nor even sent him a farewell note. It wasn't the best way to encourage a man. Why should he have written? And he'd apparently learned she was in Jujul's camp. If he didn't expect word to get through to her he wouldn't write. At least he was looking for her. Or was he? Was he only looking for Jujul and she just happened to be in the same place? She stuffed the letters, unread, in a jacket pocket, and they mounted and set out.

They rode south for a few hours until he led them through an easy pass in the range they'd been paralleling. As soon as they were through she spotted Baboquivari Peak and realized they were a hell of a lot farther north and east than she'd thought. Burns' place would be closer too. It made her feel stupid again. Much more of this, she decided, and she was going to develop a complex.

They rode east then, until the sun slipped beneath the horizon behind them and a sky, filled with broken clouds, wove itself into a quilt of twilight and flame. They stopped in the gathering darkness to share a quick meal of cold fry bread and jerked beef. It was close to ten before they reached their goal, dismounted, hitched the horses, and climbed onto the porch to knock on the Burns' front door.

Bill and Edith were amazed to see her, and very relieved. They'd begun to worry when they found out where they'd sent her. But they were in sympathy with Jujul's refusal to register his people. As soon as she assured them she was all right and had been well treated, she was able to secure their promise of silence about having seen her until she told them it was OK.

"You really ought to let that Fitzpatrick fellow know you're all right," Edith told her. "He's been well nigh crazy with worry about you." The way she said it made Mary think Edith suspected there was something between them. It also reassured her a little. What she'd believed J.D. felt was probably really there. Only that prompted guilt because she'd hardly given Larry a thought. She owed him everything but she hadn't even glanced at his letters.

So, there she was, after all that time away from both of them and no clearer about how to handle things than when she left. And this still wasn't the time or place to work it out.

Bill helped her get the pickup started. She loaded her pack and showed Jujul how to get in and out and where he should sit. He seemed delighted with the truck, like a child with a new toy. She estimated the driving time, there and back, allowed a few hours for their peace council, and told Bill and Edith to expect them back about dawn. Bill promised to feed and water their horses. He'd have them saddled and ready when they returned.

She thanked them, climbed in the truck, and pointed it down the ruts that led to Tucson.

The White Man's Village

He thought they would ride their horses straight into the White Man's village of Tucson. He was surprised when Marie told him they would be too conspicuous if they did so, that her people now almost universally got around in machines. No one rode horses in Tucson anymore.

Jujul had been curious about the machines, these things that moved themselves, since he first saw one almost twenty summers ago. Hers was the first he had ever ridden in, or even touched. It was interesting. The thing was big and heavy, with intricate mechanisms which allowed the opening and closing of its doors. And there was another handle inside which he could turn one way to raise and the other to lower the glass window beside him. Most curious, most enjoyable.

The machine had a gait very different from a horse. A horse moves with a regular rocking motion and one simply moves with it, adjusting to its rhythm, but Marie's truck moved with a motion understandable only to itself. They had hardly gone any distance before it bucked so violently he struck his head against the roof. Marie told him to hold onto the seat. He did so, and it was just as well because as their speed increased, its motions grew wilder. They pitched and bounced and rolled along in a way that, while alarming, was also exciting.

They did not move much faster than a horse, though, and Jujul began to doubt the efficiency of these machines. Not only was it just a little faster, it was confined to following a set of rutted tracks across the desert, incapable of going cross country. He though Marie's claim of how much time the truck would save them on their visit to Tucson must be exaggerated.

And then they came out on a smooth ribbon of roadway, like a path so heavily traveled over generations that even the rock it crosses is worn smooth, yet wide enough for ten men to walk abreast along its surface. It had always puzzled him why the White Men would want to build such a thing. When they turned onto it, Marie increased the truck's speed until they moved faster than he had imagined could be possible. It took his breath away. No horse could come close to this pace, and there was no longer much sense of motion to the ride. His respect for the Anglos increased.

The truck's headlights pierced the darkness, showing the path ahead for a distance that amazed him. Occasionally, out of the blackness into which they rushed, came a faint glow. It would separate into two distinct blinding flames that launched themselves toward him at a mad pace, then whooshed by Marie's side of the truck, leaving only tiny fading embers to mark the passing of another machine such as theirs. The first time it occurred Jujul would have torn open his door and leaped for his life, but he was unable to recall how the mechanism worked, and long before the memory returned the danger was safely past. After a few such encounters, it became pleasant to watch these rushing creatures of the night, to wonder whom they might contain and what important missions demanded that they hurry so across the world.

They topped a rise and a valley suddenly spread before them. It was filled with stars. He thought that when Elder Brother saved the sky from falling he must have missed part of it, and that it lay there in their path. He found he could hardly breathe. But as they continued to rush down into that valley, gradually the stars separated into individual lights, not actually stars at all, but only the artificial lights of the Anglos. He could not have been more amazed if they actually were stars and it turned out that Marie's people lived in their company. Tucson's name was derived from an *O'odham* word meaning "black foundation" for the volcanic hills against whose flanks it rested. He had expected something like that. But he had also expected a village not unlike his own. With the strange buildings of the White Men, of course, and machines in their corrals along with cattle and horses, but never had he dreamed of such a strange and magnificent place as this. It went on forever. In the space it occupied there was room for every village of the People he had ever seen, and more, far more. Buildings, not just like the strange ones at ranches, but others large beyond belief, some that spread across neatly laid-out squares and others that towered like cliffs into the darkness, pinnacles on which to prop the sky. And all of them ablaze with light, colored light, flashing light, moving light. He sought words to express his reaction to this awesome place and had none. Then a recently learned English phrase came to mind.

"Oh fuck!" he said.

Dead Men, Waiting

It was the wrong night for a movie and the wrong movie for the night. The film was a light comedy depicting the adventures of a well meaning young man who was having difficulty remaining faithful to his lovely wife, and whose life was further complicated by the arrival of a shallow cad offering sauce to the goose. It came a little too close to home to be funny, what with Larry and his redhead out there somewhere and J.D.'s earlier decision to take Mary away from him. He hadn't bothered to consider whether she might want to be taken. He was also having trouble reconciling himself with being the sort of person who would even try.

J.D. finished his popcorn and soda and walked out into the cool night somewhere in the middle of the first reel. His Ford was in a parking lot off south Stone Avenue. He walked through empty streets, ahead of the bar and theater crowds and behind the shoppers and diners. Downtown Tucson was nearly his own.

He played "she loves me, she loves me not," with a mental daisy as he strolled along, occasionally pausing to do a little wrestling with his conscience about the morality of the situation. Larry was a healthy young male, suddenly without his mate. In the same circumstances, how many men, J.D. included, could have avoided what the redhead was offering? And how significant was it, really? Did it mean he loved Mary any less? How would she deal with it if she found out? And what would it make of the man who used it as a weapon, or even a motive? Lots of questions, no satisfactory answers, the stuff of life.

J.D. was so filled with his own problems, he nearly collided with the beggar when he rounded the corner onto Ochoa Street. A pair of hollow, vacant eyes looked out at him from under the brim of a greasy hat. Ragged clothes, too big for his shrunken frame, hung from narrow shoulders. Gnarled hands held the crutches firmly in the pits of his arms. The right leg was long and skinny, the left, a stump that ended above the knee.

J.D. was momentarily frozen, unable to breathe, unable to move. The man raised an arm, reached out toward him. J.D. stumbled away. He would have fallen into the street but for the parked car he backed into.

"No," he heard someone whisper. "No." It was his own voice, harsh, almost unrecognizable with terror. And then he was running. He couldn't stop until he found the Ford. The shaking didn't end until he got home and significantly dropped the level in a bottle of scotch. Only then did he start to believe his own denial. Only then did he understand it really hadn't been Ortiz.

Questas had stopped screaming. He was only making the regular bubbling moans necessary for a man sucking air through congealing blood. The sun was gone and it was starting to get cold. J.D. watched through slitted eyes. It was too dark to see much. The moon would be coming soon. He couldn't decide whether that would make it better or worse.

There was a flat place up in the rocks. The Nationalists had set up camp there. They'd sent a couple of sentries out to guard the road before dark. He knew because one of them stepped on his hand as they went by. It hurt worse than the knife had, but he didn't move or make a sound. He was beginning to think he might survive if only Questas didn't scream anymore. If he did, J.D. was afraid he might join him. Then they would find him too and give him more reasons to scream.

There were still two men near Questas. He could see the glow of their cigarettes and hear the low murmur of their conversation. They weren't working on Questas anymore. Questas was beyond caring and that took the fun out of it, but they still sat with him, perhaps to watch him die.

J.D. moved. He had wondered if he could anymore. He flexed the fingers of his injured right hand and they rustled in the gravel. Too loud, but no one came to investigate—no one came to carve him into a likeness of Questas. He moved the hand again. All his fingers worked. Nothing was broken. He brought the hand to his belt and checked. The knife was still there. They'd been careless in their looting. It was a good knife.

He tried sitting up. His head spun a little because of the tension of lying still for so long with them all around and Questas screaming. He made hardly a sound. No one noticed. He tried getting to his knees and it was still OK. He stood. Figures around a fire up in the rocks cast huge, misshapen shadows that danced malevolently on the surrounding brush and boulders. A match flared as one of those by Questas lit another smoke. His companion muttered an indistinct comment.

J.D. took a step. Gravel crunched loudly under his boot. His heart leaped into his throat and he stopped and held his breath. His back crawled, waiting for a bullet. But the thunder of his step sounded only in his own ears. They still hadn't noticed him.

His breath came in shallow gasps he couldn't control as he bent and untied his boots and slipped them off. He tied their laces together and draped them around his neck. He tried again. Sharp stones bit through his ragged socks, but it didn't matter. He moved as softly as the night breeze. Once he stepped on something soft and yielding and nearly fell. It was only Rodolfo, who could no longer protest. After that he felt ahead with his toes before he put any weight down.

The sentries had posted themselves just outside Tres Santos where the road began to narrow and rise up into the pass. One of the guards was asleep, snoring softly. The other lounged against a rock, smoking and gazing at the stars. The sky was full of them, silent witnesses to Spain's agony.

He could have killed the sentries easily. Perhaps he should have, but it only occurred to him later, long after he was away from there. He had a knife and more than enough motive, but his feet had a will of their own. He passed them by.

He couldn't remember the journey. Just as well, he already remembered too much. They told him later that he was still going on like that, boots strung around his neck, knife clutched in his bruised hand. The bottom of his socks were worn away and he was leaving bloody footprints behind him in the dust. That was how he entered the village of Los Gatos.

Los Gatos might have been a prosperous place once, but not when J.D. reached it. It was too close to the front. Most of the population had left, and the few dozen homes and businesses that hadn't been destroyed by the regular bombing runs had been claimed by Ortiz and his band.

It they took him to see Ortiz when he arrived, he didn't remember that either. He didn't even remember finding the village. After the sentries, the first thing he remembered was waking in the night screaming. It was something he would do for quite a while.

A burly man whose hair hung over his forehead in greasy locks brought a lamp into his room and told him everything was all right, he was safe. The man needed a bath even worse than J.D. did, but he had a soothing voice. They shared a cigarette, then he left the lamp on the table and J.D. slept again. In the morning they took him to see Ortiz.

Ortiz had made his headquarters in the local *cantina*. But for the kitchens, the building remained untouched by the bombs. Ortiz sat behind a table in the back corner and in the dim interior it was hard to make him out. He was tall and gaunt, his clothes hanging loosely on him as if they had been made for a bigger man. His eyes burned with an inner fire. Perhaps he consumed himself from within and that was why he was shrunken, why his clothes no longer fit. He wore a hat that would have been fashionable in any metropolitan capital, but it was filthy. J.D. had the feeling he could tell how long Ortiz had owned it, dating it by counting the rings of salt about the band the way one counted a tree's rings.

Ortiz asked him who he was, where he came from. How he happened to come to Los Gatos with bare, bloody feet and a wound cut into his chest. It was the first J.D. realized he'd damaged his feet. He looked down and saw them swathed in bandages, painless thanks to someone's ministrations.

J.D. told him about Saturnino Martinez, of whom Ortiz had heard. He told him about their defections and how their supplies dried up as the last of their contacts with the local population left. He told Ortiz about the peasant and the aerodrome, and he told him about the trap.

He told it as if he'd witnessed it from a safe distance, not as a man to whom it had done the things it had. When he told them about Questas, Ortiz' lieutenants began to mutter among themselves and their leader emerged from behind the table. That was when J.D. discovered Ortiz had given a leg to the cause. A filthy pant leg was neatly folded and pinned not far above the knee. Ortiz grabbed his crutches in great knobby hands and swung himself across the room. There was a table there with a map under the remains of someone's supper dishes.

"They might still be there," Ortiz muttered. His lieutenants gathered around the map, and the ones who'd brought J.D. returned him to his room. Rest, they told him, recover. J.D. promised to do his best. Try not to think of it, they told him. He tried that too, but it didn't work. He woke the camp regularly with the echoes of Questas' screams.

For several days the camp was almost vacant. Those who remained came to comfort him less and less. J.D. felt them watching him cautiously from the corner of their eyes as he sat in the shade of the olive tree in front of his room. It was as if they feared his dreams were contagious.

One morning J.D. was roughly awakened by a pair of men. They told him Ortiz wanted him. He was still lost in the webs of nightmare. Questas voice called from beyond the veil of sleep. J.D. moved too slowly to suit them. One of them gave him a hard shove and he stumbled and fell.

"Wait," the other said. "Time for that later."

J.D. didn't understand. The one who pushed him was the same man who had comforted him that first night and brought the lamp.

The sun was just peeking over the hills east of the village when they led him into the *cantina*. The place looked the same as it had before, only this time most of Ortiz' band lined the walls. Ortiz sat behind his favorite table, his missing leg hidden and his eyes burning so bright that J.D. wondered briefly why anyone had bothered to light the room's lamps.

"Tell it again," Ortiz demanded. "Tell me what happened to Martinez and the others and how you got away."

J.D. wasn't healed yet. His feet and the cut across his chest were doing nicely, but his soul still held a wound that festered and wept and required treatment. He should have understood that something was wrong. He should have asked. Instead, he answered, like an automaton. He had relearned the habit of doing what people told him—not of thinking, reasoning for himself. Thinking was dangerous. Thinking took him back to the road outside Tres Santos. He avoided thinking. He did as he was told and recited it again. He may have even used the same words.

By the time J.D. finished, the thing that burned within Ortiz had drawn him erect. As J.D. spoke, Ortiz paced, tripedally, across the open floor. When J.D. stopped, so did he. He waved a crutch toward the door that had once led to the kitchens and now led to a jumble of rubble and the alley beyond.

"Bring him in," he shouted.

Two men carried in a stretcher. On it lay a form as fully bandaged as the contents of an Egyptian sarcophagus. Once it had been a man. Now it lay there and fought for air. It moaned slightly as they set it down, and J.D. knew who it was.

"Questas," he said. The horror that washed over him made his voice not much louder than a whisper. He tried to go to the shattered remnant. He wanted to beg its forgiveness, to make it understand why he had left it behind. He'd thought Questas as good as dead. Still, he should have done something. He should have killed the ones who sat beside him. He should have brought Questas out with him, or ended his suffering. The men who'd brought J.D. to the *cantina* continued to hold him by his arms. J.D. didn't have the strength to break free. They probably didn't even realize that he tried.

Questas lay in the middle of the floor where his eyes could peer up at J.D. from the depths of his shrouding.

"Do you know this man?" Ortiz asked. His voice was soft and gentle, but the eyes that watched J.D. along the raised, pointing crutch, smoldered with contempt.

"Fitzpatrick," Questas rasped.

"Tell us what he did there, in the road above Tres Santos."

"He ran," Questas answered. "They ambushed us and he broke." He had to pause and gasp for air between sentences. "Martinez tried to stop him. So did Medina. It got them both killed. Medina knocked him down. But he got up. He ran again. He was shouting and sobbing."

"No," J.D. whispered. "It was Medina who ran, not me." No one heard him. It wouldn't have mattered anyway. They wouldn't have believed him in the face of Questas' accusation. He was no longer sure he believed himself.

"I didn't think he got away," Questas continued. "But then they shot me and I didn't see him anymore. I was unconscious. Then they found me with the knife." His voice was rising. There was madness just behind it.

"You should have come back," Questas told J.D. "You should have stopped them," he cried. "You shouldn't have lived."

One of the stretcher bearers bent to his side and calmed him. It was a good thing. If he had screamed, J.D. would have joined him. Screamed his way down into some fetid pit inside his soul from which he might never again have emerged. As it was, he stood on its brink and chill terror wafted over him from its maw, paralyzing him.

"No," Ortiz agreed, looking at J.D. "He shouldn't have lived. But such errors can be remedied." He had drawn his knife and he swung slowly toward J.D. Both of them knew what he planned to do with it.

"Stop!" Questas commanded. J.D. wouldn't have thought the man could be aware of anything but his personal tortures, but the knife had caught his attention, wrenched him back. "No one deserves that," he said. "I would have run too. If I'd known what they would do to me. You weren't there. Any man might have broken. Faced with what we met, any of you might have done what he did. Believe me. There is a place inside each of us beyond which we cannot go. Force us there, and we break. We cry, we whimper, we foul ourselves. Above Tres Santos, the lucky ones died before they found that place. Fitzpatrick and I, we found it, we crossed over. Pray, each of you, that you never follow."

In a way, J.D. knew, Questas was right. Even though it was Medina who broke and ran, and in the confusion of the killing Questas had gotten them confused. Still, in the end, J.D. had broken and run too, with room in his thoughts for only himself. He felt as guilty as Questas believed him.

"I can't allow this man to live," Ortiz told Questas.

"It might be kinder if you killed us both," Questas said. "I'm not sure we can live with what we've learned about ourselves. Only do it quickly. Don't make us face that place again."

Maybe J.D. should have argued, defended himself. But he didn't. He believed Questas.

They took J.D. out and led him to a converted storage shed. There were three other men there. He didn't have to ask. He could see it in their eyes. They, too, were dead men, waiting only on the formality of the rite of passage.

They were kept there through the night and none of them slept. A boy whimpered softly to himself while a bald man knelt in the corner and prayed. Just after dawn the guards came for them. The boy begged and wet himself. The bald man fought them and tried to break free. He had to be dragged along as he cursed them and their wives and mothers and children. J.D. and the fourth wretch followed meekly.

The machine gun was set up in the shade of the east wall of the central plaza. They tied the prisoners along the opposite wall, facing into the angry sun. A small crowd bunched behind the gun, there to witness vengeance or justice, there to seek some clue to the nature of life and death, or there for want of anything better to do at sunrise in Los Gatos.

There were iron rings in the walls to tether draft animals. They worked equally well to secure those condemned to die. J.D. was tied to the ring at the north end of the wall. The boy hung limply from the one beside him and cried for his mother. The belt was in the breach of the machine gun. The gunners lounged behind it and smoked, impatient to finish and get on with the new day.

Ortiz hobbled into the plaza at the head of his lieutenants. In honor of the occasion he wore a pistol buckled on his hip. Otherwise he looked no more military than usual. He appeared a more appropriate figure for sitting in the sun with a tin cup to collect on the guilt of those who thought "better him than me."

They put blindfolds on the others, but when they began to tie one on J.D., Ortiz forbade it.

"Not that one," he called. "Let him look death in the face this time."

The bald man asked for a priest to hear his confession. Los Gatos had none. Ortiz nodded to the gunners and they cocked their weapon. A bird sang in a distant tree and the boy sobbed.

"Start at the south end," Ortiz told them. "Make Fitzpatrick the last."

The gun spoke, the gunner sweeping the barrel up and down and his assistant keeping the belt flowing smoothly. Spent brass rained onto the plaza's dusty surface. The gun traversed each body several times, until what hung from the iron ring was torn and shredded and human no more.

J.D. couldn't hear the boy over the thunder of the gun, but he felt the splatter of the youth's blood when he died, and the sting of plaster chips from the wall as the stream of lead flowed nearer. Something slammed his right side, hammer blows so massive and in such close succession he could not distinguish one agony from another. He welcomed the great darkness that swept into his mind.

Her name was Elena. She watched with the silent crowd in the plaza, one of the few with just cause to be there. The boy was her son. J.D. should have died beside him, but she wouldn't allow it.

The gun jammed. They ran it down his right side, four bullets, four holes, some fractured ribs, some massive tissue damage, a great deal of blood, but, miraculously, nothing damaged that would not heal. They had only fired about a hundred rounds. The gun had spent less than ten seconds at its task. It had not had time to overheat. A ten second burst should not have been too much to ask of it. But it was an old gun. Perhaps the tolerances critical to its function had worn. Perhaps its crew did not understand the need to keep its mechanism cleaner than they kept themselves. The cartridge that housed the round which tore away part of the muscle of J.D.'s thigh lodged in the ejector. It would not clear the way for the one which would have blown away his kneecap. Metal met metal in ways for which the gun was not designed. The thunder stopped and the hail of brass and lead ceased. But the plaza was not silent. It was filled with a distant but growing roar, previously unnoticed over the sound of the gun. Fascist airplanes. Two of them—coming low and fast, to reduce a little more of Los Gatos back to the components from which it had been formed.

The plaza cleared. Executioners and curious alike sought their own safety. They left the jammed gun behind, along with four bodies that hung, bloody ornaments to honor satisfied, upon a sunlit wall.

Her son was dead. J.D. wasn't. Oblivious to the planes and their bombs which tore at the heart of the village, she cut both of them down, placed them in a hand cart, and wheeled them out through a maelstrom of smoke and dust to the little farm, a few miles down the valley, where she lived.

Ortiz never came looking. J.D. didn't know whether he died in the bombing or thought the execution satisfactorily completed. By the time J.D. was fit enough to concern himself with such questions, the village was abandoned.

Elena seldom had much to say to him. She never asked who he was nor why he'd been against the wall. The war had taken too much from her—a husband, brothers, and her only son. She would claim whatever flotsam it washed her way, not because she cared for what she saved, but because the act denied the war yet another victory over her.

She nursed and fed him and he healed. When he was able to leave, she sent him on his way with little care for what would become of him. He was in poor condition by the time he reached Angüés. He had a fever from infection and it passed on into pneumonia. After that there were only bits and pieces, fragments of memory of the time between Angüés and the hospital not far from Baltimore. Death chewed him, then spat him out. He was not yet ripe enough. It would wait and pluck him when he was less ready to die. He slowly regained his health and his strength, but for a long time he woke in the middle of the night with Questas' screams echoing in his memory, and his own echoing in the dark hospital room.

Business and Pleasure

Mary was so surprised to hear an English profanity on the old Papago's lips that she looked away from the street to see what was wrong, and when she looked back the light had changed to red. It was late and there was barely any traffic. They got away with running it.

"I beg your pardon?" she said, then remembered to translate the phrase into *O'odham*.

"I was searching for an expression to voice my reaction to your village," he told her. "I could not find one in my own tongue, but I remembered yours. Perhaps it is not appropriate. One such as I, who is at war with your people, should be less delighted and more awed, and yet, I am delighted. Have I used the expression incorrectly?"

"No," Mary admitted. "It, or several variations, cover quite a variety of situations. You just surprised me, that's all."

"I have a good memory. It is one of the reasons I am a *Siwani Mahkai*. Our people do not have many ways to aid their memory. Knowledge is either retained or it is lost."

She hadn't paid much attention to their route, just their destination. They'd driven in on Arizona 86, cut north along Mission to Congress, and were entering downtown Tucson.

"You've never seen Tucson before, have you?" she asked, suddenly understanding what prompted the exclamation.

"No," he said. "I have not even been to Sells."

"You've never seen any other American city?"

"There are others? Yes, I suppose there must be, but surely not many are so large."

"Actually," she said, "Tucson isn't large. Only about 40,000 people here. There must be thousands of cities like this in the United States, and lots that are bigger. New York City, for instance, must be two hundred times the size of Tucson."

He said it again.

"Maybe there's something I should explain to you about that expression," she said. It would be a fine thing if it got around that the one useful bit of English he'd picked up from her was its ultimate obscenity. Her reputation for ladylike behavior was on shaky ground in too many quarters already.

J.D. lived on the north side, on East Helen. She went up Stone, took Speedway to Sixth, then turned north for a block and back east again. She glanced at her wrist to check the time but her watch was still in her pack. Unwound for a couple of months, it wouldn't have been much help. She'd been on Papago time for too long. All the same, she had a pretty good idea what time it was. The sun set about 5:30 in early January. Say about four and a half hours on horseback and then another couple for the drive, maybe a little more because the desert part of the trail was hard to follow in the dark. It was probably between midnight and one.

The lights in J.D.'s house were off but his Ford hugged the curb out front. She pulled up behind it and turned off the ignition. The neighborhood was dark and still.

"Come with me and stay quiet," she told him.

They went up the front walk across a grassy lawn flanked by a pair of date palms. Jujul looked curious and she could tell he wanted to ask questions, but he was taking her admonition to silence seriously. They weren't likely to have any problems even if they caught a curious neighbor's attention, but she didn't want to try to explain Jujul to one of Tucson's finest.

J.D.'s was a nice little bungalow on the south side of the street. It had a great view of the Catalinas and a small enough yard to give a bachelor a fighting chance. She and Larry had been there often enough for her to know where the front door was and the general layout inside. Mary tried the handle and it was unlocked. They went in and she closed the door behind them. A bit of light filtered past Venetian blinds and softly striped the living room. She found the sofa.

"Sit here and wait," she told Jujul. "I want to talk to J.D. first, before he sees you."

He sat, awkward in such an alien environment. She felt her way through the attached dining room and found the hallway beyond. It was very dark there. She knew which door led to the bathroom. The bedroom must be behind the other. She tried it.

The room was pitch dark, filled with the faint smell of whiskey and the sound of ragged breathing. She felt along the wall and found a switch. She hesitated. What if he wasn't alone? It couldn't matter, she realized, except to her. This was far too important to abandon on the possibility of shattered fantasies. She threw the switch.

The light was blinding for a moment, then there was just a bedroom, small, crowded, and a little sloppy. J.D. was sprawled on the bed, arms flung wide, sheets twisted. His face looked troubled and his eyes rolled beneath closed lids. Whatever he was dreaming wasn't pleasant.

She'd wondered what it would be like to be alone with him in this room for months, but the situation wasn't quite what she'd imagined and there was important business to attend to. She sat gently on the edge of the bed and reached out to softly stroke his brow. Business could wait a moment.

His eyes flew open. They darted about the room, desperate, haunted, then found her. "Mary!" he gasped, and she was in his arms and his lips were on hers, and she almost forgot the old man in the living room.

The instant he sensed she was trying to disengage herself, he let go. She climbed out of the bed, breathing hard and adjusting her clothes. He looked confused and uncertain, which, under the circumstances, were appropriate reactions.

"I guess that means you're glad to see me," she said.

"What? How? Why?" He stammered, sitting up in bed, fighting the sleep and booze that still fogged his mind.

They were good questions, though. Abbreviated as they were, she understood them. What was she doing there? How had she gotten away? And, why had she come to him? She went back over to the bed and took his hand. No reason she couldn't mix business and pleasure. She answered as best she could. She told him the highlights of her life in Jujul's camp, what she'd come to think of the old man and his people, how she'd managed to avoid even suspecting until Jujul chose to tell her. The only important things she left out involved her feelings for him and her persisting confusion about them. Just then it would have been too easy to succumb to her fascination, leaving logic and reason to bother her later. And there was that important business they needed to conduct first, sitting, waiting in the front room. She hadn't told him about that yet either.

"Jujul wants to meet you, J.D.," she told him. "That's one of the reasons I'm here. I agreed to arrange it, but I need to be sure you won't have to arrest him on sight. Can you still meet with him face to face, no strings attached?" It was what she had to know. J.D. might have orders to do just that by now, the sort of orders he couldn't ignore.

He rubbed at his eyes and put a hand through his sleep tousled hair while she talked, but he didn't interrupt and it was clear he was listening carefully.

"That's exactly what I've been trying to do," he said. "Larson's rasing hell and pushing for assault with intent, but my concern with the case is the federal aspect, draft resistance. If Larson's managed to hammer through an arrest warrant on his charges, I haven't been advised of it. My instructions are still to try to keep a lid on this, to bring it to a peaceful conclusion. I'd like nothing better than a chance to meet and talk to your friend. And, yes, you have my promise it'll be without strings. Wherever and whenever Jujul wants, and when we're done, he can walk away and think about what I've said, talk to his people. Whatever he needs to do. OK?"

"OK," she agreed. She got off the bed and dragged at his hand. "Come on, he's waiting in your living room."

"Living room?" he asked, as if trying to recall what part of the Southern Arizona desert that might be in.

"Living room," she repeated with a big smile. "You know, through that door and toward the front of the house."

"Living room," he said again, understanding this time. "You are one remarkable lady, you know that?"

She liked it better than being the idiot who had lived in Jujul's village for a month and a half without the glimmer of an idea as to where she was. "Come on," she said, and tugged again, and discovered why he hadn't been following her.

"Sorry," he said, pulling the sheet back up over his waist. "No clean pajamas."

She blushed. Ruth and Maggie had been right about the scars. There was a fourth one where it would be hidden by a bathing suit.

"Maybe I should go wait with your visitor," Mary suggested.

"Suit yourself," he said, grinning at her embarrassment. "I've got nothing left to hide."

She picked up a pair of slacks from where he'd left them hanging over the back of a chair and tossed them on the bed.

"Put your pants on," she commanded, "and come greet your guest. We'll play later." She was out the door before she realized what she'd said. Apparently she'd just committed herself to cheating on her husband. So much for logic and reason. She would have turned right around and gone back and made good on it if Jujul hadn't been waiting.

To Surrender

They had learned respect for each other during their protracted and deadly serious game of hide and seek. That respect carried them beyond their initial reaction to each other's alienness. They both spoke some Spanish, but Mary's ability to translate to each man's native language soon had them exchanging information and opinions with surprising comfort.

Jujul explained his side of the Larson incidents. He hinted at unsatisfactory encounters with Anglos in the past. For just a moment, Mary saw raw emotion burning in the old man's eyes like nothing she'd seen there before. But he hid it quickly and, just as quickly, acknowledged that what a man looked like on the outside had nothing to do with the person within. Good or evil could not be equated with race or language or culture.

J.D. explained the draft law. Mary had already done it, but the marshal knew far more details and could answer Jujul's probing questions. J.D. argued that the literacy requirement alone guaranteed none of Jujul's people could presently qualify to serve in America's armed forces. He reluctantly admitted that the rules might change if war actually came. Surprisingly, Jujul seemed relieved, not at the revelation but by his honesty.

J.D. explained that he had been authorized to guarantee the elimination of federal charges if Jujul would surrender to him and his people would comply with the registration process. Larson's criminal charges, unfortunately, were another matter. He promised to bring all the pressure he could on Larson to have them reduced or dropped altogether, but he had to admit it was something he might not be able to control. He couldn't guarantee that Jujul or a few of his men might not have to serve some jail time, only that he would do his best to see that it was minimal or nonexistent.

There came a time when it had all been said. Mary and J.D. exchanged a knowing glance. It was up to the old man to weigh their words, consider his impressions, and make his decision. There was nothing more they could do to influence it.

Jujul sat stiffly on the edge of J.D.'s sofa and listened to a cacophony of incomprehensible sounds—the hum of the refrigerator from the unseen kitchen, the ticking of the clock on the mantel across the room, the occasional surf of tires on pavement, and the distant call of a railroad locomotive. It seemed this monstrous village never totally slept. Painful memories wrestled with equally painful logic.

Jujul's eyes traveled slowly around the room, taking in its marvels and mysteries one last time, then came to rest on Mary. "Tell him I accept," he said, his voice almost too soft to hear. He took a deep breath and, if possible, straightened his ramrod spine just a fraction more.

"I accept," he said again, in a voice from which all doubts had been banished. "I will need three days," he told Mary as she translated. "One day to return to my village, and one to persuade my people to agree to what I have done. On the third, I will bring all my men of the appropriate age to Burns' Ranch. Will that be an acceptable place for them to register with your Selective Service and for me to surrender myself to you?"

"Whatever place and time will be most convenient," J.D. replied diplomatically. He would have a draft board registrar at the ranch and do his best to quash any outstanding warrants before Jujul's people arrived. Then, if there weren't any hitches, as soon as the registration was complete Jujul and his men could simply go home.

They shook hands. It was a custom Mary had explained to Jujul while she lived in his village. The clock on J.D.'s mantel chimed the half hour, and Mary glanced at it and the adjacent calendar. It was 3:30 A.M. on Saturday, January 4, 1941.

"We'd better get going," she told them, each in his own language. Then, just to J.D., "We've got a long drive and some riding to do. I don't know about Jujul, but I'm too old for all nighters like this."

"I'll drive you," he offered.

Mary was tempted. Maybe she could nap. But no, she was too keyed up, and, being close to J.D. would keep her talking for the whole trip.

"I don't mind, and anyway, this way I'll be there to drive you back," he said.

"Back? I'm not coming back. I'm going with Jujul. I may not get the dissertation I had in mind, but I should be able to put one together about a Papago village in crisis after all this."

"No. You can't do that," he said, taking her by the arm. "You can't disappear again."

She was touched, but she was also determined. She translated the gist of their argument to Jujul who'd been standing by, courteously quiet but obviously curious.

"She will be in no danger with us," Jujul said. "I will guarantee this. If she wants to come, to observe how we resolve our problem, it is something I owe her."

J.D. wasn't happy. He looked in her eyes and tried the most persuasive argument of all. "Please don't go," he said.

"I've got to," she told him. "It's only for three days, closer to two and a half now. I'll be there on Monday. If you can keep things quiet, there's no reason Larry needs to know I've come out then. At least not for a few days."

Shit, she thought, he hasn't offered me anything even remotely like that. What if I've misread him? What about Larry? Then she saw the answer in his smile, and none of the rest of it mattered. Desire was an easy winner over a confused blend of comfort and obligation.

They were just standing there, making eyes at each other like a couple of kids. Jujul misunderstood. He thought they might still be arguing about her safety and that J.D. didn't trust him with it.

"Tell him I will give him one further evidence of my confidence in him and assurance for your well being," he said. "Tell him my true name is Coyote Among Thistles."

She told J.D. and tried to explain what it meant for a Papago to reveal his true name, especially to someone who could be an enemy, what a powerful weapon he was placing in J.D.'s hands.

J.D. was suitably impressed. She remembered telling Jujul that J.D. had a secret name of sorts as well.

"It would be a nice gesture to give him your real name," she suggested, after explaining.

He hesitated a moment, then nodded. "OK, but it requires some explanation and it may be difficult for Jujul to understand.

"My father was a notorious and vociferous agnostic. There was nothing he liked better than casting his doubts on everyone else's religious waters. His father disowned him, off and on again, with some regularity. I gather I was conceived when Father was once again being disclaimed by the family. My grandfather apparently promised to acknowledge the prodigal, as it were, if my father would name his first born son from the books of the Bible. He'd long ago cut Father out of his will, but Father was his only offspring and he wanted, as he colorfully put it, to pass along the fruit of his labors to the fruit of his loins. If my father would agree to the bargain and promise not to change the name later, grandfather would make me his sole heir and name Father as administrator until I reached legal age. It wasn't a fortune, but it was a sizeable estate until the Depression hit. My parents were surviving well enough, but Father eventually decided he couldn't turn down an offer of security for his unborn child. He agreed, but he couldn't help turning it into a joke in the process.

"My grandfather expected me to be named Matthew John, or the like, but he reckoned without his son's perversity. My name is Judges Deuteronomy Fitzpatrick. I don't think Grandfather ever spoke to Father again after he saw the birth certificate, but the old man honored the bargain and I inherited. The greatest kindness my parents did for me, however, was in never telling anybody else what my name was. I was always just J.D. They didn't even tell *me* till I was old enough to appreciate the whys and be wary about who I shared it with. Maybe you can explain to Jujul that, from my own point of view, I've given him a weapon also, a very different sort than he's given me, but nothing casual or unimportant."

She explained it briefly to the old man, then asked him to wait for a minute in the truck. She promised to explain in detail as they drove back.

As soon as Jujul was out the door she and J.D. began their private goodbyes. She told him her own secret name and that she thought she loved him. He told her he was long past thinking about it. He was sure he loved her. She started to give him a hint of what he could look forward to on Monday, and then, before she knew what she was doing, her hands were on his buckles and buttons. They collapsed on the floor in a tangle of hastily shed clothing. It was as quick, as frantic, as any experience she'd ever had, but this time it was her need that demanded and received instant satiation. It wasn't remotely like any of her sexual fantasies, but it was infinitely better than anything she'd felt before. She wanted to try it again, with variations, but Jujul was waiting. She struggled back into her clothes and kissed him lightly on the cheek.

"Monday," she whispered in his ear, a whisper full of promise. She went out the door and ran to the truck.

A Metropolis to Rival Many Chickens

"His name's Pete but they call him Talker," Parker said as he locked the office door behind him. "Not because he's got much to say, but because he tends to brag. He was working on a ranch near Sasabe. Knifed a White Man and ran for it. He's been hiding out in a village near the east edge of the reservation. Jujul's people were passing through pretty regularly. When he figured out who they were, he tracked them."

Parker's battered Plymouth was in the lot behind his office. It looked like a car that made regular trips over unimproved desert roads. The paint was scratched from contact with stones, branches, and cactus needles. The glass was glazed from blowing sand. It had a couple of extra spares tied to a luggage rack on the trunk and a pair of canvas water bags hanging from the front bumper. Parker opened a door for him and walked around and climbed behind the wheel. The Plymouth started on the first try and sounded better than it looked.

"Little bastard likes money, wants a chance to earn more. He's trading me Jujul's whereabouts for getting him clear of a murder charge. The irony is, not only did the guy not die from the wound, he didn't even report it. Big mean bastard, I'm told, who planned to find Talker, wherever he might get to, and take care of things personally. Only he and some of his pals rolled their pickup on the way home from a drunken binge on New Year's Eve and he had the misfortune to end up in one of the places it picked to roll. I suppose I should have told Talker as soon as I found out, but he can't read maps and I might not be able to follow his directions. So, I'll wait till he takes us where we're going.

"I'm glad you happened along when you did. I've been trying to figure out what to do with this information. Only person I could think of who might be willing to pay for it was a BIA man who wouldn't have come up with near what you did. Besides, that might have hurt my conscience from time to time, and if it ever got out, wouldn't have done my reputation any good either."

They pulled around the building and paused beside the spot where Sasaki had nosed the DeSoto up near the door. "Need anything from your car," Parker asked, "or want to lock it up?"

"I've got everything I need, and locking it won't be necessary."

"No, you're right," Parker observed. "You could leave an unlocked car for a month here in Sells without anybody bothering it." Sasaki doubted that, and he'd left the keys in the ignition to make it easy for anyone who wanted to prove otherwise. Not that he expected anyone to be able to link him to it, or that it would matter if they did, once he got where he was going, but if it disappeared there would be just one less loose end.

Parker had stashed Talker in a clapboard hut on the outskirts of Sells. It looked like the first strong wind would carry it off, along with Parker's distant relatives to whom it belonged. The attorney was keeping them in moonshine in exchange for Talker's rent and, as long as the booze held out, they were willing to be accommodating and forgetful.

Talker proved to be a nervous little man without much interest in the cause of Indian rights, but plenty of interest in the ten dollars Sasaki offered for his services. The three crowded into the Plymouth and took the road toward Tucson. It wouldn't have seemed so crowded if Talker had picked up the Anglo habit of bathing regularly along with his greed.

About twenty-five miles east of Sells they turned off onto a dirt track that headed northeast. Sasaki wouldn't have noticed its existence if it hadn't been part of their route. They left a pair of swirling dust clouds in their wake, an easy spoor to follow. It didn't concern him. No one was trailing him. He'd made sure of that long ago. And if anyone was keeping an eye on either of his companions, they would leave their own smudge on the clear blue sky. Parker drove, and the only pursuers Sasaki noticed were occasional vultures. Their company seemed appropriate.

They drove through two villages and stopped to replace one flat tire before reaching the community called Many Chickens. Unless the fowl were well hidden, it was a misnomer.

Sasaki made them haggle over the price of the horses they'd have to use to go on from there. Not that he cared what the fee was, he just didn't want Parker and Talker to have any reason to think they were making a one-way trip.

They rode east until dusk and camped at the base of a stunted hill with only a forest of saguaros for company. It had been almost a year since Sasaki had last ridden a horse. The next morning he ignored a set of aches with which he'd been long unfamiliar. Climbing back in the saddle took real effort. Parker had the same problem, but he complained about it with a bad joke about building the calluses he would need for his seat at the head of the tribal council.

About mid-afternoon Talker asked whether they wanted to sneak in or not. Sasaki told him not. They rode down an incline, crossed a narrow valley, topped a rise, and there it was. A metropolis to rival Many Chickens lay at the foot of a jagged little range, one of the reservation's more impressive examples of topography. An occasional improbably verdant patch attested to the presence of sporadic water.

The citizens weren't glad to see them. Almost a dozen men hung around in the background, cradling a collection of antique rifles and shotguns in their arms as the trio rode in. None of the other villages they'd passed through had shown a need to defend themselves. Sasaki decided their guide had probably brought them to the right place.

A tall young man greeted them, if that was the right word. Parker translated.

"He's asking what we want. Says they're a poor village and can't afford to offer hospitality. Besides, they've got sickness and it's dangerous for us to stay. Red carpet treatment all the way."

"Do any of you speak English?" Sasaki called out.

A child ducked behind his mother's skirt and an old man coughed. There was no other answer, just a sullen, watchful silence. If no one could understand him, he was in trouble.

"Don't worry, Mr. Begay," Parker reassured him. "May not be anyone here who's what you'd call real fluent, but several of them will speak enough for you to get by."

"Good," Sasaki thanked him. Then louder, to his unwilling hosts, "Mr. Parker here assures me that some of you can understand me. That is important since neither you nor I can trust either of the men with me to tell you what I say. They both know this is the village of Jujul and they have sold you to me for a price. It is lucky for you that I have come as your friend and ally. But these two are enemies and cannot be allowed to leave."

Parker and Talker both looked shocked and angry, but Sasaki noticed a satisfactory shifting of weapons to cover them.

"What kind of shit is this?" Parker hissed. "I thought we had a deal. I wouldn't turn you in."

"Better safe than sorry, Mr. Parker. I'm sure you'll understand. Jujul will probably decide to move his village again, since it's clear his location has been compromised. Perhaps we can release you then. Whatever, you'll leave $500 richer. I gave you my word. The fee should be worth a little of your time."

Their conversation made them the center of attention and Talker took advantage of it. He spurred his mount straight at the nearest armed man. There wasn't time to aim or shoot before the horse brushed him aside. Other guns came up as Talker flattened himself in the saddle and rode hard for the open desert. The man who'd acted as spokesman for the village shouted something and the guns came down after a couple of wild shots. Several men ran to the nearest corral, grabbed mounts, and gave chase.

An armed man took hold of Parker's horse. Most of the remaining guns centered on him. Talker couldn't have done Sasaki a bigger favor if he'd been paid for it. The Japanese was still a stranger, but someone to believe. He'd issued a warning and in seconds it had proved accurate.

The young man who had addressed them before stepped in front of Sasaki's horse. He didn't grab the reins, just stood there looking up at him.

"Who are you?" he asked. His English was thick, awkward from lack of use, but understandable.

Sasaki looked at him and his fellows. They were a mixed bunch, some old, some fat, some young, and all together about as ignoble looking a bunch of savages as he could imagine. Their village was a poor collection of piled up rocks, mud, and branches.

"Please, who are you? What you want?" The young Indian didn't say it with impatience, only uncertainty, as if he doubted his ability to be understood.

"I am Kozo Sasaki," came the proud reply. "I am a Captain of the Imperial Army of Japan, and I have come to help you make war on your enemies."

"Holy shit!" Parker said.

Historical Footnote

"You know, hosting the surrender of America's last hostile Indians just might get us mentioned in a historical footnote somewheres," Edith Burns said as she filled J.D.'s plate with half again as many pancakes as he could normally eat in a week.

He nodded and said, "Moof," around a mouthful of omelet.

"I know I'm pretty excited about it, and so's Bill," she said, giving her husband a stack that was even bigger. Bill nodded too, though it was hard to tell whether it was the surrender or the pancakes he was excited about.

J.D. had left the office before dawn. That was pretty silly since there wasn't much chance Jujul would bring in his people before noon, if that early, but whenever it was, he wanted to be there to greet Mary. Logic wasn't his long suit where she came in. If he'd been logical he would have waited and driven out with the rest of them. If Jujul happened to come in early he'd wait, and Mary would want to see the thing through to the end. He wouldn't be able to persuade her to leave until the village was registered, and Edward Larson offered and received apologies and informed the Deputy United States Marshal of his intent to drop all charges pending in the matter. Larson was going to be having about as much fun as the guest of honor at a tar and feathering, but he was going to do it. Bill Fredericks, the Reservation Supervisor, had strongly recommended the action. It was the time of year when he sent in his annual personnel evaluations. J.D. had added a persuasive argument of his own involving the rearrangement of Larson's limbs and features, one for each day Jujul spent in jail.

They were going to have a crowd for the making of Edith Burns' historical footnote. Aside from Fredericks and Larson of the BIA, there would be at least two representatives of the local draft board. The Chairman of the Papago Tribal Council was bringing a few of his own people to do a little politicking. It all added up to a dismal failure for J.D.'s attempts to keep it quiet and out of the news. Reporters from as far away as Phoenix were coming. At least he'd made it an iron-clad condition that there be no advance publicity. If there was, he'd promised to personally stake out the offending party on the nearest anthill, or, worse, make sure they missed covering the event. He'd only have a few hours with Mary before the whole thing became public knowledge and Larry started wondering where she was. It was the best he'd been able to do. Maybe it would be enough. J.D. wondered what he'd do if she chose to go home to her husband. Would he tell her about Larry and the red-headed naiad? He didn't much like himself for not being sure he wouldn't.

Tires rolled across the gravel of the ranch yard, and J.D. stepped out of the warm house into about as uncheerful a morning as could be asked for. The sky hung low and threatening, truncating the nearby peaks and masking Arizona's normally distant horizons. The car was a black-and-white from the Pima County Sheriff's office. He'd called and left word for Jesus the night before. J.D. didn't want anyone from the sheriff's office trying to serve any warrants he didn't happen to know about. He hadn't managed to talk to Jesus personally while he was dealing with all the necessary VIPs, but he knew Jesus would want to be there at the finish. J.D. just asked the dispatcher to tell Jesus that the Deputy U.S. Marshal suggested he zigzag his way out to their favorite ranch Monday morning. He'd made the man write the message down and read it back to him to be sure he got it right. Jesus would know what it meant, but the hot shots in the sheriff's department wouldn't stand much chance of deciphering it.

Jesus climbed out of the cruiser looking very tired. He would have gotten the message at the end of his shift, and he must have driven straight out to the ranch.

"You get yourself on in here and have some breakfast, Deputy," Edith Burns called from the door behind them. "Let the marshal get back to his pancakes. He ain't hardly touched them yet."

J.D. led Jesus inside and took another shot at the pancakes. There were more than he remembered. Around mouthfuls he filled Jesus in on a slightly censored version of his midnight visit from Mary and Jujul and their agreement for today's surrender.

Jesus rubbed the sleep from his eyes and grinned. "Good," he said. "Then I won't get chewed out so bad if I don't show up for my next shift on time. And when I have to explain all the extra mileage on my vehicle I can just tell them to bill the U.S. Marshal's Office, 'cause I got commandeered."

"Hell," J.D. told him, "I'm so happy with the way this thing's going to work out, I'll cover you out of my own pocket if Uncle Sam balks."

When events seem to be going right, it's usually because you've overlooked something. J.D. had hardly finished expressing his pleasure when it started evaporating. A fresh set of tires crunched thorough the gravel outside. J.D. got up to see who else was impatient. He wasn't expecting anyone from the official party until close to noon. It was his experience that bureaucrats always take at least twice as long to do anything as can be reasonably expected.

When he saw the Auburn Speedster the zest went right out of his day and he felt like a middle-aged man who'd just spent another sleepless night in what had become a succession of far too many. Larry Spencer wheeled the car up to the porch and climbed out.

"What're you doing here, Larry?" J.D. asked. He could hardly have been less delighted to see anyone. Larry seemed a little hurt at the coolness of J.D.'s greeting, but he held onto a bit of righteous indignation just the same.

"What's going on out here?" he countered. "You never returned my calls, then a reporter phones me looking for background information on the woman who's helping bring in Jujul's band and it's Mary he's talking about. I finally pried out of him that something was happening out here today and when my efforts to find you weren't successful, I just came on out. What's the deal? Where's Mary, what's she got to do with Jujul? I've got a right to know, J.D. She is my wife."

"I wasn't sure you were still aware of that," J.D. snarled. Larry went bright crimson. For just a moment J.D. thought Larry might swing at him, and hoped so because he wanted to hit someone or something real badly just then. The moment passed.

"Please, J.D., I still love her. I've got to know what's going on. If she's in danger...."

"Yeah," J.D. said through a wave of guilt. "OK." He reluctantly admitted to himself that Larry might still care, and what she did or what happened to her could still hurt him.

J.D. ushered Larry into the dining room. Edith Burns immediately set a huge mug of steaming coffee under his nose and began surrounding it with platters of pancakes, sausages, and omelets from the cornucopia of her kitchen. He sat and listened as J.D. went through it again, and once he understood Mary wasn't in danger, he started shoveling it in.

Things were getting complex. Mary's arrival was transforming itself from pleasant fulfillment to frightening uncertainty. On the other hand, J.D. couldn't think of anything else that could go wrong. But he was counting his wrongs before they hatched.

One of Burns' hands came in the front door and bent to whisper in his boss's ear. Burns' eyes got big and he stopped dead in the middle of his third stack of pancakes.

"Jujul's here," he announced, answering his guests' inquiring gazes. "But something's wrong. He ain't got but about twenty men with him, and Mary ain't there."

They cleared the dining room table simultaneously, the words pulling them out from under their meal like the trick with the table cloth, leaving steaming plates and platters miraculously behind. J.D. was closest to the door, so he was the first one through, but the mob was on his heels.

Burns' ranch house sat on a little terrace above a normally dry stream bed. Dry on the surface, but Burns' well didn't have to be very deep. Gentle slopes rose up to normal desert on both sides, but only on the west was that rise clearly visible. Cottonwoods and mesquites along the water course blocked the view in the opposite direction.

Jujul and a band of horsemen sat along the top of the ridge that divided desert from valley, strung out against the slate grey sky. They looked like a flock of cheap extras for a Hollywood Western.

When he saw them on the porch, Jujul left the others and brought his roan down the slope. He only came about halfway before he stopped and sat his mount, waiting. J.D. noted the butt of the infamous Sharps protruding from a saddle holster, and he could see how solemn the man looked. There was no sign of Mary.

"The rest of you stay here," he commanded. "Jesus, come with me." To his surprise, everyone obeyed.

He suppressed a need to charge head long up that slope and start choking "where is she"s out of the old man. The morning had taken on a hard, crystalline edge. A wrong move might shatter it and the shards could fall in lots of dangerous ways, impossible to reassemble again. Jujul dismounted as they reached him and held out a hand. J.D. took it. The grip was hard. Sad, angry eyes bored out of the old man's face. Before J.D. could tell Jesus to ask him about Mary, Jujul started.

"I gave you my word, Fitzpatrick," he said, through the deputy. "As far as I am able, I keep it. First, I promised to surrender myself to you today. I do that now. When you hear the rest you must decide what to do with your prisoner, but I urge that you release me, so that you and I may accompany each other."

J.D. wanted to interrupt him, wanted answers to the only important question. But the Indian was getting to it in his own way, and the marshal knew he wasn't going to like what he was about to hear.

"When Marie and I returned to where my village is hidden we discovered it had been found by three men. Two of them were *O'odham*, the third claims to be an officer of an army not yet at war with, but opposed to your own. He says he represents a place I have not heard of, a land of the rising sun.

"There is not time for details now, but he had been very persuasive in my absence. He has convinced most of the young men of the village, those whose blood still runs hot and who lack the maturity to make sound judgements, that he could lead them on a successful campaign against your people. I managed to impress on some how foolish this was, how mighty your nation and how hopeless our cause, but he has promised to arm them with weapons equivalent to your own. He says a boat comes from his distant land, a boat that travels beneath the sea, and it will bring them all they need to fight you.

"My return divided the young men of the village. But our people have a tradition which allows a war chief to be independent of our normal leadership. Whoever wishes to make a fight proclaims himself, and those who sympathize with his cause or desire plunder or adventure may join him as they wish. I could not dissuade them all, so I thought, perhaps, I might win them back by challenging their new chief to single combat. I am a foolish old man. He knew many tricks and he beat me easily." For the first time J.D. noticed the bruises on the side of his face.

"He left me unconscious in the dirt. When I woke, I found he had taken his followers and gone. He had also taken one of the men who came with him, the other ran away. And he took Marie.

"He left word that he took Marie and the other to insure our silence. If the rest of us would not cooperate with him, then at least we could not tell you, not if we valued the safety of the White Woman or the lawyer John Parker. We should not honor my promise to surrender. We should stay hidden as long as possible and keep ourselves out of both his way and yours.

"He has thirteen of our young men with him. Seven of their women have gone along as well. There are twenty-three all together. If we leave now we may catch them before they reach the sea.

"I can offer you only myself and six other old men. The rest I have brought with me are men of the age for this registration thing. I bring them here for that purpose. When they are done they may go home. I do not think they would be of much value in our search. Too many of them have sympathies which lie with those who have followed this stranger. But we can take their horses and provisions for you and as many men as you wish to bring, and we will go and find the man who has stolen Marie, and, with her, my honor.

"You may decide not to trust me, since part of my word to you has been broken, but I beg you to do so. If I and the other old men from our village are there, we may be able to keep our young men from fighting against you. It is one thing for them to choose to make war on Anglos, another for them to fight their fathers and uncles. What do you say?"

J.D. said, "Jesus, Jesus!" pronouncing it both ways. "A Japanese spy, a submarine, hostages! No way Jujul could be making all that up. Tell him we're coming. Let me go think up some lies to tell the others and borrow an arsenal from Bill Burns. You pick us out a couple of the best horses."

Jesus relayed the information to Jujul as J.D. sprinted back down the slope. Bill, Edith, Larry, and half a dozen ranch hands stood waiting impatiently on the porch. He wished he could take Burns aside and explain it to him, but there simply wasn't time. There wasn't time to concoct any convincing stories either. What could he tell them? That Jujul had brought in part of his people, the rest were coming, Mary with them, and Jesus and he would like to borrow some guns so they could do a little hunting with the old man and a few of his friends to pass the morning? Nobody would be buying that bridge.

He told them the basics. He left out the part about the mysterious stranger who claimed to be Japanese, and he left out the part about the other hostage. It just complicated things, would take too long to explain. And he didn't want them telling the officials and reporters who should be descending on them in a few hours. Maybe the guy wasn't really Japanese. Even if he was, they didn't need to start a war scare. Too many Arizonans already expected the yellow hordes to come pouring into the United States momentarily by way of Mexico. Oriental Americans had enough problems without their neighbors suddenly having reason to think each and every one of them might be a potential spy. And, if you added Indian allies....

"I'll come," Bill said. "And I can mount a dozen armed hands in no time, give us a numerical advantage."

"No," J.D. told him. "Thanks, but no. I trust the old man. The fewer outsiders get mixed in, the less apt we are to come to any shooting. I really think we stand a better chance without you."

Burns sucked on the cigarette he'd just lit off the butt of its predecessor as he fought his disappointment. He might not like it, but he understood.

"And I need you to keep the heat off with the press and officials who come in later. Make a big deal out of the members of the village who are here to register. Play down the fact that there's a problem. Don't even hint Mary's a captive. Tell them Jujul is having trouble convincing a few diehards and we've gone back to his village to help negotiate."

"We'll do it," Burns said, happier now that he had something to do.

"I'm coming with you," Larry said.

"Jesus, Larry!" J.D. exploded. "Don't be an ass. You'll just slow us down, and if there's a problem out there I'll have you to worry about as well as Mary."

"God damn it, J.D.," he said. "I've got to come. She's my wife. I can't stand around here pretending nothing's wrong and making happy faces for a bunch of reporters and bureaucrats, and I sure as hell can't go back to Tucson and calmly wait by the phone. Either you take me along, or I head back to town and spread the word and get a real rescue effort mounted."

J.D. should have talked him out of it. He should have found something that seemed useful for Larry to do that also kept him out of the way and off the front pages. But he couldn't think of anything under the pressure of the moment, especially after the threat to go public. The only alternative was to punch Larry's lights out, bind and gag him and have Bill and Edith keep him out of sight until they got back. It was a good idea, except for involving the Burnses in a felony.

"All right," he agreed. "Bill, find him a gun too, maybe a shotgun and some double-ought so he's got a chance of hitting what he aims at."

Larry tried to thank him, but J.D. was already on his way back up the slope toward Jesus and Jujul. He'd just noticed the gentle rain that was beginning to sweep across the ranch yard. If it kept up, they could lose the trail.

Out of Our Jurisdictions

They put Larry up on a big skittish brown colt where he tried to look right at home, not like someone who hadn't been on a horse since his mid-teens and then only the old mare that refused to hurry even for her feed bag. There was a roll of blankets and supplies tied up behind him and a twelve-gauge automatic shotgun in a saddle holster within easy reach of his right hand in case he proved brave enough to let go of the reins. A bandolier of shells hung over his shoulder. It was obvious he thought he cut a dashing figure and J.D. almost changed his mind and left him behind when Larry wished out loud for someone with a camera to record the scene.

They rode hard, with Larry riding harder than the rest. Everyone else was a natural extension of their animal. Larry held on for dear life, bouncing and swaying and wearing blisters in unnatural places.

They stopped after a couple of hours. J.D. was cold and sore, the steady drizzle had soaked him. He was ready for a rest but it was too soon. He was glad when Larry, not he, started to climb down from the saddle only to be stopped by Jesus.

"We've cut their trail," Gonzales said. "Stay where you are. The Papagos are studying it. This rain's going to make them damned hard to follow. We need to memorize any peculiarities now, while they're relatively fresh. We'll move on again in a minute."

Larry started to protest, but he noticed J.D.'s cold scrutiny and shut up. He might be in pain, but he still had his pride.

The Papagos leaned far out of their saddles studying the damp earth. J.D. couldn't see what they were looking at and couldn't see what they were following when they started out again.

They kept it up all day. So did the rain—slow, steady, soaking, and cold as death. When they stopped, Jesus had to tell J.D. several time before he reined his animal in. He'd ceased functioning in the normal fashion. Everything was on automatic pilot while the real J.D. curled up somewhere inside and hid until it was over.

"Too dark to follow a trail anymore," Jesus said. "Might as well climb down and eat something. Try to get some sleep. We'll start again at first light."

Larry unhooked his foot from the stirrup, swung back over the saddle, and ended up flat on the ground, confused about how he got there. He tried to get up and couldn't.

J.D. fumbled through his wet saddle bags and dug out a flashlight Burns had sent along.

"Look at the blood," Jesus said.

"Shit. Stupid kid's ridden himself raw."

"No way he'll sit a horse tomorrow. He's through."

"We can't just leave him out here and we can't stop." J.D. finally had someone to focus his anger on. It helped him forget his own pain. "If there really is a submarine and they get weapons and explosives and slip back into the States, we're going to have a real mess on our hands. Not just what they might cause, but the reaction of vigilante groups. Some of our locals, given an excuse, would be delighted to make the slaughter at Camp Grant seventy years ago look like a fucking picnic."

"Maybe we could leave one of the Papagos with him."

"We're too few already."

The argument went on and Larry lay there and listened. Something about it struck him as humorous and he giggled.

"He's delirious," J.D. said.

Hands fumbled with Larry's belt. He thought it was the redhead and protested that this was neither the time nor place. When he tried to stop her, more hands held his arms. They turned him over and pulled down his pants and shorts and it felt like they took along part of his rump with them, but the cold air and rain were soothing. He lay there, bare ass pointed at the sky. Something symbolic there, J.D. thought.

Jujul began rubbing something on the raw spots and Larry came unglued. J.D. looked away and decided not to mention his own blisters. They finished and covered Larry up again and turned him back over. Another Papago spooned some food in him and wrapped him in blankets.

J.D. shared some of the cold gruel the Papago were handing out, then crawled in his own bedroll and tried to find a way to get comfortable. He knew he wasn't going to sleep and that thought was still fresh in his mind when Jesus shook him by the shoulder and told him, "Time to get up."

He didn't answer. When he sat up he didn't hurt as bad as he should have. It was the middle of the night, or so he first thought. Then he realized he could see people moving, packing the horses. He could see a little desert too, and make out the edges of bits of the surrounding geography. It had stopped raining. Low, broken clouds made a misty pilgrimage toward where he thought Tucson might be. Between the clouds were patches of paling stars and dusky sky. One of the Indians handed him a plate of cold food and he ate it, neither recognizing nor caring what it was. Another Papago roused Larry, fed him, saddled his horse and packed up his blankets. When he finished eating Larry climbed to his feet. He could still walk. Well, more like waddle, actually. He hobbled a few steps into the desert and relieved himself. When he came back they were all waiting for him.

"Can you ride?" J.D. asked.

"Only one way to find out," Larry replied grimly, launching himself toward his tall brown instrument of torture. One of the Papagos had been wearing a fleece-lined jacket the day before. During the night it had been cut up and made into a pad for the top of his saddle. It sat there, fleece side up, and made Larry want to cry at the breadth of human kindness. The man had sliced a blanket and was wearing it serape style.

"Thanks," Larry muttered, damp-eyed.

He climbed aboard and forced himself to accept the agony.

"I shouldn't have let you come," J.D. told him, riding alongside and watching the grimaces come and go.

Larry agreed, but didn't say so. He was afraid it might come out a whimper. J.D. spurred ahead and Larry made himself do the same.

J.D. had slept better than he had any right to, probably because he'd missed too much sleep lately. He still didn't feel up to fighting his way out of a paper bag, much less taking on the wild bunch they were trailing, and maybe a Japanese submarine as well. The Papagos, not one of whom could have been under fifty, looked fresh, but then a day's ride in the rain and a night in a cold camp probably wasn't that unusual for them. Jesus looked better than J.D. felt. Larry looked like death had changed mounts, giving up a pale horse for a tall brown one.

"You think this is the Jap the FBI was looking for?" J.D. asked the deputy.

"Occurred to me," Jesus replied. "We happen across an agent, I'll ask." Strain and fatigue were shortening everyone's tempers.

"Where the hell are we?" J.D. wondered. The landscape had taken on a nightmarish quality, rugged, rocky, barren. In comparison, the desert around Tucson was lush and garden-like.

"We're both a little out of our jurisdictions, if that's what you mean."

"When?" The conversation kept J.D. from thinking about what they were going to do if they actually managed to catch anybody.

"This morning sometime. I saw the marker maybe a quarter mile off on a hillside."

"How can you follow a trail through this?" J.D. asked, gesturing at nature's exercise in surrealism, the entrance to which should have born a Dantesque, "abandon hope," warning.

"What, you kidding? Trail? I lost it before we crossed the border. Since then I haven't seen so much as a hint that anybody else has ever been here before."

"These guys must be really good then," J.D. said. "Compliment them for me will you."

"Sure," Jesus agreed, and put together a string of sounds that made about as much sense to J.D. as his life had so far. The old men looked at each other and smiled. Jujul rode back alongside them. He and Jesus exchanged a few pleasantries, then Jesus turned to the marshal.

"They've lost it too," he said. "Makes me feel better about my tracking. I thought these guys must be real wonders myself."

"Lost the trail," J.D. shouted, losing something of his own. "Then what the fuck are we doing out here?"

"Take it easy, J.D.," Jesus advised. "These guys know what they're doing. I noticed it too. They were headed pretty straight.

No attempts to mask where they're going. Probably thought nobody would follow them, especially before yesterdays's rain washed it out. Anyway, we've just been heading in the same direction. Jujul figures to let Larry rest at the base of those hills up ahead while he and the others fan out and look for fresh signs. We should have passed where they camped last night. If they haven't headed off at a right angle, we'll pick them up easy enough. Wait to get excited till they get a chance to be proved wrong."

"OK, OK," J.D. agreed. "Only tell them to start now. We'll look after Larry and wait at the base of those hills. We can't waste any time in case they really are meeting a sub."

They compromised. J.D. took Larry to where a lonely organ pipe cactus stood guard at the base of the hills, and Jesus chose better company and rode out with the Papagos.

J.D. was frantic about Mary. He had worried about her all that time when she'd been fine and his concerns were groundless. And then, just when she was going to walk out, safe and sound, she was suddenly engulfed in real danger. Who was this supposed Jap? Was he a real agent or was he just some psycho? And which was better? Which one kept Mary an unharmed prisoner and not a corpse along side the trail?

And what about Parker? Was he a co-conspirator or another hostage?

Then there was Larry. He was a doubly unneeded complication. If J.D. managed to get Mary out of this, how was Larry's presence going to affect what happened next? Larry, especially in the condition in which he would arrive, was clear evidence that what happened to Mary still mattered to him. It could be a stunning indictment to their indiscretion. J.D. was willing to fight for her, but if he used his most effective weapon, the redhead, he'd be making himself into someone he wasn't sure he could live with anymore. And if he didn't like himself, how could Mary?

At the cactus, J.D. helped Larry off his horse and lay him, face down, on a smooth surface. Larry went right to sleep. He didn't get much of a nap though. Jesus and the *O'odham* rode up within half an hour. They'd found the trail. Clear enough even J.D. could follow it, they claimed. Jujul gave Larry's posterior another treatment and they got him back on his horse and moving. Glassy-eyed and wobbly, Larry somehow managed to stay aboard.

A Race of Warriors

J.D. is coming. Mary kept telling herself that over and over.
She remembered his long, lean body. She remembered the scars.
He'd been a hero in Spain, right? If anybody could get her out of
this it would be J.D. He'd be looking for her by now. He would
have begun when they didn't show up at Burns' ranch on time.
But where would he look? He hadn't been able to find Jujul's
village. Even with all the things she'd told him about its location,
he might still take a lot of time getting there. She needed J.D.
now. She didn't want to die. No matter how she tried to deny it,
she expected Sasaki to kill them.

She and Jujul had separated before going back to the village.
The old man had seen his riders out where he hadn't expected
them. Something unusual was going on. He decided it was best for
them to maintain the fiction, and she went back to the women's hut.

She had just changed and hidden her gear when two of the
young men came for her. She was surprised. It wasn't proper, but
she didn't have any reason not to accompany them, not then.

She didn't know who Sasaki was when she first saw him. He
was just a skinny stranger ranting in English, but he'd already
worked some kind of miracle. The man was a zealot, a true believer.
She recognized the type. She'd seen fundamentalist preachers
accomplish the same thing, or the occasional Fascist dictator on a
larger scale. Get that fire in their eyes and that ring in their voice
and suddenly people would do anything they asked. It didn't matter
whether they understood or not, just so they could be part of the

general hysteria, swept along on the monumental tides of the leader's evangelical ego.

That's how it was with this one, and Jujul's villagers were too simple, too naive to realize what was happening. Sasaki laid into them with a fervor Herr Hitler would have admired. "We, the Mongoloid Race, the sons and grandsons of Asia, are the rightful inheritors of the Earth. The Whites are usurpers. They must be stopped, driven from the lands that belong by sacred right to our peoples so that we, the people who know and understand the land, might make it ours again."

He told them how noble and just their cause was. They liked that, even if most of them hadn't realized they had one till then. He told them how the Whites were evil and had no right to impose their will on the Papago. They liked that too, though they were remote enough that few of them realized anyone else had the final say until the draft registration law brought it home to them.

There were two strangers. The second turned out to be the Papago Attorney, John Parker. J.D. had told her about him. Parker must have argued with Sasaki before she arrived. He seemed thoroughly cowed and a little rivulet of blood streaked one side of his chin.

Someone had told Sasaki she was there. When her guards brought her back he ignored her until he felt confident enough of his hold on the village. She had been too shocked to say a word. That was what he finally warned her about.

"You'll speak only with my permission," he told her, "and only in English. If you disobey, I'll tear out your tongue and eat it for my supper."

Nobody complained when he threatened her. Some of the young men laughed.

Then Jujul came back. Mary had wondered where he was. Probably Sasaki had too.

Jujul rode up on his big roan and demanded to know what was going on, who the strangers were. Somebody told him and he lost his temper and the argument began. An hour earlier and it might have made a difference, but Sasaki had told them what they wanted to hear and suddenly, unexpectedly, Jujul was telling them the opposite. He had started this little rebellion, and now he was saying they had to quit, go give themselves up to a federal marshal, because he, Jujul, had arranged it, given his word. It wasn't a popular course to advocate. Most of them had expected him to welcome the persuasive stranger who'd come to help them make war on the Anglos. Instead, out of the blue, he wanted to surrender.

The village didn't take it well. A matter of such importance should be decided by the council, a mandate of the elders.

"There was no time," Jujul told them. "There still is not. I am *Siwani Mahkai*. I have decided. I have given my word and I will keep it. I will take my people in. You may follow me or replace me, those are your options."

Rat Skin angrily suggested Jujul's sudden conversion must be the doing of the White Woman. "We should never have let the Anglo witch into our village."

When it was translated for Sasaki he ordered that she be bound. Someone started to obey but the old man stopped him. Sasaki countered with insults—Jujul was too old, he had become a woman and was unfit to lead a race of warriors. He baited the old man, laying down a verbal challenge that couldn't be ignored. Jujul had to pick it up, make it physical or step aside and acknowledge that a new bull was dominant male in this herd.

Jujul seemed to realize exactly what Sasaki was doing. Surprisingly, he seemed pleased it was coming to this. He went at the stranger like a man goes after vermin, businesslike, determined only that it should not escape him. It didn't. Mary had heard of the oriental art of unarmed combat, but she'd never seen it before. The villagers hadn't even heard of it. What happened must have seemed nearly miraculous to them. The old man never had a chance. Sasaki took him easily, tormenting and humiliating him before his people. And then, before shame might be transformed to pity, Sasaki finished it.

With Jujul lying, bleeding and unconscious, Sasaki let the women treat him. Sasaki was smart enough to know he couldn't just walk in and kill the old man. He could push things only so far. It was a delicate balance.

They tied Mary's hands behind her and someone held onto the end of the rope. Sasaki went back to his sermon. His audience was less certain now, especially as he became more specific. They believed in him, agreed with him, but there were old loyalties, habits, and a degree of natural timidity. Mary was impressed when

Sasaki finally managed to persuade thirteen to accompany him. Twenty with their women. It was an amazing accomplishment, but she could sense Sasaki's disappointment.

She felt like Alice on the trail of a white rabbit. The insanity of the outside world had somehow reached into the heart of the People's land to replace their gentleness with savagery. She was a prisoner of war, hostage to a man who claimed to be a Japanese officer. She was going with an Indian war party to meet a submarine. None of it could be real.

Sasaki got them organized. The warriors and their women gathered mounts, provisions, and prisoners in response to his orders. Parker probably wondered what the hell a woman anthropologist was doing in Jujul's village, but he was too busy spitting blood to ask. Sasaki was obviously surprised to find her there as well, but he evidently wasn't the curious sort. He had a job to do and she was just another problem to solve.

The villagers who weren't going stood around and watched, quiet, like mourners at a funeral. My funeral, and maybe Parker's, she thought. They didn't do anything to help the ones who were leaving, but they didn't do anything to stop them either.

They rode southwest. They rode well into the night, though they didn't ride hard or make any particular effort to mask their trail. Mary guessed Sasaki wasn't concerned about being followed. He thought Jujul was the only one who might come after him and the old man hadn't looked like he would be capable of that sort of thing for weeks. And he would think, if Jujul went to the authorities, no one would believe his wild tale. It sounded absurd to Mary, and she was there.

They stopped late that first night. The Papagos built a fire and Sasaki preached his war to them over supper. Mary doubted if he knew it, but the war chief was expected to sing songs predicting victory in such a situation. Unintentionally, he was doing what the Papagos expected. It was effective.

Sasaki kept Mary and Parker apart from the others. Each prisoner's feet were tied, as were their hands, and they were staked out so they couldn't move very far in any direction or talk to each other without being loud enough to catch his attention. When the coals died, Sasaki bedded them down, one on each side of him, roped so any movement would wake him.

She was frightened but exhausted. Even the strain and danger couldn't keep her from dozing.

She woke in the middle of the night. She didn't know why. Sasaki was breathing regularly but she could see that Parker's eyes were open. She could also see that he was moving, edging closer to the Japanese so he wouldn't pull on the ropes. It was hard to move in the blankets and with his hands and feet tied, but he finally found a rock. Not sharp, but heavy, big enough to crush a skull.

Parker twisted and contorted, and finally sat upright beside his target, the stone in his lap. He grasped it in both hands and twisted to raise it over the pale face beside him. Mary realized with sudden horror that Sasaki's eyes were open, watching, his lips faintly smiling. Parker slammed the rock down but Sasaki wasn't there anymore. It thumped heavily in the dirt where he'd been.

Sasaki was up, standing over them, a ghostly figure in the dim starlight. He was grinning now. The Papagos slept soundly, except for a rat-faced youth with a knife who mysteriously turned away and slipped from sight. She didn't recognize him, but she didn't have time to think about it. Sasaki uncoiled like a striking snake, his boot slammed into Parker's face producing an explosion of blood and broken teeth.

She woke Parker in the morning. When she tried to feed him, he couldn't eat. He could hardly move his mouth at all. His nose was broken, clogged with dried blood. His tongue was so swollen he had trouble getting air.

Sasaki told his followers what had happened. No one seemed surprised. No one seemed concerned at the result, except Mary. And the lesson wasn't lost on her. She asked him, politely, in English, if she might tend Parker's wounds. He allowed it. He owned them.

"Very foolish, Mr. Parker," he said, speaking not just to Parker, but for Mary and the Papagos as well. "I suppose you were afraid I would kill you. I can understand that. But neither you nor this woman are our enemies. We won't kill noncombatants. You're safe with us. When we meet the submarine, I'll turn you over to its commander. I'm afraid you'll have to remain prisoners for a time. I can't have you talking about me to the authorities until war comes or our own fight is won, but you'll be well treated. And, when this is over, you can both come home."

Mary thought Sasaki was overestimating the band's sensibilities. He seemed to think they might abandon him if he killed his prisoners. Back when the Papago made war on the Apache, they regularly killed women and children. There'd been no noncombatants. She didn't know how these people felt about her, certainly not strongly enough to insist she be freed, and none of them seemed to know Parker at all or have any reason to care what Sasaki did with him. They were under the Oriental's spell, and leaving his prisoners' corpses to rot probably wouldn't turn any of them away.

They rode again. The day blurred, all that remained was her terror. Sasaki watched her. Lots of men had watched her, their lust clear, but his lust was different. If he wanted her, she thought it was just for the pleasure of taking her life. When he looked at her, he wasn't undressing her with his eyes, he was reveling in the power he held over her, and imagining how to exercise it. They camped again and she cried a little, quietly so he couldn't see.

On Monday morning the sky clouded and wept for her and the attorney. They rode on, methodically, monotonously, southwest.

Once, when she and Parker were more or less alone, she whispered to him. "Do you think he'll really send us on the submarine?" She tried to sound hopeful, but she didn't get the answer she wanted.

His tongue worked a little by then. He was hard to understand, but, unfortunately, not impossible. "We're dead," he told her. She tried telling herself J.D. was coming, but she no longer believed it.

They camped again. She slept again. By morning it had stopped raining. Broken clouds ran after the fleeing storm. Parker finally managed to eat a little, but it started his mouth bleeding and he had to quit. They rode on. By midday she could smell the sea.

The Grandfather of All Sharks

They weren't hard to follow. Their trail, left fresh after the rain, was as clear as a big neon arrow. They wouldn't have been hard to find anyway. They'd just headed straight for the gulf. Anyone in pursuit, even without expert trackers, would have only had to search a little coastline.

A blade of moon sliced its way down a royal purple sky toward sunset's last ruddy bruise. The makeshift posse rode over a ridge of rock and sand and suddenly there were two moons, one sinking toward where its twin rose from the Sea of Cortez. They had arrived.

Their quarry had lit three fires. The big one was on the right, the two small ones just south of it. They were visible for miles inland. From the sea they'd be visible a lot farther.

"They seem to be expecting company," Jesus said.

"Not as much as they're going to get," J.D. replied.

Sasaki's band was in a little cove on a beach that would have done any picture postcard proud. Only the lack of a lush background of coconut palms spoiled the effect. Instead, there were rocks and sand and scrub brush, and a dry arroyo that would carry rare runoff down to the welcoming sea.

"How do we go in?" Jesus asked.

"Carefully," J.D. said. Then, "Shit, I don't know. Ask Jujul. But we need to hit them soon, before that damn sub gets here, and we've got to catch him away from his prisoners, where we can pick him off or pin him down while we snatch them."

Jesus asked.

"We will leave the horses and this one," Jujul said, indicating Larry, "here. I will send Raven ahead to scout, to see how they have arranged themselves, how he holds the hostages, and whether we can take them by surprise. The rest of us should move closer, down the arroyo, and wait for Raven."

Jesus translated while a Papago melted into the darkness. J.D. wanted to warn the man to be careful, but he was already gone without J.D. noticing. It reassured him a little when Jesus pointed that out.

"I couldn't get close to them if they've posted sentries," Jesus explained. "Neither could you. Jujul thinks Raven can. This is his desert and most of them down there are his people. I figure they're the ones who should call the shots from here on."

"Yeah," J.D. agreed, "just so they realize keeping Mary safe is our first priority."

Jesus nodded toward Jujul. "You think he doesn't know that? He gave you his word. What's happened violates his sense of honor. He'll give his life to get her back safely if he has to."

"Yeah, sorry. I understand. Just edgy, nervous, you know." His palms were damp and his guts were sending messages to his brain suggesting they go do something else.

They got Larry off his horse and under some blankets. He was feverish, hallucinating again. He closed his eyes and murmured to himself for a few moments before his breathing got deep and regular.

They made a picket line for the horses, gathered guns and ammunition, and quietly threaded their way into the arroyo. Jujul led the way with J.D. right behind him, a band of shadows, sliding through a tortured landscape. J.D. could see them moving, but could hear only Jesus and himself, and then, faintly, the soft pulse of a gentle surf.

There was a place where the wash tumbled suddenly from the rocks to fall a few yards across smooth stone into a hollow bowl before continuing its rush to the sea. It was wide there, with soft sand to rest on. It was where Jujul chose to wait.

J.D. checked his clip twice and rubbed the polished wood of the rifle's stock nervously. Jujul and his men sat cross-legged on the sand. For all their apparent emotion, they might have been waiting for supper, not the outbreak of hostilities between the two great powers of the Pacific.

J.D. must have jumped half a foot when Raven reappeared. He started to swing his barrel up hard toward the Papago but Jujul caught it on the way.

"It is only Raven," Jujul said in Spanish. J.D. relaxed and looked sheepish. No one had to translate that.

"They've posted guards," Raven told them, with Jesus whispering the gist of what he said in J.D.'s direction. "There are three in the rocks just above where they've camped on the beach. They do not seem particularly alert, but their positions are well chosen. They will be hard to approach.

"There may be a fourth, one who is moving, changing locations with extreme stealth, but his actions do not fit with the others. It may only have been a coyote. Twice I thought I saw movement, another form, but I may have been wrong. I couldn't chance getting close enough to be sure.

"Most of them are by the southernmost fire. Some are dozing, some talking, some watching the sea. The stranger has two of them looking after the fires, collecting driftwood and scrub and seeing that they continue to burn. He has staked out his horses at the mouth of this arroyo, where a little fresh water from the storm is standing in a pool. One of the guards is stationed just above there. He has placed the hostages between the fires and the sea, well away from the others. It appears that their hands and feet are tied, and they are staked out in such a way as to allow them only a little movement. The stranger mostly stands near them, peering at the ocean, but from time to time he checks on his guards or speaks to the others."

"Is there a sure way to take them?" Jujul asked.

"If these were not our sons and nephews," Raven replied, "this would be easier. The stranger has placed them well and they outnumber us."

"Still, there are always options," Jujul stated.

"I can swim," J.D. told the old man. "Maybe Jesus could cover me while I sneak in and free Mary and Parker. Then we could take Sasaki at our leisure. It puts the risk where it should be, on Jesus and me. This is our job. If we do it right and get a little lucky, we should be able to avoid getting any of your people, on either side, hurt."

Jujul rubbed a hand through his beard as he thought about their options. He didn't get much of a chance to consider them. One of their companions had been keeping watch from the rocks above, and he suddenly dropped back into the arroyo.

"There is a great shark," he said. "The grandfather of all sharks has come to this place."

They clambered up among the rocks and peered out across the gulf. A long, low, ugly shadow swam slowly toward the shore, its massive dorsal fin reflecting the glow of the three fires. The submarine was there.

There's a time for logic. A time for reason. A time when good sense should prevail over rash acts. This wasn't it.

"Aw shit!" J.D. said.

The Papago muttered equivalents and Jesus said something in Spanish about somebody's mother.

"Come cover me," J.D. told Jesus, letting himself make the decisions because it didn't matter anymore whether they were right or wrong, just so long as they started doing something. "You and me down to the beach, north side of the horses. Tell Jujul everybody up here holds their fire till somebody else shoots. Won't matter whether it's us or not. Then tell them to throw as much lead down there as they can. And to shout. Try to talk their kin into staying out of it. Shoot and shout, but wait till somebody else starts it."

Jesus relayed J.D.'s instructions, then followed the marshal down hill. The two scrambled through the rocks while Jujul's men fanned out on the high ground. The lawmen made a lot of noise, but the guard above the horses was going to have his attention riveted on the strange shape out in the bay. It was something the like of which he had never seen. He wasn't going to be paying proper attention to what went on behind him. At least that was what J.D. hoped.

Luck, good or bad, was master of the situation. Bad was the first one to pay them any attention. J.D. had led Jesus far enough north for them to have a good chance of making the beach without catching a sentry's attention. They were scrambling down the slope, trying to stay low and in the shadow of the rocks because the submarine was still in clear view. Dark figures swarmed its hull, launching a pair of inflatable rafts and loading them with crates and boxes. If anyone aboard was watching the shore, the fires should help blind them, but J.D. still chose a path that kept them as invisible as possible. They avoided the smooth talus slopes and stayed in the rocks.

Between what remained of the moon and a sky full of stars, there was a surprising amount of light, but it wasn't as much as they needed. J.D. was descending the almost sheer face of a small cliff, feeling for places to put his feet, testing them with some weight, then moving a hand to a lower hold. It was maddeningly slow, but not because he wasn't pushing himself for all he was worth. Showers of gravel rained on him as Jesus followed. And then he heard a gasp, and the shower became an avalanche. Something big and dark and heavy glanced off his shoulder and nearly tore him from the rock. It plummeted into the shadows below. There was a soft thud, a sickening snap, and a low moan. He knew it was Jesus and that he must be hurt. J.D. half fell, half climbed down to where the deputy lay, another shadow among many. He could see the clenched white of Jesus' teeth and the jagged white of broken bone protruding through flesh and cloth just below his knee. J.D. knew it was all Jesus could do to keep from crying out, especially while he helped him move a little to get the weight off the injured leg. He stretched out Jesus as comfortably as the rocks would allow and made sure blood wasn't pumping from a severed artery. Jesus' face was pale, his skin clammy, and his breath coming in ragged gasps. J.D. thought he would probably lose consciousness soon.

"Go on," Jesus hissed.

"I will," J.D. told him. "Don't try to move. Don't try to do anything. Just hang on. I'll come back for you. You'll be all right."

He would be, too, if they could get him to a doctor soon enough. If infection didn't set in and turn to gangrene before he got help. If anybody survived this crazy night to find him.

Jesus nodded vaguely, waving him toward the beach. He didn't say anything more. He was keeping his jaws clamped tight to try and keep a lid on the voice that wanted to surrender to the pain. J.D. wondered what it must have cost him to keep from crying out as he fell, when he hit. He wondered if he could have done it. It didn't feel right leaving such a man, but there weren't any available choices.

By the time J.D. reached the shore the two rafts had landed. Sailors and Papagos had pulled them from the sluggish surf onto the sand and were unloading the contents. It was too late for him to take a swim. He worked his way as close as he dared, found a good shooting station—one that gave plenty of cover and screened the fires from his view. He could see Mary and Parker clearly among a cluster of dim figures and the stack of boxes. He could see more people on the submarine's deck and tower. Plenty of targets.

He didn't let himself think about how slim their chances of stopping the Japanese had become, nor how unlikely it was that Mary would survive.

Slit Their Throats

The sub's captain was unimpressed. It was clear from the way he looked at Sasaki's little band, though he didn't say anything. Sasaki couldn't blame him. He wasn't that impressed himself.

Scratch any group and you'll uncover its malcontents and sociopaths. That's what Sasaki had come away with. Jujul's village contained more than fifty adult males. Sasaki had thirteen of them, none very mature, as well as a few camp followers. It wasn't what he'd envisioned. He'd thought the whole village would be interested in what he had to offer and he'd certainly never expected the man who'd led them out, actually employed force of arms against the United States, to be so ready to give up. Fortunately, neither had his people. All things considered, Sasaki knew he was lucky to have what he did. He'd make the best of them. More than that, he'd make them better, a legend. Their numbers would grow. They had to.

"You are reasonably prompt," the captain complimented him. "I'm pleased."

Sasaki expected he was. This was a narrow body of water, an easy place to be trapped. Mexico wasn't likely to become a belligerent, nor did they have a navy capable of threatening a Japanese submarine, but this place was very close to the American border. If any hint of a Japanese presence leaked out, America's naval forces might exhibit an uncomfortable curiosity.

When Kira originally outlined the plan and its schedule to Sasaki in Tokyo, the arrival of the submarine seemed decidedly premature. Now he was glad to see it. It reinforced his authority over this small band of Papagos, an assistance which might be almost as valuable as the arms it brought. Five nights, Kira had told him. Five successive nights, beginning Monday, January 6. "If you haven't managed to contact the rebels by then, go south of the border and make the rendezvous alone. Cache the weapons and go back for them when it's convenient. You'll find the border surprisingly open and easy to cross." Kira had been right about that.

"What do you have for me?" he asked the captain. The sailors unloaded boxes and stacked them while the Papagos got in their way and jabbered at each other in excited tones.

The captain gestured toward the growing pile. "The long box is a bazooka. The one next to it, a machine gun, an old Vickers, I believe. There are two cases of rifles, two cases of submachine guns, and one of pistols. Assorted manufacturers and nationalities, none Japanese, none traceable. There are also crates of ammunition. I have another half-dozen waiting to come ashore with more ammunition and a variety of explosives."

"Very good," Sasaki told him. "And I have something for you." He indicated his captives, huddled on the sand nearby.

"Don't be ridiculous," the captain replied, gesturing at his boat. "We have no facilities for prisoners."

"I don't care what you do with them," Sasaki said, impatiently. "Let your crew use the woman if you want. Or just put them overboard somewhere at sea. They know who I am and that makes them dangerous, but their removal must be handled delicately. My Indians might resent it. I've told them I'm sending the prisoners into safe detention with you."

The captain glared at Sasaki with unconcealed disgust. Sasaki had seen the look before. The smug contempt of the officer who does his killing from a distance while keeping his hands clean. The captain's eyes seemed to mock him, to question how such an incompetent could have been put in charge of this operation. What sort of fool would have let his nationality become known, then confirm it with a view of this boat? Sasaki wondered if the man knew he was a half-breed, if he blamed that for the mistakes.

"I won't kill them for you," the captain said, disdainfully. "Nor will my men. If you want them dead, do it yourself."

Sasaki considered striking him. This officious little man would be easy enough to maim or kill. He resisted the temptation. The man controlled the submarine and its crew, and they still had most of his ammunition and explosives. Maybe later. Maybe after the war.

"All right," he said. It wasn't that he objected to doing it himself. Not at all. He just hadn't wanted to let the Papagos out of his sight. But they'd be OK for a few minutes. The unopened crates and the promise of more would keep them until he got back.

"In that case you'll transport me and my prisoners out to your ship. You'll find me something to weight their bodies with. While your men load the rest of my cargo, I'll take them behind the conning tower and slit their throats." His tone indicated that these were instructions which were not to be questioned. He stared into the captain's eyes until the man looked away.

"Get them then," the captain said. "Launch the rafts," he shouted to his men. He didn't like being a part of this and it made him angry.

Sasaki told the Papagos he must personally take the prisoners to the submarine. He would be back in a few moments with more crates. They must remain vigilant and wait for him to return. The Indians happily agreed. They looked at the stack of boxes and touched them reverently but didn't try to open any. They were excited. They were pleased. If they suspected what was about to happen, they didn't seem to care.

Sasaki released the man and woman from where he had staked them. "You see," he reassured them. "The submarine is here, just as I said. Now I'll escort you to it. You'll be prisoners for a while but the worst of your ordeal is over."

The girl wanted to believe him. Parker was too tired, too hurt, to care much, until Sasaki stuffed five $100 bills into his pocket. It would buy a brief return of hope and make his final collapse into despair so much more satisfying. If Sasaki had to kill them himself, he planned to enjoy it.

"Your money, Counselor," he said with a gentle smile. I promised you'd have it when we parted company.

They stumbled down to the boats and found their places. The captain, aloof, outwardly untouched by Sasaki's intentions, put himself in one boat with four sailors to row. Sasaki and his prisoners took the other, more crowded with its own four oarsmen.

They dragged the boats into the lazy surf and began to pull for the long dark shadow of the submarine. They were only a few yards from shore when Sasaki heard someone shout from back above the beach. The sound froze him. The voice shouted in English.

Threads That Frayed

There was enough light from the fires for the shot. It was a long one, and J.D.'s target rocked with the gentle surge of the gulf. It was especially tough because Sasaki sat between his prisoners. A sudden wave, a miss—he could destroy what he'd come to save.

He couldn't do it. He couldn't make himself squeeze the trigger. He should have test fired the borrowed Remington, made sure it was sighted in before its accuracy became such an urgent concern. Would it shoot true? He didn't know and he was afraid. While he lay indecisive on the sand behind a tumble of time worn boulders, his target gradually drew away. The shot became increasingly difficult. If he didn't make it, didn't take the chance, she'd be gone, torn out of his life forever. He didn't think his life could stand another gap of such magnitude.

He made a conscious effort to relax. He closed his eyes for a moment and wiped away the sweat that threatened to blind him. He settled himself more comfortably and tried it again. The rubber raft bounced and swayed, and his target bobbed and weaved with it. He let his body feel for the rhythm, become one with the global forces that caused it. The sight began to stay on Sasaki. His finger began to tighten. And suddenly the target had half jumped to his feet, staring back toward the beach. The sailors stopped rowing. It was Mary in his sight and not her captor.

Larry's voice came to him, loud, clear, completely nonsensical. "Who knows what evil lurks in the hearts of men?" he cried

Larry couldn't be there. The impossibility of his presence, shouting the opening lines from a radio drama contributed to J.D.'s increasing sense of unreality. He wormed around the boulders until he could see Larry coming down the slope, dragging the shotgun beside him. He was walking, a funny, mincing walk—a Charlie Chaplin I-just-sat-in-the-glue walk. No more time, no more surprise. Now or never.

J.D. rolled back behind the rocks, raised the Remington and found Sasaki. The man had a pistol. It was pointed in Larry's direction. In his half-standing position, Sasaki swayed even more wildly than before. At least he was clear of Mary. J.D. squeezed. There was an explosion that didn't come from the Remington and he jumped, involuntarily. Sasaki was gone from his sights again. Larry must have fired the shotgun. J.D. didn't let himself think about alternatives. He found Sasaki again, steadier now, both arms raised and extended, taking aim. J.D. caressed the trigger until the Remington kicked him solidly in the shoulder just as another gun, very close, also erupted. It spoiled his concentration. When he looked back at the boat he saw that Sasaki was down, but whether it was because he'd been accurate or because the man was taking cover from a near miss, he couldn't tell. Everyone in the boat seemed to be ducking. A jumble of anxious faces peered back toward the fires. Weapons began appearing where moments before there were only oars. The night came alive with the reports of all manner of small arms.

Sink the raft, he thought. That's the answer. Sink them both. He could put bullets into a portion of the craft away from Mary, keep her relatively safe, and dump all of them and all those guns in the water. Make them swim for it while he went after Mary and pulled her out. Surely she could stay afloat long enough for him to get to her, even though her hands were tied.

New target, easier this time, less worry over the rhythm. Squeeze again. A little geyser appeared just short of the raft. He worked the bolt, sliding another round into the breach while the hot brass rang as it followed its predecessor into the rocks.

And then he couldn't move. The cry that had haunted him, stalked his dreams and threatened his sanity since Spain, howled maniacally, victoriously, in his ears. SCREAMING!

"Questas?" he whispered.

More shots, more cries and shouts, but J.D. only heard one voice, one sound. SCREAMING! He lost his grip on the gun. His hands were numb, sweating. He slowly curled up behind the rocks, drawing knees to chest. His hand went into his mouth and he bit down on it. He tasted something warm and salty that flowed down his wrist. Blood. There was blood in his mouth. He didn't care what was there so long as it wasn't the scream.

He bit harder, teeth clamping down on the last threads of sanity, threads that frayed and unraveled as the scream claimed him, grabbed him up and carried him with it, plunging into a bottomless void of foul, obscene corruption and eternal, hopeless horror.

An Awful Intimacy With Mortality

It was like a nightmare, crazy, impossible, insane. They were in the raft, the Japanese sailors rowing toward the submarine, and Mary was wishing for a miracle but expecting to be dead in a few minutes. Then, there was Larry. Larry, of all people, shouting nonsense, strolling down toward the beach waving a gun. And then there were shots. Larry's, and lots of others.

Sasaki jumped up and drew a pistol. He tried to balance himself in the rocking boat and aim toward where Larry was standing. The officer from the submarine was roaring orders from the adjacent raft. He had also unholstered a pistol. His men, in both boats, dropped their oars and produced machine pistols. The officer had already begun shooting, adding the flat crack of his revolver to the volleys to be heard from the beach and above, then the machine pistols joined the explosive chorus. Muzzle flashes blossomed on the terrace above the beach as an unknown enemy returned a smaller barrage. The results whined and splashed around them.

Sasaki had squeezed off several rounds. He had the pistol up, aiming it and then he was in her lap, looking dazed, his left elbow shattered, dripping blood down her leg into the shallow sea water that lapped at her feet. There was something sticky on her face and salty in her mouth and she realized it must be part of what had been his elbow. She thought she would gag.

Everyone was ducking and the sailors were firing frantically. Larry began screaming, a terrible, agonized wail that ripped at her heart. Sasaki tried to claw his way back upright, using her as a means of leverage and covering her with fresh gore. There was more shooting. The shrill staccato cries of the machine pistols dominated the pandemonium until the boat exploded under them in a geyser of spray and torn rubber and they were all in the sea.

She surfaced only a few yards from the other raft. She heard a sound like an express train and one of the sailors slammed back into his officer. Where the man's right shoulder had been, there was only a crimson ruin that spattered his commander's crisp uniform. The sailor kicked spasmodically, his eyes rolled, and he was still, dead from the shock of whatever had struck him, not from the damage it had done, though that might have killed him eventually. Another gunner emptied his clip in the direction of that bright flash and thunder clap. It came again and she never knew just where the second sailor was hit because he somersaulted out of the raft, fountaining blood as he went. The bullet that killed him must have grazed the officer's thigh because she saw him drop his revolver and grab himself there. It also tore through the side of the raft. There was a sharp hiss as the air bladder emptied and then everyone from that boat was also in the water.

Her hands were still tied in front of her but her legs had been freed to make her easier to transport. She could kick well enough to stay up and breathe. Parker breached beside her, sputtering sea water and clawing at the air with his bound hands. She realized he couldn't swim, at least not well enough to do it with his hands tied. She caught him as he came up the second time, grabbing his hair from behind. She kicked out with a steady rhythm that kept them up and took them away from the bobbing Japanese heads. He fought her until he realized he could get the air he needed again, then he calmed down and even tried to help.

It was quiet for a moment. The force on shore couldn't be sure who anyone was in the water, and they had stopped shooting as a result. The sailors had stopped firing too, their guns abandoned in favor of the practical need to swim for their lives.

A new, bigger gun opened up from the submarine, covering the Japanese sailors' slow, soaked retreat. She listened to the slugs tear through the air and thought they sounded remarkably like the ones that had killed the two men in the raft, only these flowed steadily, one so quickly after the next that they blended into a continuous roar. She followed the arc of the tracers and watched them tear into the rocks from which the flashes had come. Even in the dim light she could see the clouds of dust and debris they raised. Another brilliant flash from the middle of that inferno answered and the machine gun ceased its angry howl. When she looked back at the sub, the gun was rotating crazily on its pivot. There was fresh blood on the tower near it. The gunner wasn't there anymore. No one rushed to take his place. No one went to man the deck gun. The crew took aboard survivors and disappeared from the submarine's hull as its engines roared to life. Its nose turned to point out of the bay, its tanks blew, and it began to sink. The boxes still on its foredeck shifted and fell aside as the water closed over them. When there was nothing left to see out there she started paying attention to which way the shore lay and aimed for it.

The waves gave her a direction. So did the fires, now well down the beach. Larry's cries still carried to her, quieter now, more infrequent, but no less terrible. She concentrated on kicking and pulling and keeping her head above water. When they hit the surf and the first wave broke over them she thought they might be in trouble. Parker panicked again and fought her and she breathed in a lot more water than is good for someone without gills, but as she tried to find the surface she discovered the water was only waist deep. She stood and dragged Parker erect and they waded wearily onto the beach.

All the shooting had stopped. The fires were smaller, dying, starving for lack of fuel. No one was visible near them. She couldn't hear Larry anymore, just Parker gasping as he knelt in the sand, just herself quietly sobbing, uncontrollably, now that they were safe.

She wondered if she should try to do something for Parker, then decided she didn't know what would help. He would probably be OK anyway. It was Larry who was hurt and needed her. She started along the beach. She would have run, but she didn't have the strength. She might have called out to him, but there weren't any words. Her mind was a confused jumble of emotions—relief, fear, gratitude, and maybe even love.

She almost stepped on Sasaki before she saw him. What remained of the fires had blinded her as she tried to look behind them for the spot where she'd last seen Larry. She jumped back but his hand snaked out and caught her heel and she went down hard.

She screamed. She had thought she was safe, thought he was dead and it was over, but he was still there, still between her and safety, haunting her, offering an awful intimacy with mortality.

His left arm dragged in the sand at an unnatural angle as he pulled himself to his knees. He looked at her and smiled. There was madness in his eyes.

She tried to crawl away from him but she was too terrified, too tired, too slow. He was on his feet beside her, above her.

"Get up," he commanded.

She screamed again. He kicked her in the face, opening wounds where her cheek slammed against teeth, flooding her mouth with enough blood to choke off the scream.

"Get up," he said again. She spat blood on the sand and tried to obey.

Parker came out of the dark. He had found a piece of driftwood somewhere. It was clasped in his bound hands and raised over his head. He slashed it at Sasaki with enough force to turn the man's brains to jelly, but Sasaki slipped aside and Parker fell, carried off balance by his momentum. Sasaki kicked him, much harder than he'd kicked Mary. Parker's head shot up spraying blood and saliva. Sasaki stepped behind him and drove his good hand into the back of Parker's neck. There was a sickening snap and Parker slammed face first into the beach, his body slowly following, unaware that it was already dead.

Another figure rushed him. Sasaki must have half seen it. He nearly pivoted out of its way but it struck him a glancing blow and they both fell. Sasaki hissed with pain as his left arm hit the sand, but he rolled out from under the larger figure, and the two of them scrambled to their feet and faced each other. Mary turned to flee, her limbs possessed of a sudden ability to run she hadn't believed possible. She would have stayed to help but Sasaki had become a personal demon. She was as overwhelmed by her own terror as Fitzpatrick had been only moments before. Her mind would no longer accept any option other than escape. And so she ran.

Three paces. And then Sasaki whirled and turned and lashed out with his foot and she felt something give and she was falling, her arms and legs wouldn't obey her anymore and the world was getting darker. She never felt herself land.

Not With Terror, With Rage

Screams took J.D. to hell. Screams brought him back. Mary's screams. She was in trouble, she needed him. Nothing else mattered, not even Questas.

J.D. ached. He felt like he'd been sick for a long time and was just beginning to recover. He was weak and his head reeled as he climbed to his feet.

The cries came from behind him. He turned toward them as they were choked off. He felt himself wanting to scream again but this time, not with terror, with rage. He wanted to feel his hands on the man who was hurting Mary. He wanted to take him apart.

J.D. ran. Somewhere, deep inside, he found a well of strength and tapped it. His long, quiet strides ate up the darkened beach. He saw the foreigner, saw the crumpled form at his feet and thought it was Mary. He threw himself at the man. No plan, no what ifs, nothing but a need to kill.

Sasaki must have heard him at the last moment, caught sight of him out of the corner of an eye. Sasaki started to turn and throw himself aside, raising an arm to ward J.D. off, but it was the wrong one. The arm that might have saved him hung limply at his side and seeped down his fingers to drip on the pristine sand. Only the sand was already spoiled by the dead thing at his feet.

J.D. hit Sasaki a glancing blow, his shoulder rammed ribs. He clutched at the man but couldn't hold on. His momentum, more that Sasaki's efforts, tore them apart. They both hit the sand and J.D. rolled and came up, ready. Sasaki was up almost as fast, mouth wide in grin or grimace. Air hissed between his lips. J.D. could see the man's left arm was useless, shattered at the elbow. Sand stuck to the wound. Sasaki had fallen on it and J.D. could tell he'd hurt him.

The corpse on the beach wasn't Mary. Mary's face was bleeding, but she was on her feet nearby. She looked at the Japanese with such horror that J.D. knew just killing him wouldn't be enough. He would have to make him suffer. His death would need to be slow, prolonged, demeaning.

Mary dashed up the beach toward safety, and J.D. started to relax a little. She would be OK now, even if J.D. somehow failed, but he wouldn't. He had a ravenous hate to help him, inhuman in its intensity. Surely nothing could stand before it—especially not a little man with only one good arm.

Sasaki bounced back, whirled, kicked, and J.D. saw Mary fall. He didn't give the Oriental time to strike her again. He bored in, but Sasaki spun and kicked him in the chest and he couldn't breathe. Sasaki danced across the sand toward where the American fell, but J.D. rolled just in time to avoid another kick and somehow, this time, got hold of the man's foot. Sasaki lost his balance and went down, close enough for J.D. to grab one of his legs. He fought the paralysis in his chest and scrambled toward the Japanese, determined to get a firm enough grasp on the leg to break it. Sasaki's other foot slammed off the side of his face as J.D. pulled his head back at the last moment, but the sky erupted in iridescent glows that were behind J.D.'s eyes instead of in front and he lost his grip.

J.D. rolled blindly, looking for distance, listening to his opponent's frenzied movements. He stopped when he could see again. The Japanese was on his feet, but he was pale and he paused long enough to touch his damaged elbow with his good hand.

J.D. got to his feet, expecting Sasaki to try something while he was still down, but the man only waited, watched. When J.D. was back up Sasaki gave him a small formal bow. "You are an unexpected pleasure," he said. J.D. didn't understand, didn't care, and it didn't matter because Sasaki was coming at him again and Mary wasn't moving and he had to finish this and get to her, see just how seriously she was hurt.

J.D. expected another kick, but Sasaki only feinted this time and slammed an open hand at his throat. J.D. blocked it with his left forearm and heard something snap. His arm went numb. No pain yet, but there would be, later, if there was a later. J.D. countered with a hard right uppercut that caught Sasaki just under the ribs. The Oriental began to double over, but as he did he charged and butted J.D. in the stomach. Both men went down in a confused pile. J.D. couldn't get a good hold on him because his bad arm was in the way, but Sasaki's hindered him as well. They rolled free of each other, but not before J.D. bit off part of Sasaki's ear.

They were on their feet again. J.D. could move his left arm a little, but not enough to be useful. He could feel something dripping down his cheek from where he'd been kicked and his right eye was narrowing, swelling shut. He wasn't sure how much longer he would be able to see out of it. He went for Sasaki again, and this time tried using his feet. It must have surprised Sasaki. The Japanese tried to block it reflexively with his left arm, but the arm didn't work and J.D. caught him, not in the crotch as he'd intended, but on the hip as the man rolled away. Sasaki's right hand went for J.D.'s eyes but missed and took away a hand full of hair. J.D. slipped in another hard right to the rib cage and avoided the counter, this time bringing up a knee into Sasaki's face. He heard Sasaki's nose go against his knee. Sasaki straightened up, his face a bloody, misshapen mask, and faked with his hand again and J.D. walked into the foot that followed it and cracked his ribs and drove a small, jagged splinter into his lung. Breathing became agony. Scarlet froth accompanied each exhalation, but he'd got hold of Sasaki's foot and he held on with a strength born of desperation. Sasaki lost his balance and fell, and J.D. twisted the captive leg as he followed and felt it snap as he landed on it.

Sasaki was on his face and J.D. was above him but the Oriental put an elbow into J.D.'s jaw and forced him off. J.D.'s right hand somehow got pinned under him and Sasaki got his good hand on the back of J.D.' head and jammed his face into the sand. J.D. fought, but Sasaki had his full weight on him. J.D. couldn't break free and he couldn't breathe because of the rib and the blood in his lung and the sand that blocked his mouth and nostrils. His struggles grew weaker, spasmodic. A crimson mist swept out of the dark and engulfed him. It gradually ceased to matter that Sasaki still held him and kept his face jammed in the sand. He hardly heard the soft footsteps that approached them, no longer cared who they belonged to.

Whatever Future There Might Be

Sasaki's life had narrowed down to a single focus—victory, glorious victory. He would finish this worthy opponent.

He was so intent on completing his conquest that he didn't hear Talker coming. Talker hit him on the back of the head with the butt of his knife. He had to do it three times to make Sasaki stop.

That left four inert forms on the sand. Talker checked Parker first. He was just as dead as he looked. There was a wad of soggy bills in one of the attorney's pockets and Talker transferred them to his own without looking at them. The woman wasn't wearing anything but a soaked cotton shift. It was obvious she had nothing of value so he didn't bother with her. The White Man seemed in danger of drowning in his own blood. Talker turned him over and started going through his pockets. When he found the badge he quit.

He went back to Sasaki. The Jap was unconscious, messed up bad from the fight. He didn't seem likely to be a problem for a while, but he'd killed the only man Talker believed could restore his dreams. Now, whatever future there might be for him depended on what he'd taken from Parker and the roll of bills he knew this man had been carrying in the wallet inside his jacket.

Sasaki was still alive but his face looked like ground beef. Little bubbles frothed in the blood oozing from the corner of his mouth. Talker checked his coat. The billfold was still there. It was soaked, but it was thick with American currency, mostly in denominations he'd never seen before. Talker put it in his pouch. He might have a future after all.

Sasaki's hand shot up and grabbed Talker by the neck. His grip was vice-like. Sasaki's eyes were wide. His mouth was drawn back in a rictus of contempt. Talker didn't bother fighting him. He just ran his blade across Sasaki's throat. The man's eyes registered surprise, denial. The artery pulsed a fountain onto the sand. The flow grew weaker and Sasaki's eyes clouded, his arm went slack and the hand fell away. Talker cleaned his blade on Sasaki's jacket, sheathed it, and went up into the rocks where he would be hard to follow. His horse wasn't far.

Beginnings and Endings

Someone told Jujul the world was round. That seemed appropriate. A great circle, without beginning or end. He liked that. But the world was not like a man's life. A life was more like a line drawn in the sand, however crookedly. A life had clear beginnings and endings. Those weren't the important parts, though. The middle was what mattered. There, one could exercise a little control. He knew the line that was his own life was nearing its end. It didn't matter. Parts of the middle had been very good indeed.

He had spent all his days in a land of distant horizons and great emptiness, a place with few people and little water. It was strange and a little frightening to find himself somewhere so different. Following his conviction he was sent by train to a city called Los Angeles, and, truly, it dwarfed Tucson the way Sells dwarfed *Stohta U'uhig*. It was a fabulous journey, filled with the White Man's wonders. He was driven from the railroad station to a place called Terminal Island. It was difficult to comprehend. It consisted of a chunk of earth completely surrounded by water. No wonder, he decided, there is so little water in the People's land when there is so much here.

The place they called a prison was intended, if he understood it, to be a punishment for crimes committed against others. He found a sense of implausibility in the concept. The prison provided him with a room called a cell. It was larger than any home he remembered, brighter, and less subject to the effects of weather. The cot they gave him was the softest bed Jujul had ever known.

He understood his fellow prisoners found the food especially dull and monotonous, but, to Jujul, it was a constant adventure of new and exotic tastes. He never before ate so well or regularly. The White Men must be a very rich people indeed, to find such treatment a punishment.

Each prisoner was assigned a job. The prison officials discovered Jujul had some experience at cultivation, so they put him to work in the warden's garden. From there he could watch the ocean and the parade of boats that drifted about its surface, each proceeding majestically on some mysterious errand. And he discovered previously inconceivable forms of vegetation. Imagine, having the time and water to grow flowers, things with no value beyond their beauty. That was his greatest delight, even if these blooms were nothing like the ones from his visions. Every reward he might have dreamed of finding when he journeyed to the world of the dead was provided in the place he was sent to be punished. Most strange, most curious, these White Men.

It was not perfect, of course. First, he was confined. It was hard to be near so many wonders and be unable to explore them. Having lived in a world not even bounded by distant horizons, it was difficult to be suddenly closed in by walls and bars and guards. An even greater problem was language. Jujul knew so little English and no one spoke *O'odham*. The few who spoke Spanish seldom spoke it with him. Initially, one of his guards learned a few phrases with which to communicate certain basic things to him, but the man often confused them and asked Jujul to eat when he wanted him to go someplace or asked if he wished to relieve himself when he meant to say it was time to return to his cell. Jujul decided to learn English.

It was hard work, and it failed to relieve the oppressive sense of loneliness he felt. The art of communication and persuasion had been the hub around which his life was centered. Now, even when he puzzled out a word, he had difficulty understanding the concepts on which it was based. His fellow prisoners shared so few common experiences with him and held such a different view of the world. He tried to talk to them, but only a few made an effort to understand, or be understood. In the midst of more people than he had once believed inhabited the earth, he was lonelier than he had ever been.

The man who might have been most helpful was the prison chaplain. Because of the similarities in their professions and the abundance of free time they shared, they should have found a common ground from which communication might spring. Unfortunately, the chaplain had a mind far narrower than his portly body. He tried to tell Jujul about Jesus, and the old man listened attentively though without much comprehension. In return, he courteously tried to explain about Elder Brother, but the dumpy little man became as stiff as his collar and stormed off to shepherd a more conventional flock.

It was the warden who helped Jujul decipher the occasional letters Jesus and Marie sent. They had tried hard to aid him against the charges the BIA man, Larson, made sure were brought against him, but Jujul never joined the contest. He understood. Someone had to pay for all the damage done and the lives lost. He was the logical candidate, especially when he was allowed to trade his own acquiescence for the dismissal of charges against his fellow villagers, even those who followed Sasaki into Mexico. Marie and the deputy told him that Sasaki's existence was his strongest defense, but it was like a knife that was pointed at both ends. It might cut him free, but it would wound his people in the process. Agents from some investigation bureau persuaded all of them to stay silent about Sasaki. They tried to explain it to him. The United States was on the verge of war with Sasaki's country. Some Americans had originally immigrated from that same nation. If it became known that Japan had sent someone to sabotage and kill in Arizona, those people would suffer from the fear and suspicion of their fellows. Perhaps even random acts of violent revenge might occur. The O'odham were equally in peril if the facts were known. Jujul did not understand all the subtleties, especially as they involved peoples other than his, but the concept of the sacrificial goat wasn't hard to fathom.

And he was guilty. He had underestimated the Americans, then Sasaki. The Japanese was dead. The attorney was dead. Marie and her husband and the deputy, Gonzales, were hurt, and J.D. Fitzpatrick....The marshal was still alive, but he had barely survived the journey back to Sells and none of the letters had mentioned him for some time. Jujul didn't know just where or how J.D. might be anymore. The world was much bigger than Jujul had thought. He could understand how a man might become lost in it.

With the warden's aid, Jujul sent replies containing the half-truth that he found jail most fascinating and hardly a punishment at all. And so his days passed, each very much like the one before, until the world chose to interfere again.

It was early in the month the Anglos called December, in their year of 1941, when word came that the Japanese had attacked the United States at a place named Pearl Harbor.

The prisoners were to be moved. A mood prevailed which bordered on hysteria, a nightmarish fear that hordes of Japanese would soon pour down on California from out of the sunset. Terminal Island was to become a military base. The prisoners would be evacuated inland to a place called Fort Leavenworth in the distant land of Kansas. Everything was rushed. The Japanese might come at any moment.

Jujul wondered what would become of those citizens of Japanese descent Gonzales and Marie had been so worried about, now that war had truly come. He felt sorry for them, but was glad he had helped prevent the People from sharing their fate.

A federal order commuting Jujul's sentence reached the warden in the midst of the evacuation. There wasn't time to carry it out. He forwarded it to Fort Leavenworth, but for all the good it did he could have sent it straight to Oz.

The prisoners were loaded on a train at dusk. Jujul was excited, curious what strange new country he might see from the train and what the mysterious Kansas would be like.

The railroad car was cold and drafty. Dust and soot sifted in through broken windows and cracked floorboards. It was crowded, cramped, and the car rocked violently, making a regular metallic complaint as it rolled toward the sunrise. Jujul wasn't the only one who found it impossible to sleep.

They stopped shortly after first light. Outside lay a desert not unlike the one Jujul had known most of his life. Some plants were different and it was colder than he was used to, but the horizons were where they should be, the rocks and mountains gaunt, spare reminders of the world Elder Brother had left for the People.

They stopped in the middle of nowhere, at a place where the engine could be resupplied with coal and water, and where a simple breakfast was made available for the convicts and their guards. It was a place with nowhere for the former to run and nowhere for the latter to lose them.

Jujul was glad of the excuse to stretch his aching limbs. He was feeling his age. All his old wounds ached. He limped down off the train, dragging the chains that linked his wrists and ankles and kept his pace unnaturally short. He shuffled aside, uninterested in breakfast. A guard said something to him, probably ordering him back in line, then turned his attention elsewhere and Jujul ignored him, breathing the fresh cold air, savoring the sense of a world without artificial limits. He felt a different hunger, an ache he would have found difficult to define.

Sagebrush and sand stretched toward a horizon just this side of forever. That vast emptiness was something he needed far more than the thin oatmeal, biscuits, and coffee being served nearby.

There was a low spot just north of the tracks that caught the rays of the morning sun and held them, making it seem somehow warmer and more hospitable than what surrounded it. The place probably would have escaped his notice if it weren't for the vegetation that grew near its center. It was a thistle with an unlikely cluster of exploding blossoms. He had never seen a plant like it before and yet he recognized it instantly. When he was a child he had dreamed of an earlier version with a single stalk on which only two flowers bloomed. When he told his mother about the dream she explained that he must have dreamed of her, for Two Flowers was her secret name. It was the first evidence of his calling to become a *Mahkai*. He saw the plant in his mind again when he fasted and consulted his crystals to find a name for the daughter of Raven and Grey Leaves, the child who would later become his second wife. There were more blossoms on it then. He'd seen it many times since, including for Marie, and each time more buds had opened. And now, here it was. The dream which had affected so much of his life was reality.

The guard was getting old. He'd been big once, a powerful giant of a man. Now his body seemed to be falling in on itself. Where before he'd strained his shirt with his shoulders and chest, now he strained it with his belly. He had a toothache that had kept him from getting much sleep before they left and a night on the train hadn't helped. He was tired and his jaw throbbed. It made him even more short-tempered than usual. He kicked one prisoner, booted him in the seat of the pants, for trying to crowd into the chow line. As he hustled the man to the rear of the column he realized his bladder needed to be emptied yet again, another unkind reminder of how the years weighed on him. He took a few steps into the desert, opened his fly and aimed at the clump of weeds at his feet. It took much longer than it used to. When he finished he turned and began stuffing himself back inside his pants. One of the prisoners was standing nearby, watching him intently. It was a tall, slender, old man with skin almost as dark as the stock of the rifle the guard had laid on the ground beside him.

Jujul was offended. It felt almost like a personal violation when the guard began urinating on the flowers he recognized. They had been of such great significance to his life. He reminded himself that the man could not know what he was doing and that the plant would hardly care. Still, it felt like an insult and he stood and glared as the guard turned around.

There was something about the man that was familiar.

"What you starin' at, old timer?" the guard grumbled, fumbling unsuccessfully with his pants. He looked back down to see why he was having a problem.

Jujul's mouth dropped. That face had been seared into his memory with agonizing incandescence. The man stood above the clump of many flowers that he had defiled, just as, decades ago, he had stood above Jujul's beautiful young bride, Many Flowers, to whom he had done much worse. Jujul was moving before he realized it. He had sworn he would find the man. He had vowed to make him pay.

The guard glanced back up. He couldn't believe it. The skinny old codger was rushing him. What could he hope to accomplish? There was no place for him to go out here, even if the guard wasn't going to reach down and pick up his rifle and blow his damn fool face off.

The guard bent, reached for his weapon. There was something about the prisoner. Something familiar. He touched the gun's stock and looked back up. The prisoner was an Indian. He'd never known any Indians. And this one looked mad enough to kill him. Looked like that brave down along the border back about the time Villa raided Columbus, New Mexico.

The rifle slipped from his fingers but he couldn't look away from the Indian's eyes. Sweet Jesus! It was him. It was that damned buck who'd come at him with that big rifle, and then a knife, and tried so hard to kill him once when both of them were younger.

Jujul saw recognition in the guard's eyes. He lunged and wrapped the chain between his wrists around the man's neck and yanked. The guard's head snapped up and his pants slipped off his bloated waist and slid down his thighs. Jujul added his cry to those of his women, still clear in his ears across the decades. Only, this time, they cried out in triumph. The guard nearest to them looked up and shouted.

Jujul didn't recognize the words. It didn't matter. He kept pressure on the chain and the man who had raped his wife flailed wildly and managed to put an elbow in Jujul's ribs. Jujul hardly felt it.

Prisoners and guards were turning, looking around in wonder at where one old man howled as he strangled another. The guard who had shouted raised his rifle. He thought he had the angle. He though he was a marksman. Jujul didn't let it matter, he twisted and thrust the rapist between them.

The end of his line. Jujul was there, but he was not afraid. He had always wondered why he had seen blood among the flowers, and why its existence did not trouble him.

The shot tore through the old guard's face. It extracted the tooth that had been annoying him and, with the assistance of the chain, it broke his neck.

Jujul almost heard the shot. He almost felt the blow from a bullet with just enough force left to exit the back of the guard's neck and then penetrate his own brain case. It tore the last thoughts from his mind and dropped him, just as his secret name predicted—Coyote Among Thistles.

In that last moment, just before the bullet struck him, it occurred to Jujul that his life was like a circle after all, looping back at the end to this unfinished business. A circle, not a line. A revelation. And suddenly, other things he had only partially understood before also became blindingly clear. Flowers of insight blossomed in his soul. It was magnificent, wondrous. He remembered an English expression. "Oh fuck!" he whispered into the guard's ear, and he began to smile.

See Spot Run

Mary was at the typewriter when the telephone rang, pounding out a blazing sixty words a minute because this was just a rough draft and she had a handle on what she wanted to say and felt it was important enough to say it. Larry must have been into something himself because he let it ring five times before he got it and that made her lose concentration as she thought about making a last second dash for the phone.

Larry said "Hello," and "I don't think I should disturb her right now." She nearly had the thread back when his voice got very quiet and he almost whispered into the phone, "Yeah, I heard about it, but she doesn't know yet. I'll tell her, but I was going to let her finish today's work on the dissertation first." That tore her away from further consideration of the role of the *Mahkai* in traditional *O'odham* society. She found herself paying close attention to a silence that went on for several minutes while Larry listened to further details of something he didn't want to disturb her with. She got up and went into the living room. She hooked her thumbs in the pockets of her faded old Levis and leaned up against a bookshelf while Larry glanced at her and looked guilty, but kept nodding to the person who couldn't see him from the other end of the line.

"OK," she asked, after he thanked that someone for calling and put the phone down, "what's going on?"

He got up from the couch and limped over and put his hands on her shoulders. Except around the house, he was still using a cane because of what the bullet had done to his pelvis.

"Jujul's dead," he said. "I should have told you, would have, but you were being so productive and I knew it would upset you and, besides, there's nothing you can do about it."

She slipped out from under his grasp and went over and sat on the sofa and held her face in her hands.

"How?" she asked.

He'd hidden yesterday's newspaper under a stack of archaeological texts on the end table next to his favorite chair. He handed it to her. It was already folded open to the appropriate page. The story was in back of all the latest disasters from the Pacific, just above an ad for a Christmas sale at one of the downtown department stores and a notice that *The Maltese Falcon* would soon be opening in Tucson.

"Papago Chief Murders Guard, is Slain in Escape Attempt!" the headline cried. The article didn't say much more. It just gave his name, Jujul, and mentioned his trial in Tucson in the spring for assault on BIA agent Edward Larson, then gave spare facts and lurid hints about events the reporter clearly didn't understand.

Mary didn't want to believe it. She knew Jujul wouldn't hurt anyone without a reason. It didn't make any sense.

"There's more," Larry said. "That was the attorney who defended Jujul last spring. Jesus Gonzales read this same article yesterday. Then he decided to go pay a personal visit on Larson. I guess he thought it was all Larson's fault. They're holding Jesus down at the county jail. The attorney tells me Larson's in about the same shape as the banks were after the crash of '29. He's probably going to be a mouth breather unless they can surgically undeviate his septum while they're setting his jaw and doing something with his broken cheekbones. He needs a dentist too."

"I'm going down to the jail," she said. "You stay here. See if you can find out anything more about what happened to Jujul. Maybe try to call J.D., make sure he knows about Jesus."

She grabbed her keys from a bowl on the mantel and sprinted out the door.

It was a cool grey day, the streets still damp from a morning shower, the sky still heavy with the threat of more. With less than two weeks till Christmas, holiday decorations had appeared in most downtown merchants' windows, but they seemed more forlorn than cheerful, reflecting prevailing fears and doubts instead of conventional joy.

Mary aimed the Auburn toward the Pima County Courthouse. She loved the dome, thought it was one of the few pieces of modern architecture in Tucson that dared show any character of its own.

She found a vacant parking place a couple of blocks south on Church, abandoned her vehicle, and started north on foot, sidestepping a profusion of puddles on the uneven sidewalk. She glanced up just in time to see J.D. cross Broadway and duck into a bar on the corner. It didn't surprise her, but it made her a little sad. By the time she got to the bar her feet were soaked. Her mind was on other things than avoiding puddles.

⟶

"Good Spot, good boy," Mary said, slipping between the fence rails and into the pen.

Spot snorted and pawed at Stephanie's jacket again. He wasn't the cute, adorable calf she'd helped raise anymore. He'd grown up, turned into the foundation bull for one of the finest herds of Holstein cattle in the state of Ohio.

Daddy had let her pick the silly name. It fit. He was predominately white but covered with the big, black blotches that had inspired her.

Stephanie was her best friend, and had been most of their lives. She was the daughter of the couple Daddy had hired to help raise her after her mother and baby brother failed to survive the ordeal of a breech birth. Stephanie's mom had been Mary's surrogate mother for as long as she could remember, as well as Daddy's housekeeper and cook. Steph's dad was their chief hired hand.

Mary and Steph had grown up like sisters, closer even, since Steph was only seven months older. Like sisters, their friendship sometimes waxed and waned, though the bond between them had remained steady. Just recently, it was stretching a little thin.

Steph's jacket was in the pen because Larry had tossed it there. That's what adolescent boys did to the girls they wanted to impress—tease them, pester them, annoy them.

Larry Spencer's parents lived just across the road and Larry had been the third member of their trio through most of their childhood. There weren't any other nearby farms with kids their age. The three had played together whenever Larry's parents allowed, or Steph and Mary weren't busy with chores. Steph had always been number three in the trio. She was the most reticent to take a dare or play rough and tumble, the way pre-adolescent boys and tomboys preferred. But strange and dramatic things were happening to their bodies, Steph's especially. Larry had suddenly begun to perceive them as girls instead of friends. It was weird.

Larry was cutting up and showing off for them. They were the sort of silly, boy things that Mary usually enjoyed beating him at, before Steph became their prime target.

Larry claimed he'd sneaked into the tent and watched the hootchie kootchie girls at the county fair. He demonstrated the strip tease he'd seen, peeling off his jacket, then dared Steph and Mary to try it themselves. Mary was planning to refuse, only Larry didn't bother pressing her. He concentrated on Steph instead and Steph finally agreed. She did a surprisingly slinky imitation that had Mary considering getting a bucket of cold water to throw over both of them, or telling them to just get fucked, though she wasn't clear exactly what that ultimate obscenity meant.

Steph got the jacket off, but Larry wanted it as a prize. He tore it out of her hands and made her chase him, squealing like some silly, well, girl, around the pens behind the barn, then tossed it into Spot's pen. That was too much and Steph instantly metamorphosed from flirty *femme* to ice virgin.

Steph had started after her coat until Spot noticed. He turned and she broke and headed for the nearest fence. They could all see Spot run at her, his intent apparently serious until she vaulted the rails.

Steph quickly climbed back to the top one. The fence she'd hopped was between Spot and some of his offspring, several young bulls Daddy was planning to take to the next cattle sale in Columbus.

"Larry Spencer," Steph demanded, shaking a pretty fist, and, incidentally, the bosoms Mary didn't have yet, "you get my jacket out of there right now. And you get me out of here too, or I'm gonna tell Pa you were trying to take my clothes off."

Steph's Dad was a big Swede with remarkable red hair, and, occasionally, a matching temper. Larry hurried to obey, only Spot wasn't offering much encouragement. He was out there butting the jacket around, pawing at it with his hooves, and glaring at Larry like he though Larry had designs on his feed trough. Larry paused and turned pale. Mary thought he was considering whether Spot or Steph's dad was the bigger threat. Was he better off dead, or with his privates ripped off by an irate father.

"Oh, you're such a baby," she told Larry. "I'll get it." Actually, Mary thought he was showing a sensible bit of discretion, but she was hardly going to tell him that. Spot was used to Larry, but only on the other side of fences. She, on the other hand, had handled him all his life.

Only, once she was closer to most of a ton of Holstein bull than the fence, she noticed Spot wasn't treating her with much more respect than he'd shown Steph and Larry. At least he wasn't stomping on the jacket anymore, but he was pawing the earth, throwing up muddy clods like a track star digging in for the start to the hurdles. There was nothing out here to hurdle, except maybe Mary or the fence. She was more likely to be able to clear the fence, but she wasn't going to get to it before he got to her, if he wanted.

Mary recalled her father's warnings. "Spot's no fucking calf anymore," he'd told her. "He's a full-size, grown-up bull who gets testy and mean when he's not ballin' the ladies."

"Spot, you cut it out," she commanded. Spot took a step back, tossing his head and blowing a little spittle.

A couple more steps and she would be there. Spot bawled, a noise that sounded like a warning.

"Don't you even think it," she said, steadily advancing. She bent slowly, retrieved the jacket. Trust Steph and Larry to put her in front of a bull with a bright red cloak.

Mary began to retreat. Spot began to advance. Mary stopped. Spot didn't. He lowered his head and drove toward her as if he wanted to do some real damage. Mary flicked the coat to one side and tried to dodge to the other. Spot didn't buy it. He hit her in the pit of her stomach and she felt her legs come flying off the ground as he snapped his head up and tried to run through her. She heard somebody scream and knew it wasn't her because she didn't have any air in her lungs to scream with. She flipped over his back and came down hard in the mud and manure with that terrible feeling you get when the wind's been knocked out of you. Just as she managed to gasp in a little air, there was Spot, jamming his head into her again, apparently trying to push right through her and splatter her guts all over his pen.

"What the fuck!" she heard Daddy roar. Daddy never took the Lord's name in vain but he had a fondness for a host of obscenities that Mary had already appropriated as her own. Spot pulled back and she could see that Daddy had jumped into the pen. Steph had left the back rail and was in the pen too. Daddy looked at her and he looked at Steph. Spot looked at all of them. Daddy ran over and scooped Steph up and carried her to safety. Spot came back and stuck his head in Mary's gut again and shoved. Being up to her ass in mud and bullshit, she slid. She was near the fence. She felt a hand reach through and grab her arm. She got hurt worse being yanked between the boards of the fence than by Spot, in spite of both intentions. She was surprised to discover it was Larry who had pulled her from danger. Daddy still held a thoroughly hysterical Steph in his arms.

For a while, Mary thought Daddy was going to turn Spot into about a year's worth of hamburger. He didn't though. Spot was too valuable. Mary wasn't surprised anymore. Her world had shifted. It no longer revolved around her. Daddy had saved Steph and abandoned her. She didn't get too upset when she discovered Larry and Steph skinny dipping in the creek a couple of years later. Larry had rescued her. After that, she could forgive him almost anything. She owed him. When Larry came back to her, the way he always did, she agreed to be his steady girl, and she said yes when he asked her to marry him. She hardly gave the succession of other girls he fooled with a second thought, and never dreamed of doing anything similar...until J.D.

The Sincerest of Emotions

The bartender had curly white hair, a full jolly face with dimpled cheeks and a red nose, and, if he'd only had a beard, would look exactly like Santa Claus. He'd bring you what you asked for, too, and never inquire whether you'd been naughty or nice. J.D. wanted a double and innkeeper Claus set it in front of him with a hearty smile and reduced the stack of silver J.D. had placed on the long wooden bar.

His drink glowed warm and amber in the glass and then it started to glow inside J.D. too and the awful sense of failure he'd been carrying since he woke up in the hospital dulled a little.

He'd just finished typing up his report on the Japanese battle flag that had been found atop the pole in front of Old Main on the University of Arizona campus the morning after Pearl Harbor. Some local Japanese Americans were suspected, but they turned out to be among the most patriotic citizens J.D. had met, even now, when neighbors they'd known for years had suddenly stopped speaking to them. He had come out of their house to find the guy next door standing guard on his porch with a shotgun. J.D. showed the man his badge and told him what to expect if anything should happen to the family he'd just visited.

Things were getting out of hand. They'd be rounding up the Japanese soon, putting them in camps, and then they'd start drafting them, the ones who didn't volunteer first, but not for service in the Pacific.

He knew about the flag. It was a fraternity prank. He even had a pretty good idea which fraternity, but Tucson had been so outraged that no one was talking now and he couldn't prove it.

J.D. had been planning to buy a bottle and see if maybe Jesus might want to drive out to the reservation with him and look up some of the old men they'd ridden to Mexico with. Share their memories, and their pain. A last minute request for surveillance of yet another Japanese family had canceled his plans last night. This was his first chance to wash the bad taste of the duty from his soul.

Claus came back down the bar and stood there and smiled and said "What'll it be?" J.D. found that curious because he thought he was the only customer in the place and there was still plenty of whiskey in his glass.

"Do you have any coffee?" she asked. Her voice opened the door on a huge empty space inside him, so big he didn't think anything could ever fill it.

She sat on the stool beside him while the bartender went to get her order. She looked tired. The scar on her cheek where Sasaki had kicked her was only a few shades paler than her skin. It should have made her less beautiful, but the flaw only added a hint of vulnerability and contrasted with her otherwise perfect features. He wanted to reach out and touch her so he reached out and touched the whiskey instead.

"You never called," she said, "or wrote. You didn't even open my letters, just sent them back."

"I'm sorry," he said. "You'd made your choice. I couldn't think of anything appropriate to say." At least he hadn't brought up the redhead. He shrugged and sipped his drink again.

When she spoke her voice was tight, lots of suppressed emotion just under the surface. "You know, when they released you from the hospital, the doctor called me like I asked him. I wanted to know where you were going and he said I should aim myself in the general direction of your house and try the first bar. It's been over a month now, I'm glad to see you've gotten this close to home."

J.D. shoved a coin in the direction of the arriving coffee and Santa snatched it, paused to briefly twinkle his eyes at her, and returned to the cash register. He cranked the handle, it played jingle bell, and he dropped the nickel in the drawer.

She nodded toward J.D.'s glass. "That make it any better?"

"Fills a little emptiness, masks a little pain."

"Fuck that!" she said.

Santa looked up from polishing glasses. J.D. glared at him and he turned away.

"Listen," she said, "if I hurt you when I went back to Larry, I'm sorry. I'm not sure it was the right thing to do. I'm not even sure he needs me more than you. But he'll let me live with my flaws. I don't think you can do that. Since you have to be perfect, how could anyone you share your life with ever be anything less?"

He reached for the bourbon and took a deep sip. It burned its way down his throat and helped relieve the sting of her words, but not enough.

"You're not going to find what you need in there either. You spent more than nine months in that hospital. You were hurt bad enough that you almost died, but you should have been out a long time before you were. They told me you didn't commit yourself to living again. You didn't give up, exactly, but you wouldn't make up your mind to face things either."

She sighed and sipped her coffee and ran her hand through her thick dark hair. "What happened out there really scared me. I thought I was going to die and then all of a sudden Larry was there. I guess I always knew he cared, I just forgot how much, or how much it mattered to me. It means a lot that you came after me too, but then so did Jujul and Jesus, and, in some way, the three of you had to. Larry didn't.

"When I woke up we were each on a travois on our way to Sells and I was even more scared because I could hardly move my arms and I couldn't move my legs at all. I was afraid I might be paralyzed. And you and Larry and Jesus were all hurt too. I didn't know if any of us would make it.

"After they moved us to Tucson and I could get around again, I spent the next couple of weeks sitting either by your bed or Larry's. I don't know if you remember that. I hadn't decided yet, not then, but Larry responded to me and you didn't and the doctors told me they didn't think you would. It felt like you abandoned me. So, when they sent Larry back to Ohio, I went with him, and I didn't come back till Jesus told me I might do some good as a character witness at Jujul's trial. You didn't respond much then either.

"Larson was characterizing Jujul as some kind of savage and the only two people who ever had any control over Larson were you and Fredericks, and Fredericks had just had his stroke. The FBI was telling us we had to keep our mouths shut about Sasaki, that it might make things better for Jujul, but it sure as hell would fuck things up for his people and we needed you. God damn you, we needed you to sort things out or pull some strings or throw your weight around a little. We needed you to help us keep the old man out of jail and you just lay there and waited to see if you were going to die."

J.D. watched the tear slide down her cheek and catch on the scar.

"I'm sorry," he said. "That's the trouble. People keep needing me and I keep letting them down."

She turned, shaking her head. Her rich mahogany curls took turns hiding one side of her collar and then the other. "That's why I'm with Larry. You still don't understand, do you J.D.? You think you're to blame. All those people in Spain, you think it's your fault they died. That things came apart out there in the desert. That a bunch of us ended up with battered bodies and bruised psyches—all your fault. Shit, Fitzpatrick, the only person you've ever failed is yourself.

"Don't you get it! We won. Sasaki died, not us. There isn't any rebellion out there on the reservation anymore. Parker may be dead, but he got that way all by himself, not because of you. You're the one who made it possible for us to need you again. Maybe we still do."

"Won? Haven't you heard about Jujul?" he asked. "Don't you know? He died!"

"Yeah, I know. It's terrible and I don't understand it. I always thought you could help him, if you only tried. I still think you could have. But you know, he made choices too. They say he attacked that guard. I thought, as far as he was concerned, his life ended when he took the rap and went to jail. Everything after was just waiting around to die. Maybe he took all he could, then made them finish it for him. But now, here you are, indulging in a private wake that's probably more for yourself than Jujul, while another person who thought you were his friend sits behind bars. He always did what he could for Jujul, but he didn't have the connections, didn't have the political clout. He never got anywhere trying, but he never quit either. When he heard what happened to the old man he didn't just open the nearest bottle. Maybe what he did wasn't right, but there's some justice in it."

J.D. took another sip. "What are you talking about?"

"Jesus drove out to the reservation yesterday afternoon. I guess he made a mess of Larson's face, and his own career, before they stopped him." She nodded toward the bourbon. "You keep hitting that stuff as hard as you are and you'll do a number on your career too, only the gesture won't have been as dramatic and by then, there may not be anybody left to care.

"I haven't stopped loving you, you know," she said. She was digging through her purse for tissues and Santa was doing his best to pretend he wasn't listening. "I'm not sure I ever will, but I love Larry too, and Larry needs me for more than just sharing his self-pity. I'm afraid, if you ever get past that, you may not need anybody for anything else at all."

She spun off the barstool and headed for the entrance. She wasn't hurrying but she was gone before J.D. could decide whether he wanted to respond, to say nothing of where to start. He wasn't even sure she was wrong.

He watched her go and felt the hollow place in his soul start to ache again. Draining the rest of his drink didn't fill it, so he ordered another.

"You know," Santa observed while refilling his stocking, "at least self-pity is the sincerest of emotions."

J.D. picked up the glass and rotated it slowly in front of his eyes, watching the amber liquid swirl and distort whatever he viewed through it. "You're a real comfort," he muttered. He wasn't talking to innkeeper Claus.

He felt guilty, all right. Jujul was dead because he hadn't acted quickly enough. But she was wrong. He had acted.

He'd gone to the FBI, the same agent who'd convinced her and Larry and Jesus to keep their mouths shut, the one who'd arranged the deal that sent the old man to jail in exchange for Larson dropping charges against the other Papagos, the one who stood beside J.D.'s hospital bed while he floated on the tenuous edge of consciousness and told him the public record would show that all their injuries resulted from an automobile accident that occurred after Jujul was captured, and, as a federal officer, he was expected to make sure no one ever suspected anything else.

J.D. only had one thing to bargain with, a threat to go public. At first the agent didn't believe he'd do it, and told him so, and was even kind enough to wonder who would believe an alcoholic, shell-shock case from Spain anyway. But, in the end, the Bureau decided not to take the chance. All the silence they'd arranged to protect the Papago and Americans of Japanese descent also covered the Bureau's ass. As long as it held, they didn't have to explain how they'd lost track of a Japanese secret agent who'd killed and kidnapped American citizens. Not needing to explain that was worth something—clemency for Jujul. He got their guarantee a few days after Pearl. Obviously, he got it too late.

It was warm in the bar, not like the chilly gloom outside. The place radiated an artificial sense of goodwill and the assurance of pleasant forgetfulness. It smelled of tobacco smoke and beer and whiskey, comforting smells, as welcome as a greeting from an old friend. J.D. sat and experienced the place, inhaled it into his innermost self to see if it might diminish the void he still felt there, listened to its promises and tried to believe. He couldn't quite do it.

Winter Forever

J.D. stuffed his hands into his pockets as he walked back. A pair of the army bombers that were becoming increasingly common at Davis-Monthan droned by overhead, skimming the bottom of clouds that hung as cheerful as lead. The crowds of Christmas shoppers seemed equally joyous, their faces down, concentrating on puddles, hidden by turned up collars and turned down brims. The afternoon was becoming colder, hinting that even Tucson, in spite of claims by the chamber of commerce, couldn't avoid winter forever.

The collection of recruiting posters by the entrance to the federal building looked more festive than downtown's Christmas decorations and suggested conflict might prove similarly enjoyable. J.D. knew better.

He went briskly up the stairs and though he only went to the second floor, he was breathing a little hard by the time he got there. He walked down to the end of the hall and into the office that housed the only FBI agent a backwater like Tucson rated. He waved his badge at a secretary who made a desperate attempt to intercept him before he could disturb her boss, but was through the second door without benefit of knocking before she could get there. He closed it in her face as the startled agent looked up from a desk full of paperwork.

"You still owe me one," J.D. told him.

"Shit, Fitzpatrick!" the agent complained. "It's not my fault the old bastard tried to make a break for it. Jesus! What do you want from me now?"

"That's right," J.D. said enigmatically. "That's exactly who I want, only you've got the pronunciation wrong."

Afterword and Acknowledgments

On October 16, 1940, an attempt was made to arrest a *Tohono O'odham* Chief named Pia Machita. He had refused to allow his people to be registered for the newly instituted military draft. A beaten and bloodied posse was run out of his village, after which the recalcitrant Papago and his people disappeared into the desert. Despite the best efforts of tribal and federal authorities, they remained at large, and in what was effectively a state of war with the United States and the Bureau of Indian Affairs, until they were captured in May 1941.

The concept for *The Grey Pilgrim* is based on that incident, chronicled by Elmer W. Flaccus in his article, "Arizona's Last Great Indian War," *The Journal of Arizona History*, Vol. 22, No. 1, 1981. Though an attempt to capture the mood of the people, places, and times in which Pia Machita's rebellion occurred may have produced other similarities, this is an imaginative work, not a fictional account of historic events.

I would like to apologize to the *Tohono O'odham* for having created a fictional rival to a fascinating and complex individual who steadfastly followed the dictates of his own grey pilgrim, and for any misrepresentations of their culture inadvertently made.

I owe so much to Kathryn A. Munday, George Michael Jacobs, and Dr. Gary Orin Rollefson, special friends who allowed themselves to be imposed upon for reaction to and assistance with various phases of the original story. My pilgrimage might never have begun but for Dr. Karl H. Schlesier, who first introduced me to Jujul (under many other names). The first version of the novel could not have been completed without the guidance of Martha Gore and Peter Rubie, and the suggestions of Thomas J. Riste and David Yetman.

Not many authors have the opportunity to revise a novel after it has been published. Most probably wouldn't want to. Perhaps they are wiser than I.

Barbara Peters, owner of the Poisoned Pen Mystery Bookstore in Scottsdale, reviewed the original and liked it well enough to feature it at her store, despite feeling it was out of balance. She is now Editor for the Poisoned Pen Press, and with her kind assistance, I have been given the opportunity to restore some material cut from the previous version. This edition combines what I believe are the best of both, with a little polishing and a few minor additions and deletions—lessons learned in the subsequent decade. I hope it's a significantly better read.

Along with Barbara Peters, thanks also to Robert Rosenwald, Louis Silverstein, and all the folks at Poisoned Pen Press. If they hadn't loved good mysteries so much that they had to begin publishing the ones that, otherwise, might be out of, or never in, print, this pilgrimage might have ended long ago. And, I would have missed some *great* reading.

Thanks to Paige Wheeler, my agent, for believing in, and putting up with, yet another quirky author. Many friends and family, including some who may not think so, were invaluable to the process.

Finally, special thanks to my wife, also a Barbara, but for whom the support of all the rest would have been insufficient.

For any errors or failures in the novel, I alone am responsible.

J.M. Hayes
Tucson, Arizona

To receive a free catalog of other Poisoned Pen Press titles, please contact us in one of the following ways:

Phone: 1-800-421-3976
Facsimile: 1-480-949-1707
Email: info@poisonedpenpress.com
Website: www.poisonedpenpress.com

Poisoned Pen Press
6962 E. First Ave. Ste 103
Scottsdale, AZ 85251